# The Wanderer by Frai

## or Female Difficulties

## Volume I of V

Frances Burney was born on June 13th, 1752 in Lynn Regis (now King's Lynn). By the age of 8 Frances had still not learned the alphabet and couldn't read. She now began a period of self-education, which included devouring the family library and to begin her own 'scribblings', these journal writings would document her life and cover the next 72 years.

Her journal writing was accepted but writing novels was frowned upon by her family and friends. Feeling that she had been improper, she burnt her first manuscript, The History of Caroline Evelyn, which she had written in secret.

It was only in 1778 with the anonymous publication of Evelina that her talents were available to the wider world. She was now a published and admired author.

Despite this success and that of her second novel, Cecilia, in 1785, Frances travelled to the court of King George III and Queen Charlotte and was offered the post of "Keeper of the Robes". Frances hesitated. She had no wish to be separated from her family, nor to anything that would restrict her time in writing. But, unmarried at 34, she felt obliged to accept and thought that improved social status and income might allow her greater freedom to write.

The years at Court were fruitful but took a toll on her health, writing and relationships and in 1790 she prevailed upon her father to request her release from service. He was successful.

The ideals of the French Revolution had brought support from many English literates for the ideals of equality and social justice. Frances quickly became attached to General Alexandre D'Arblay, an artillery officer who had fled to England. In spite of the objections of her father they were married on July 28th, 1793.

On December 18th, 1794, Frances gave birth to their only child, a son, Alexander.

Frances's third novel, Camilla, in 1796 earned her £2000 and was enough for them to build a house in Westhumble; Camilla Cottage.

In 1801 D'Arblay was offered service with the government of Napoleon in France, and in 1802 Frances and her son followed him to Paris, where they expected to remain for a year. The outbreak of the war between France and England meant their stay extended for ten years.

In August 1810 Frances developed breast cancer and underwent a mastectomy performed by "7 men in black". Frances was later able to write about the operation in detail, being conscious through most of it, anesthetics not yet being in use.

With the death of D'Arblay, in 1818, of cancer, Frances moved to London to be near her son. Tragically he died in 1837. Frances, in her last years, was by now retired but entertained many visits from younger members of the Burney family, who gathered to listen to her fascinating accounts and her talents for imitating the people she described.

Frances Burney died on January 6th, 1840.

## Index of Contents

DEDICATION

TO DOCTOR BURNEY, FRS and correspondent to the institute of France [1]

The earliest pride of my heart was to inscribe to my much-loved Father the first public effort of my pen; though the timid offering, unobtrusive and anonymous, was long unpresented; and, even at last, reached its destination through a zeal as secret as it was kind, by means which he would never reveal; and with which, till within these last few months, I have myself been unacquainted.

With what grateful delight do I cast, now, at the same revered feet where I prostrated that first essay, this, my latest attempt!

Your name I did not dare then pronounce; and myself I believed to be 'wrapt up in a mantle of impenetrable obscurity [2].' Little did I foresee the indulgence that would bring me forward! and that my dear father himself, whom, even while, urged by filial feelings, and yet nameless, I invoked, [3] I thought would be foremost to aid, nay, charge me to shun the public eye; that He, whom I dreaded to see blush at my production, should be the first to tell me not to blush at it myself! The happy moment when he spoke to me those unexpected words, is ever present, and still gay to my memory.

The early part of this immediate tribute has already twice traversed the ocean in manuscript: I had planned and begun it before the end of the last century but the bitter, and ever to be deplored affliction with which this new era opened to our family, in depriving us of the darling of our hearts, [4] at the very moment—when—after a grievous absence, we believed her restored to us, cast it from my thoughts, and even from my powers, for many years. I took with me, nevertheless, my prepared materials in the year 1802, to France; where, ultimately, though only at odd intervals, I sketched the whole work; which, in the year 1812, accompanied me back to my native land. And, to the honour and liberality of both nations, let me mention, that, at the Custom-house on either—alas!—hostile shore, upon my given word that the papers contained neither letters, nor political writings; but simply a work of invention and observation; the voluminous manuscript was suffered to pass, without demur, comment, or the smallest examination.

A conduct so generous on one side, so trusting on the other, in time of war, even though its object be unimportant, cannot but be read with satisfaction by every friend of humanity, of either rival nation, into whose hands its narrative may chance to fall.

Such, therefore, if any such there be, who expect to find here materials for political controversy; or fresh food for national animosity; must turn elsewhere their disappointed eyes: for here, they will simply meet, what the Author has thrice sought to present to them already, a composition upon general life, manners, and characters; without any species of personality, either in the form of foreign influence, or of national partiality. I have felt, indeed, no disposition, I ought rather, perhaps, to say talent, for venturing upon the stormy sea of politics; whose waves, for ever either receding or encroaching, with difficulty can be stemmed, and never can be trusted.

Even when I began;—how unconsciously you, dear Sir, well know, what I may now, perhaps, venture to style my literary career, nothing can more clearly prove that I turned, instinctively, from the tempestuous course, than the equal favour with which I was immediately distinguished by those two celebrated, immortal authors, Dr Johnson and the Right Honourable Edmund Burke; whose sentiments upon public affairs divided, almost separated them, at that epoch; yet who, then, and to their last hours, I had the pride, the delight, and the astonishment to find the warmest, as well as the most eminent supporters of my honoured essays. Latterly, indeed, their political opinions assimilated; but when each, separately, though at the same time, condescended to stand for the champion of my first small work; ere ever I had had the happiness of being presented to either; and ere they knew that I bore, my Father! your honoured name; that small work was nearly the only subject upon which they met without contestation[5]:—if I except the equally ingenious and ingenuous friend whom they vied with each other to praise, to appreciate, and to love; and whose name can never vibrate on our ears but to bring emotion to our hearts;—Sir Joshua Reynolds.

If, therefore, then, when every tie, whether public or mental, was single; and every wish had one direction; I held political topics to be without my sphere, or beyond my skill; who shall wonder that now, united, alike by choice and by duty, to a member of a foreign nation, yet adhering, with primæval enthusiasm, to the country of my birth, I should leave all discussions of national rights, and modes, or acts of government, to those whose wishes have no opposing calls; whose duties are undivided; and whose opinions are unbiased by individual bosom feelings; which, where strongly impelled by dependant happiness, insidiously, unconsciously direct our views, colour our ideas, and entangle our partiality in our interests.

Nevertheless, to avoid disserting upon these topics as matter of speculation, implies not an observance of silence to the events which they produce, as matter of act: on the contrary, to attempt to delineate, in whatever form, any picture of actual human life, without reference to the French Revolution, would be as little possible, as to give an idea of the English government, without reference to our own: for not more unavoidably is the last blended with the history of our nation, than the first, with every intellectual survey of the present times.

Anxious, however, inexpressibly!—to steer clear, alike, of all animadversions that, to my adoptive country, may seem ungrateful, or, to the country of my birth unnatural; I have chosen, with respect to what, in these volumes, has any reference to the French Revolution, a period which, completely past, can excite no rival sentiments, nor awaken any party spirit; yet of which the stupendous iniquity and cruelty, though already historical, have left traces, that, handed down, even but traditionally, will be sought with curiosity, though reverted to with horrour, from generation to generation.

Every friend of humanity, of what soil or what persuasion soever he may be, must rejoice that those days, though still so recent, are over; and truth and justice call upon me to declare, that, during the ten eventful years, from 1802 to 1812, that I resided in the capital of France, I was neither startled by any species of investigation, nor distressed through any difficulties of conduct. Perhaps unnoticed, certainly unannoyed, I passed my time either by my own small—but precious fire-side; or in select society; perfectly a stranger to all personal disturbance; save what sprang from the painful separation that absented me from you my dearest Father, from my loved family, and native friends and country. To hear this fact thus publicly attested, you, dear Sir, will rejoice; and few, I trust, amongst its readers, will disdain to feel some little sympathy in your satisfaction.

With regard to the very serious subject treated upon, from time to time, in this work, some, perhaps many, may ask, Is a Novel the vehicle for such considerations? such discussions?

Permit me to answer; whatever, in illustrating the characters, manners, or opinions of the day, exhibits what is noxious or reprehensible, should scrupulously be accompanied by what is salubrious, or chastening. Not that poison ought to be infused merely to display the virtues of an antidote; but that, where errour and mischief bask in the broad light of day, truth ought not to be suffered to shrink timidly into the shade.

Divest, for a moment, the title of Novel from its stationary standard of insignificance, and say! What is the species of writing that offers fairer opportunities for conveying useful precepts? It is, or it ought to be, a picture of supposed, but natural and probable human existence. It holds, therefore, in its hands our best affections; it exercises our imaginations; it points out the path of honour; and gives to juvenile credulity knowledge of the world, without ruin, or repentance; and the lessons of experience, without its tears.

And is not a Novel, permit me, also, to ask, in common with every other literary work, entitled to receive its stamp as useful, mischievous, or nugatory, from its execution? not necessarily, and in its changeless state, to be branded as a mere vehicle for frivolous, or seductive amusement? If many may turn aside from all but mere entertainment presented under this form, many, also, may, unconsciously, be allured by it into reading the severest truths, who would not even open any work of a graver denomination.

What is it that gives the universally acknowledged superiority to the epic poem? Its historic truth? No; the three poems, which, during so many centuries, and till Milton arose, stood unrivalled in celebrity, are, with respect to fact, of constantly disputed, or, rather, disproved authenticity. Nor is it even the sweet witchery of sound; the ode, the lyric, the elegiac, and other species of poetry, have risen to equal metrical beauty:—

'Tis the grandeur, yet singleness of the plan; the never broken, yet never obvious adherence to its execution; the delineation and support of character; the invention of incident; the contrast of situation; the grace of diction, and the beauty of imagery; joined to a judicious choice of combinations, and a living interest in every partial detail, that give to that sovereign species of the works of fiction, its glorious pre-eminence.

Will my dear Father smile at this seeming approximation of the compositions which stand foremost, with those which are sunk lowest in literary estimation? No; he will feel that it is not the futile presumption of a comparison that would be preposterous; but a fond desire to separate, with a high hand!—falsehood, that would deceive to evil, from fiction, that would attract another way;—and to rescue from ill opinion the sort of production, call it by what name we may, that his daughter ventures to lay at his feet, through the alluring, but awful tribunal of the public.

He will recollect, also, how often their so mutually honoured Dr Johnson has said to her, 'Always aim at the eagle!—even though you expect but to reach a sparrow!'

The power of prejudice annexed to nomenclature is universal: the same being who, unnamed, passes unnoticed, if preceded by the title of a hero, or a potentate, catches every eye, and is pursued with clamorous praise, or, its common reverberator!—abuse: but in nothing is the force of denomination more striking than in the term Novel; a species of writing which, though never mentioned, even by its supporter, but with a look that fears contempt, is not more rigidly excommunicated, from its appellation, in theory, than sought and fostered, from its attractions, in practice.

So early was I impressed myself with ideas that fastened degradation to this class of composition, that at the age of adolescence, I struggled against the propensity which, even in childhood, even from the moment I could hold a pen, had impelled me into its toils; and on my fifteenth birth-day, I made so resolute a conquest over an inclination at which I blushed, and that I had always kept secret, that I committed to the flames whatever, up to that moment, I had committed to paper. And so enormous was the pile, that I thought it prudent to consume it in the garden.

You, dear Sir, knew nothing of its extinction, for you had never known of its existence. Our darling Susanna, to whom alone I had ever ventured to read its contents, alone witnessed the conflagration; and—well I remember!—and wept, with tender partiality, over the imaginary ashes of Caroline Evelyn, the mother of Evelina.

The passion, however, though resisted, was not annihilated: my bureau was cleared; but my head was not emptied; and, in defiance of every self-effort, Evelina struggled herself into life.

If then, even in the season of youth, I felt ashamed of appearing to be a votary to a species of writing that by you, Sir, liberal as I knew you to be, I thought condemned; since your large library, of which I was then the principal librarian, contained only one work of that class;[6] how much deeper must now be my blush, now, when that spring of existence has so long taken its flight, transferring, I must hope, its genial vigour upon your grandson![7]—if the work which I here present to you, may not shew, in the observations which it contains upon various characters, ways, or excentricities of human life, that an exterior the most frivolous may enwrap illustrations of conduct, that the most rigid preceptor need not deem dangerous to entrust to his pupils; for, if what is inculcated is right, it will not, I trust, be cast aside, merely because so conveyed as not to be received as a task. On the contrary, to make pleasant the path of propriety, is snatching from evil its most alluring mode of ascendency. And your fortunate daughter, though past the period of chusing to write, or desiring to read, a merely romantic love-tale, or a story of improbable wonders, may still hope to retain, if she has ever possessed it, the power of interesting the affections, while still awake to them herself, through the many much loved agents of sensibility, that still hold in their pristine energy her conjugal, maternal, fraternal, friendly, and, dearest Sir!—her filial feelings.

Fiction, when animating the design of recommending right, has always been permitted and cultivated, not alone by the moral, but by the pious instructor; not alone to embellish what is prophane, but to promulgate even what is sacred, from the first æra of tuition, to the present passing moment. Yet I am aware that all which, incidentally, is treated of in these volumes upon the most momentous of subjects, may HERE, in this favoured island, be deemed not merely superfluous, but, if indulgence be not shewn to its intention, impertinent; and HERE, had I always remained, the most solemn chapter of the work, I will not anticipate its number, might never have been traced; for, since my return to this country, I have been forcibly struck in remarking, that all sacred themes, far from being either neglected, or derided, are become almost common topics of common discourse; and rather, perhaps, from varying sects, and diversified opinions, too familiarly discussed, than defyingly set aside.

But what I observed in my long residence abroad, presented another picture; and its colours, not, indeed, with cementing harmony, but to produce a striking contrast, have forcibly, though not, I hope, glaringly tinted my pen.

Nevertheless, truth, and my own satisfaction, call upon me to mention, that, in the circle to which, in Paris, I had the honour, habitually, to belong, piety, generally, in practice as well as in theory, held its just pre-eminence; though almost every other society, however cultured, brilliant, and unaffectedly good, of which occasionally I heard, or in which, incidentally, I mixed, commonly considered belief and bigotry as synonymous terms.

They, however, amongst my adopted friends, for whose esteem I am most solicitous, will suffer my design to plead, I trust, in my favour; even where my essays, whether for their projection, or their execution, may most sarcastically be criticised.

Strange, indeed, must be my ingratitude, could I voluntarily give offence where, during ten unbroken years, I should, personally, have known nothing but felicity, had I quitted a country, or friends, I, could have forgotten. For me, however, as for all mankind, concomitant circumstances took their usual charge of impeding any exception to the general laws of life.

And now, dear Sir, in leaving you to the perusal of these volumes, how many apprehensions would be hushed, might I hope that they would revive in your feelings the partial pleasure with which you cherished their predecessors!

Will the public be offended, if here, as in private, I conclude my letter with a prayer for my dearest Father's benediction and preservation? No! the public voice, and the voice of his family is one, in reverencing his virtues, admiring his attainments, and ardently desiring that health, peace of mind, and fulness of merited honours, may crown his length of days, and prolong them to the utmost verge of enjoyable mortality!

F. B. d'ARBLAY. March 14. 1814

[Footnote 1: To which honour Dr Burney was elected, by the wholly unsolicited votes of the members des beaux arts. His daughter brought over his diploma from Paris.]

[Footnote 2: Preface to Evelina.]

[Footnote 3: Inscription of Evelina, 'O Author of my being!' &c.]

[Footnote 4: Susanna Elizabeth Phillips.]

[Footnote 5: So strongly this coincidence of sentiment was felt by Mr Burke himself, that, some years afterwards, at an assembly at Lady Galloway's, where each, for a considerable time, had seemed to stimulate the other to a flow of partial praise on Evelina and—just then published—Cecilia; Mr Burke, upon Dr Johnson's endeavouring to detain me when. I rose to depart, by calling out, 'Don't go yet, little character-monger!' followed me, gaily, but impressively exclaiming, 'Miss Burney, die to-night!']

[Footnote 6: Fielding's Amelia.]

[Footnote 7: Alexander Charles Lewis d'Arblay.]

VOLUME I

CHAPTER I

During the dire reign of the terrific Robespierre, and in the dead of night, braving the cold, the darkness and the damps of December, some English passengers, in a small vessel, were preparing to glide silently from the coast of France, when a voice of keen distress resounded from the shore, imploring, in the French language, pity and admission.

The pilot quickened his arrangements for sailing; the passengers sought deeper concealment; but no answer was returned.

'O hear me!' cried the same voice, 'for the love of Heaven, hear me!'

The pilot gruffly swore, and, repressing a young man who was rising, peremptorily ordered everyone to keep still, at the hazard of discovery and destruction.

'Oh listen to my prayers!' was called out by the same voice, with increased and even frightful energy; 'Oh leave me not to be massacred!'

'Who's to pay for your safety?' muttered the pilot.

'I will!' cried the person whom he had already rebuffed, 'I pledge myself for the cost and the consequence!'

'Be lured by no tricks;' said an elderly man, in English; 'put off immediately, pilot.'

The pilot was very ready to obey.

The supplications from the land were now sharpened into cries of agony, and the young man, catching the pilot by the arm, said eagerly, ''Tis the voice of a woman! where can be the danger? Take her in, pilot, at my demand, and my charge!'

'Take her in at your peril, pilot!' rejoined the elderly man.

Rage had elevated his voice; the petitioner heard it, and called—screamed, rather, for mercy.

'Nay, since she is but a woman, and in distress, save her, pilot, in God's name!' said an old sea officer. 'A woman, a child, and a fallen enemy, are three persons that every true Briton should scorn to misuse.'

The sea officer was looked upon as first in command; the young man, therefore, no longer opposed, separated himself from a young lady with whom he had been conversing, and, descending from the boat, gave his hand to the suppliant.

There was just light enough to shew him a female in the most ordinary attire, who was taking a whispering leave of a male companion, yet more meanly equipped.

With trembling eagerness, she sprang into the vessel, and sunk rather than sat upon a place that was next to the pilot, ejaculating fervent thanks, first to Heaven, and then to her assistant.

The pilot now, in deep hoarse accents, strictly enjoined that no one should speak or move till they were safely out at sea.

All obeyed; and, with mingled hope and dread, insensible to the weather, and dauntless to the hazards of the sea, watchful though mute, and joyful though filled with anxiety, they set sail.

In about half an hour, the grumbling of the pilot, who was despotic master of the boat, was changed into loud and vociferous oaths.

Alarmed, the passengers concluded that they were chaced. They looked around, but to no purpose; the darkness impeded examination.

They were happily, however, mistaken; the lungs of the pilot had merely recovered their usual play, and his humour its customary vent, from a belief that all pursuit would now be vain.

This proved the signal to general liberty of speech; and the young lady already mentioned, addressing herself, in a low voice, to the gentleman who had aided the Incognita, said, 'I wonder what sort of a dulcinea you have brought amongst us! though, I really believe, you are such a complete knight-errant, that you would just as willingly find her a tawny Hottentot as a fair Circassian. She affords us, however, the vivifying food of conjecture, the only nourishment of which I never sicken!—I am glad, therefore, that 'tis dark, for discovery is almost always disappointment.'

'She seems to be at prayers.'

'At prayers? She's a nun, then, depend upon it. Make her tell us the history of her convent.'

'Why what's all this, woman?' said the pilot, in French, 'are you afraid of being drowned?'

'No!' answered she, in the same language, 'I fear nothing now—it is therefore I am thankful!'

Retreating, then, from her rude neighbour, she gently approached an elderly lady, who was on her other side, but who, shrinking from her, called out, 'Mr Harleigh, I shall be obliged to you if you will change places with me.'

'Willingly;' he answered; but the young lady with whom he had been conversing, holding his coat, exclaimed, 'Now you want to have all the stories of those monks and abbesses to yourself! I won't let you stir, I am resolved!'

The stranger begged that she might not incommode any one; and drew back.

'You may sit still now, Mr Harleigh,' said the elderly lady, shaking herself; 'I do very well again.'

Harleigh bit his lip, and, in a low voice, said to his companion, 'It is strange that the facility of giving pain should not lessen its pleasure! How far better tempered should we all be to others, if we anticipated the mischief that ill humour does to ourselves!'

'Now are you such a very disciple of Cervantes,' she replied, 'that I have no doubt but your tattered dulcinea has secured your protection for the whole voyage, merely because old aunt Maple has been a little ill bred to her.'

'I don't know but you are right, for nothing so uncontrollably excites resistance, as grossness to the unoffending.'

He then, in French, enquired of the new passenger, whether she would not have some thicker covering, to shelter her from the chill of the night; offering her, at the same time, a large wrapping coat.

She thanked him, but declared that she was perfectly warm.

'Are you so, faith?' cried the elderly man already mentioned, 'I wish, then, you would give me your receipt, Mistress; for I verily think that my blood will take a month's thawing, before it will run again in my veins.'

She made no answer, and, in a tone somewhat piqued, he added, 'I believe in my conscience those outlandish gentry have no more feeling without than they have within!'

Encreasing coldness and darkness repressed all further spirit of conversation, till the pilot proclaimed that they were halfway over the straits.

A general exclamation of joy now broke forth from all, while the new comer, suddenly casting something into the sea, ejaculated, in French, 'Sink, and be as nothing!' And then, clasping her hands, added, 'Heaven be praised, 'tis gone for ever!'

The pilot scolded and swore; every one was surprised and curious; and the elderly man plumply demanded, 'Pray what have you thrown overboard, Mistress?'

Finding himself again unanswered, he rather angrily raised his voice, saying, 'What, I suppose you don't understand English now? Though you were pretty quick at it when we were leaving you in the lurch! Faith, that's convenient enough!'

'For all I have been silent so long,' cried the old sea officer, 'it has not been for want of something to say; and I ask the favour that you won't any of you take it ill, if I make free to mention what has been passing, all this time, in my mind; though it may rather have the air of a hint than a compliment; but as I owe to being as much in fault as yourselves, I hope you won't be affronted at a little plain dealing.'

'You are mighty good to us, indeed, Sir!' cried Mrs Maple, 'but pray what fault have you to charge Me with, amongst the rest?'

'I speak of us in a body, Madam, and, I hope, with proper shame! To think that we should all get out of that loathsome captivity, with so little reverence, that not one amongst us should have fallen upon his knees, to give thanks, except just this poor outlandish gentlewoman; whose good example I recommend it to us all now to follow.'

'What, and so overturn the boat,' said the elderly man, 'that we may all be drowned for joy, because we have escaped being beheaded?'

'I submit to your better judgment, Mr Riley,' replied the officer, 'with regard to the attitude; and the more readily, because I don't think that the posture is the chief thing, half the people that kneel, even at church, as I have taken frequent note, being oftener in a doze than in a fit of devotion. But the fear of shaking the boat would be but a poor reason to fear shaking our gratitude, which seems to me to want it abundantly. So I, for one, give thanks to the Author of all things!'

'You are a fine fellow, noble Admiral!' cried Mr Riley, 'as fine a fellow as ever I knew! and I honour you, faith! for I don't believe there is a thing in the world that requires so much courage as to risk derision, even from fools.'

A young man, wrapped up in flannels, who had been undisguisedly enjoying a little sneering laugh, now became suddenly grave, and pretended not to heed what was passing.

Mrs Maple protested that she could not bear the parade of saying her prayers in public.

Another elderly lady, who had hitherto seemed too sick to speak, declared that she could not think of giving thanks, till she were sure of being out of danger.

And the young lady, laughing immoderately, vowed that she had never seen such a congress of quizzes in her life; adding, 'We want nothing, now, but a white foaming billow, or a shrill whistle from Boreas, to bring us all to confession, and surprise out our histories.'

'Apropos to quizzes,' said Mr Riley, addressing the hitherto silent young man, 'how comes it, Mr Ireton, that we have not had one word from you all this time?'

'What do you mean by aprôpos, Sir?' demanded the young man, somewhat piqued.

'Faith, I don't very well know. I am no very good French dictionary. But I always say aprôpos, when I am at a loss how to introduce any thing. Let us hear, however, where you have been passing your thoughts all this time. Are you afraid the sea should be impregnated with informers, instead of salt, and so won't venture to give breath to an idea, lest it should be floated back to Signor Robespierre, and hodge-podged into a conspiracy?'

'Ay, your thoughts, your thoughts! give us your thoughts, Ireton!' cried the young lady, 'I am tired to death of my own.'

'Why, I have been reflecting, for this last hour or two, what a singular circumstance it is, that in all the domains that I have scampered over upon the continent, I have not met with one young person who could hit my fancy as a companion for life.'

'And I, Sir, think,' said the sea officer, turning to him with some severity, 'that a man who could go out of old England to chuse himself a wife, never deserves to set foot on it again! If I knew any worse punishment, I should name it.'

This silenced Mr Ireton; and not another word was uttered, till the opening of day displayed the British shore.

The sea officer then gave a hearty huzza, which was echoed by Harleigh; while Riley, as the light gleamed upon the old and tattered garments of the stranger, burst into a loud laugh, exclaiming, 'Faith, I should like to know what such a demoiselle as this should come away from her own country for? What could you be afraid of, hay! demoiselle?'—

She turned her head from him in silence. Harleigh enquired, in French, whether she had escaped the general contagion, from which almost all in the boat had suffered, of sickness.

She cheerfully replied, Yes! She had escaped every evil!

'The demoiselle is soon contented,' said Riley; 'but I cannot for my life make out who she is, nor what she wants. Why won't you tell us, demoiselle? I should like to know your history.'

'Much obliged for the new fellow traveller you have given us, Mr Harleigh!' said Mrs Maple, contemptuously examining her; 'I have really some curiosity myself, to be informed what could put into such a body's mind as that, to want to come over to England.'

'The desire of learning the language, I hope!' cried Harleigh, 'for I should be sorry that she knew it already!'

'I wish, at least, she would tell us,' said the young lady, 'how she happened to find out our vessel just at the moment we were sailing.'

'And I should be glad to discover,' cried Riley, 'why she understands English on and off at her pleasure, now so ready, and now answering one never a word.'

The old sea officer, touching his hat as he addressed her, said, 'For my part, Madam, I hope the compliment you make our country in coming to it, is that of preferring good people to bad; in which case every Englishman should honour and welcome you.'

'And I hope,' cried Harleigh, while the stranger seemed hesitating how to answer, 'that this patriotic benevolence is comprehended; if not, I will attempt a translation.'

'I speak French so indifferently, which, however, I don't much mind,' cried the Admiral, 'that I am afraid the gentlewoman would hardly understand me, or else I would translate for myself.'

The stranger now, with a strong expression of gratitude, replied in English, but with a foreign accent, 'It is only how to thank you I am at a loss, Sir; I understand you perfectly.'

'So I could have sworn!' cried Riley, with a laugh, 'I could have sworn that this would be the turn for understanding English again! And you can speak it, too, can you, Mistress?'

'And pray, good woman,' demanded Mrs Maple, staring at her, 'how came you to learn English? Have you lived in any English family? If you have, I should be glad to know their names.'

'Ay, their names! their names!' was echoed from Mrs Maple by her niece.

The stranger looked down, and stammered, but said nothing that could distinctly be heard.

Riley, laughing again, though provoked, exclaimed, 'There! now you ask her a question, she won't comprehend a word more! I was sure how 'twould be! They are clever beings, those French, they are, faith! always playing fools' tricks, like so many monkies, yet always lighting right upon their feet, like so many cats!'

'You must resign your demoiselle, as Mr Riley calls her, for a heroine;' whispered the young lady to Mr Harleigh. 'Her dress is not merely shabby; 'tis vulgar. I have lost all hope of a pretty nun. She can be nothing above a house-maid.'

'She is interesting by her solitary situation,' he answered, 'be she what she may by her rank: and her voice, I think, is singularly pleasing.'

'Oh, you must fall in love with her, I suppose, as a thing of course. If, however, she has one atom that is native in her, how will she be choaked by our foggy atmosphere!'

'And has our atmosphere, Elinor, no purifying particles, that, in defiance of its occasional mists, render it salubrious?'

'Oh, I don't mean alone the foggy air that she must inhale; but the foggy souls whom she must see and hear. If she have no political bias, that sets natural feelings aside, she'll go off in a lethargy, from ennui, the very first week. For myself I confess, from my happiness in going forth into the world at this sublime juncture, of turning men into infants, in order to teach them better how to grow up, I feel as if I had never awaked into life, till I had opened my eyes on that side of the channel.'

'And can you, Elinor, with a mind so powerful, however—pardon me!—wild, have witnessed....'

'Oh, I know what you mean!—but those excesses are only the first froth of the cauldron. When once 'tis skimmed, you will find the composition clear, sparkling, delicious!'

'Has, then, the large draught which, in a two years' residence amidst that combustion, you have, perforce, quaffed, of revolutionary beverage, left you, in defiance of its noxious qualities, still thus....' He hesitated.

'Inebriated, you would say, Albert,' cried she, laughing, 'if you blushed not for me at the idea. But, in this one point, your liberality, though matchless in every other, is terribly narrowed by adhesion to old tenets. You enjoy not therefore, as you ought, this glorious epoch, that lifts our minds from slavery and from nothingness, into play and vigour; and leaves us no longer, as heretofore, merely making believe that we are thinking beings.'

'Unbridled liberty, Elinor, cannot rush upon a state, without letting it loose to barbarism. Nothing, without danger, is suddenly unshackled: safety demands control from the baby to the despot.'

'The opening essays here,' she replied, 'have certainly been calamitous: but, when all minor articles are progressive, in rising to perfection, must the world in a mass alone stand still, because its amelioration would be costly? Can anything be so absurd, so preposterous, as to seek to improve mankind individually, yet bid it stand still collectively? What is education, but reversing propensities; making the idle industrious, the rude civil, and the ignorant learned? And do you not, for every student thus turned out of his likings, his vagaries, or his vices, to be new modelled, call this alteration improvement? Why, then, must you brand all similar efforts for new organizing states, nations, and bodies of society, by that word of unmeaning alarm, innovation?'

'To reverse, Elinor, is not to new model, but to destroy. This education, with which you illustrate your maxims, does it begin with the birth? Does it not, on the contrary, work its way by the gentlest gradations, one part almost imperceptibly preparing for another, throughout all the stages of childhood to adolescence, and of adolescence to manhood? If you give Homer before the Primer, do you think that you shall make a man of learning? If you shew the planetary system to the child who has not yet trundled his hoop, do you believe that you will form a mathematician? And if you put a rapier into his hands before he has been exercised with foils, what is your guarantee for the safety of his professor?'

Just then the stranger, having taken off her gloves, to arrange an old shawl, in which she was wrapt, exhibited hands and arms of so dark a colour, that they might rather be styled black than brown.

Elinor exultingly drew upon them the eyes of Harleigh, and both taking, at the same instant, a closer view of the little that was visible of the muffled up face, perceived it to be of an equally dusky hue.

The look of triumph was now repeated.

'Pray, Mistress,' exclaimed Mr Riley, scoffingly fixing his eyes upon her arms, 'what part of the world might you come from? The settlements in the West Indies? or somewhere off the coast of Africa?'

She drew on her gloves, without seeming to hear him.

'There!' said he, 'now the demoiselle don't understand English again! Faith, I begin to be entertained with her. I did not like it at first.'

'What say you to your dulcinea now, Harleigh?' whispered Elinor; 'you will not, at least, yelep her the Fair Maid of the Coast.'

'She has very fine eyes, however!' answered he, laughing.

The wind just then blowing back the prominent borders of a French night-cap, which had almost concealed all her features, displayed a large black patch, that covered half her left cheek, and a broad black ribbon, which bound a bandage of cloth over the right side of her forehead.

Before Elinor could utter her rallying congratulations to Harleigh, upon this sight, she was stopt by a loud shout from Mr Riley; 'Why I am afraid the demoiselle has been in the wars!' cried he. 'Why, Mistress, have you been trying your skill at fisty cuffs for the good of your nation? or only playing with kittens for your private diversion?'

'Now, then, Harleigh,' said Elinor, 'what says your quixotism now? Are you to become enamoured with those plaisters and patches, too?'

'Why she seems a little mangled, I confess; but it may be only by scrambling from some prison.'

'Really, Mr Harleigh,' said Mrs Maple, scarcely troubling herself to lower her voice as, incessantly, she continued surveying the stranger, 'I don't think that we are much indebted to you for bringing us such company as this into our boat! We did not pay such a price to have it made a mere common hoy. And without the least enquiry into her character, too! without considering what one must think of a person who could look out for a place, in a chance vessel, at midnight!'

'Let us hope,' said Harleigh, perceiving, by the down-cast eyes of the stranger, that she understood what passed, 'that we shall not make her repent her choice of an asylum.'

'Ah! there is no fear!' cried she, with quickness.

'Your prepossession, then, is, happily, in our favour?'

'Not my prepossession, but my gratitude!'

'This is true practical philosophy, to let the sum total of good outbalance the detail, which little minds would dwell upon, of evil.'

'Of evil! I think myself at this moment the most fortunate of human beings!'

This was uttered with a sort of transport that she seemed unable to control, and accompanied with a bright smile, that displayed a row of beautifully white and polished teeth.

Riley now, again heartily laughing, exclaimed, 'This demoiselle amuses me mightily! she does, faith! with hardly a rag to cover her this cold winter's night; and on the point of going to the bottom every moment, in this crazy little vessel; with never a friend to own her body if she's drowned, nor an acquaintance to say a word to before she sinks; not a countryman within leagues, except our surly pilot, who grudges her even life-room, because he's afraid he shan't be the better for her: going to a nation where she won't know a dog from a cat, and will be buffetted from pillar to post, if she don't pay for more than she wants; with all this, she is the most fortunate of human beings! Faith, the demoiselle is soon pleased! She is, faith! But why won't you give me your receipt, Mistress, for finding all things so agreeable?'

'You would be sorry, Sir, to take it!'

'I fear, then,' said Harleigh, 'it is only past suffering that bestows this character of bliss upon simple safety?'

'Pray, Mr Riley,' cried Mrs Maple, 'please to explain what you mean, by talking so freely of our all going to the bottom? I should be glad to know what right you had to make me come on board the vessel, if you think it so crazy?'

She then ordered the pilot to use all possible expedition for putting her on shore, at the very first jut of land; adding, 'you may take the rest of the company round, wherever you chuse, but as to me, I desire to be landed directly.'

She could not, however, prevail; but, in the panic which had seized her, she grew as incessant in reproach as in alarm, bitterly bewailing the moment that she had ever trusted herself to such an element, such a vessel, and such guides.

'See,' said Harleigh, in a low voice to the stranger, 'how little your philosophy has spread; and how soon every evil, however great, is forgotten when over, to aggravate the smallest discomfort that still remains! What recompence, or what exertion would any one of us have thought too great, for obtaining a place in this boat only a few hours ago! Yet you, alone, seem to have discovered, that the true art of supporting present inconvenience is to compare it with past calamity, not with our disappointed wishes.'

'Calamity!' repeated she with vivacity, 'ah! if once I reach that shore, that blessed shore! shall I have a sorrow left?'

'The belief that you will not,' said he, smiling, 'will almost suffice for your security, since, certainly, half our afflictions are those which we suffer through anticipation.'

There was time for nothing more; the near approach to land seeming to fill every bosom, for the instant, with sensations equally enthusiastic.


CHAPTER II

Upon reaching the British shore, while Mrs Maple, her niece, the elderly lady, and two maid-servants, claimed and employed the aid of the gentlemen, the Incognita, disregarding an offer of Harleigh to return for her, darted forward with such eagerness, that she was the first to touch the land, where, with a fervour that seemed resistless, she rapturously ejaculated, 'Heaven, Heaven be praised!'

The pilot, when he had safely disembarked his passengers, committed the charge of his vessel to a boy, and, abruptly accosting the stranger, demanded a recompence for the risk which he had run in saving her life.

She was readily opening her work bag to seek for her purse, but the old sea officer, approaching, and holding her arm, gravely asked whether she meant to affront him; and, turning to the pilot, somewhat dictatorially said, 'Harkee, my lad! we took this gentlewoman in ourselves; and I have seen no reason to be sorry for it: but she is our passenger, and not your's. Come to the inn, therefore, and you shall be satisfied, forthwith, for her and the rest of us, in a lump.'

'You are infinitely good, Sir,' cried the stranger, 'but I have no claim—.'

'That's your mistake, gentlewoman. An unprotected female, provided she's of a good behaviour, has always a claim to a man's care, whether she be born amongst our friends or our foes. I should be ashamed to be an Englishman, if I held it my duty to think narrower than that. And a man who could bring himself to be ashamed of being an Englishman, would find it a difficult solution, let me tell you, my good gentlewoman, to discover what he might glory in. However, don't think that I say this to affront you as a foreigner, for I hope I am a better Christian. I only drop it as a matter of fact.'

'Worthy Admiral,' said Mr Harleigh, now joining them, 'you are not, I trust, robbing me of my office? The pecuniary engagement with the pilot was mine.'

'But the authority which made him act,' returned the officer, 'was mine.'

A bright smile, which lightened up the countenance of the Incognita, again contrasted her white teeth with her dingy complexion; while dispersing the tears that started into her eyes, 'Fie upon me!' she cried, 'to be in England and surprised at generosity!'

'Gentlewoman,' said the Admiral, emphatically, 'if you want any help, command my services; for, to my seeming, you appear to be a person of as right a way of thinking, as if you had lisped English for your mother-tongue.'

He then peremptorily insisted that the boat's company should discharge the pilot, without any interference on the part of the lone traveller, as soon as it had done with the custom-house officers.

This latter business was short; there was nothing to examine: not a trunk, and scarcely a parcel, had the hurry and the dangers of escape hazarded.

They then proceeded to the principal inn, where the Admiral called all the crew, as he styled the party, to a spacious room, and a cheering fire, of which he undertook the discipline.

The sight of this meanly attired person, invited into the apartment both by the Admiral and Mr Harleigh, with a civility that seemed blind to her shabby appearance, proved so miraculous a restorative to Mrs Maple, that, rising from a great chair, into which, with a declaration that she was half dead from her late fright and sickness, she had thrown herself, she was endowed with sudden strength of body to stand stiffly upright, and of lungs to pronounce, in shrill but powerful accents, 'Pray, Mr Harleigh, are we to go on any farther as if we were to live all our lives in a stage coach? Why can't that body as well stay in the kitchen?'

The stranger would hastily have retired, but the Admiral, taking her softly by the shoulder, said, 'I have been a commanding officer the best part of my life, Gentlewoman; and though a devil of a wound has put me upon the superannuated list, I am not sunk into quite such a fair weather chap, as to make over my authority, in such a little pitiful skiff's company as this, to petticoat government;— though no man has a better respect for the sex, in its proper element; which, however, is not the sea. Therefore, Madam,' turning to Mrs Maple, 'this gentlewoman being my own passenger, and having comported herself without any offence either to God or man, I shall take it kind if you will treat her in a more Christian-like manner.'

While Mrs Maple began an angry reply, the stranger forced herself out of the apartment. The Admiral followed.

'I hope, gentlewoman,' he was beginning, 'you won't be cast down, or angry, at a few vagaries—' when, looking in her face, he saw a countenance so gaily happy, that his condolence was changed into pleased astonishment. 'Angry!' she repeated, 'at a moment such as this!—a moment of so blessed an escape!—I should be the most graceless of wretches, if I had one sensation but of thankfulness and joy!'

'You are a very brave woman,' said the Admiral, 'and I am sorry,' looking at her tattered clothing, 'to see you in no better plight: though, perchance, if you had been born to more glitter without, you might have had less ore within. However, if you don't much like the vapouring of that ancient lady, which I have no very extraordinary liking to myself, neither, why stay in another room till we have done with the pilot; and then, if I can be of any use in helping you to your friends, I shall be glad to be at your service. For I take it for granted, though you are not in your own country, you are too good a woman to be without friends, as I know no worse sign of a person's character.'

He then joined his fellow-voyagers, and the stranger went on to enquire for the master of the house.

Sounds from without, that seemed to announce distress, catching, soon after, the attentive ear of Harleigh, he opened the door, and perceived that the stranger was returned to the passage, and in evident disorder.

The sea officer briskly advanced to her. 'How now!' he cried, 'disheartened at last? Well! a woman can be but a woman! However, unless you have a mind to see all my good opinion blown away— thus!—in a whiff, you won't think of drooping, now once you are upon British ground. For though I should scorn, I hope, to reproach you for not being a native born, still, not to be over-joyed that you can say, Here I am! would be a sure way to win my contempt. However, as I don't take upon me to be your governor, I'll send your own countryman to you, if you like him better, the pilot?'

'Not for the universe! Not for the universe!' she eagerly cried, and, darting into an empty room, with a hasty apology, shut the door.

'Mighty well, indeed!' said Mrs Maple, who, catching the contagion of curiosity, had deigned to listen; 'so her own countryman, the only person that she ought to belong to, she shuts the door upon!'

She then protested, that if the woman were not brought forth, before the pilot, who was already paid and gone, had re-embarked, she should always be convinced that she had lost something, though she might not find out what had been taken from her, for a twelve-month afterwards.

The landlord, coming forward, enquired whether there were any disturbance; and, upon the complaint and application of Mrs Maple, would have opened the door of the closed apartment; but the Admiral and Harleigh, each taking him by an arm, declared the person in that room to be under their protection.

'Well, upon my word,' cried Mrs Maple, 'this is more than I could have expected! We are in fine hands, indeed, for a sea officer, and an Admiral, that ought to be our safe-guard, to take part with our native enemy, that, I make no doubt, is sent amongst us as a spy for our destruction!'

'A lady, Madam,' said the Admiral, looking down rather contemptuously, 'must have liberty to say whatever she pleases, a man's tongue being as much tied as his hands, not to annoy the weaker vessel; so that, let her come out with what she will, she is amenable to no punishment; unless she take some account of a man's inward opinion; in which case she can't be said to escape quite so free as she may seem to do. This, Madam, is all the remark that I think fit to make to you. But as for you, Mr Landlord, when the gentlewoman in this room has occasion to consult you, she speaks English, and can call you herself.'

He would then have led the way to a general retreat, but Mrs Maple angrily desired the landlord to take notice, that a foreigner, of a suspicious character, had come over with them by force, whom he ought to keep in custody, unless she would tell her name and business.

The door of the apartment was now abruptly opened by the stranger, who called out 'O no! no! no!—Ladies!—Gentlemen!—I claim your protection!'

'It is your's, Madam!' cried Harleigh, with emotion.

'Be sure of it, Gentlewoman!' cried the old officer; 'We did not bring you from one bad shore to another. We'll take care of you. Be sure of it!'

The stranger wept. 'I thought not,' she cried, 'to have shed a tear in England; but my heart can find no other vent.'

'Very pretty! very pretty, indeed, Gentlemen!' said Mrs Maple; 'If you can answer all this to yourselves, well and good; but as I have not quite so easy a conscience, I think it no more than my duty to inform the magistrates myself, of my opinion of this foreigner.'

She was moving off; but the stranger rushed forth, and with an expression of agonized affright, exclaimed, 'Stay! Madam, stay! hear but one word! I am no foreigner, I am English!'—

Equal astonishment now seized every one; but while they stared from her to each other, the Admiral said: 'I am cordially glad to hear it! cordially! though why you should have kept secret a point that makes as much for your honour as for your safety, I am not deep enough to determine. However, I won't decide against you, while I am in the dark of your reasons; though I own I have rather a taste myself for things more above board. But for all that, Ma'am, if I can be of any use to you, make no scruple to call upon me.'

He walked back to the parlour, where all now, except Harleigh, assembled to a general breakfast, of which, during this scene, Riley, for want of an associate, had been doing the honors to himself. The sick lady, Mrs Ireton, was not yet sufficiently recovered to take any refreshment; and the young man, her son, had commanded a repast on a separate table.

Harleigh repeated to the stranger, as she returned, in trembling, to her room, his offer of services.

'If any lady of this party,' she answered, 'would permit me to say a few words to her not quite in public, I should thankfully acknowledge such a condescension. And if you, Sir, to whom already I owe an escape that calls for my eternal gratitude, if you, Sir, could procure me such an audience—'

'What depends upon me shall surely not be left undone,' he replied; and, returning to the parlour, 'Ladies,' he said, 'this person whom we have brought over, begs to speak with one of you alone.'

'Alone!' repeated Mrs Maple, 'How shocking! Who can tell what may be her designs?'

'She means that we should go out to hold a conference with her in the passage, I suppose?' said Mrs Ireton, the sick lady, to whom the displeasure raised by this idea seemed to restore strength and speech; 'or, perhaps, she would be so good as to receive us in the kitchen? Her condescension is really edifying! I am quite at a loss how I shall shew my sense of such affability.'

'What, is that black insect buzzing about us still?' cried her son, 'Why what the deuce can one make of such a grim thing?'

'O, it's my friend the demoiselle, is it?' said Riley; 'Faith, I had almost forgotten her. I was so confoundedly numbed and gnawn, between cold and hunger, that I don't think I could have remembered my father, I don't, faith! before I had recruited. But where's poor demoiselle? What's become of her? She wants a little bleaching, to be sure; but she has not bad eyes; nor a bad nose, neither.'

'I am no great friend to the mystical,' said the Admiral, 'but I promised her my help while she stood in need of my protection, and I have no tide to withdraw it, now that I presume she is only in need of my purse. If any of the ladies, therefore, mean to go to her, I beg to trouble them to carry this.' He put a guinea upon the table.

'Now that she is so ready to tell her story,' said Elinor, 'I am confident that there is none to tell. While she was enveloped in the mystical, as the Admiral phrases it, I was dying with curiosity to make some discovery.'

'O the poor demoiselle!' cried Riley, 'why you can't think of leaving her in the lurch, at last, ladies, after bringing her so far? Come, lend me one of your bonnets and your fardingales, or what is it you call your things? And twirl me a belt round my waist, and something proper about my neck, and I'll go to her myself, as one of your waiting maids: I will, faith!'

'I am glad, at least, niece Elinor, that this once,' said Mrs Maple, 'you are reasonable enough to act a little like me and other people. If you had really been so wild as to sustain so glaring an impostor——'

'If, aunt?—don't you see how I am scalding my throat all this time to run to her?' replied Elinor, giving her hand to Harleigh.

As they re-entered the passage, the stranger, rushing from her room with a look the most scared and altered, exclaimed, that she had lost her purse.

'This is complete!' cried Elinor, laughing; 'and will this, too, Harleigh, move your knight-errantry? If it does—look to your heart! for I won't lose a moment in becoming black, patched, and pennyless!'

She flew with this anecdote to the breakfast parlour; while the stranger, yet more rapidly, flew from the inn to the sea-side, where she carefully retraced the ground that she had passed; but all examination was vain, and she returned with an appearance of increased dismay.

Meeting Harleigh at the door, his expression of concern somewhat calmed her distress, and she conjured him to plead with one of the ladies, to have the charity to convey her to London, and thence to help her on to Brighthelmstone. 'I have no means,' she cried, 'now, to proceed unaided; my purse, I imagine, dropt into the sea, when, so unguardedly! in the dark, I cast there—' She stopt, looked confused, and bent her eyes upon the ground.

'To Brighthelmstone?' repeated Harleigh; 'some of these ladies reside not nine miles from that town. I will see what can be done.'

She merely entreated, she said, to be allowed to travel in their suite, in any way, any capacity, as the lowest of attendants. She was so utterly reduced by this dreadful loss, that she must else beg her way on foot.

Harleigh hastened to execute this commission; but the moment he named it, Elinor called out, 'Do, pray, Mr Harleigh, tell me where you have been secreting your common sense?—Not that I mean to look for it!—'twould despoil me of all the dear freaks and vagaries that give zest to life!'

'Poor demoiselle!' cried Riley, throwing half a crown upon the table, 'she shall not be without my mite, for old acquaintance sake.'

'What! has she caught even you, Mr Cynical Riley?' cried Elinor; 'you, who take as much pleasure in lowering or mortifying your fellow-creatures, as Mr Harleigh does in elevating, or relieving them?'

'Every one after his own fashion, Miss Nelly. The best amongst us has as little taste for being thwarted as the worst. He has, faith! We all think our own way the only one that has any common sense. Mine, is that of a diver: I seek always for what is hidden. What is obvious soon surfeits me. If this demoiselle had named herself, I should never have thought of her again; but now, I'm all agog to find her out.'

'Why does she not say who she is at once?' cried Mrs Maple. 'I give nothing to people that I know nothing of; and what had she to do in France? Why don't she tell us that?'

'Can such a skin, and such a garb, be worth so much breath?' demanded Ireton, taking up a news-paper.

Harleigh enquired of Mrs Ireton, whether she had succeeded in her purposed search, of a young woman to replace the domestic whom she had left in France, and to attend her till she arrived at her house in town.

'No, Sir,' she answered; 'but you don't mean, I presume, to recommend this vagabond to be about my person? I should presume not; I should presume you don't mean that? Not but that I should be very sensible to such a mark of distinction. I hope Mr Harleigh does not doubt that? I hope he does not suspect I should want a proper sensibility to such an honour?'

'If you think her a vagabond, Madam,' replied Harleigh, 'I have not a word to offer: but neither her language nor her manners incline me to that opinion. You only want an attendant till you reach your family, and she merely desires and supplicates to travel free. Her object is to get to Brighthelmstone. And if, by waiting upon you, she could earn her journey to London, Mrs Maple, perhaps, in compassion to her pennyless state, might thence let her share the conveyance of some of her people to Lewes, whence she might easily find means to proceed.'

The two elderly ladies stared at each other, not so much as if exchanging enquiries how to decline, but in what degree to resent this proposition; while Elinor, making Harleigh follow her to a window, said, 'No, do inform me, seriously and candidly, what it is that urges you to take the pains to make so ridiculous an arrangement?'

'Her apparently desolate state.'

'Now do put aside all those fine sort of sayings, which you know I laugh at, and give me, instead, a little of that judgment which you so often quarrel with me for not giving to you; and then honestly tell me, can you really credit that any thing but a female fortune-hunter, would travel so strangely alone, or be so oddly without resource?'

'Your doubts, Elinor, are certainly rational; and I can only reply to them, by saying, that there are now and then uncommon causes, which, when developed, shew the most extraordinary situations to be but their mere simple effect.'

'And her miserable accoutrement?—And all those bruises, or sores, and patches, and bandages?—'

'The detail, I own, Elinor, is unaccountable and ill looking: I can defend no single particular, even to myself; but yet the whole, the all-together, carries with it an indescribable, but irresistible vindication. This is all I can say for befriending her.'

'Nay, if you think her really distressed,' cried Elinor, 'I feel ready enough to be her handmaid; and, at all events, I shall make a point to discover whom and what she may be, that I may know how to value your judgment, in odd cases, for the future. Who knows, Harleigh, but I may have some to propose for your decision of my own?'

The Admiral, after some deliberation, said, that, as it was certainly possible that the poor woman might really have lost her purse, which he, for one, believed to be the simple truth, he could not refuse to help her on to her friends; and, ringing for the landlord, he ordered that a breakfast should be taken to the gentlewoman in the other room, and that a place should be secured for her in the next day's stage to London; for all which he would immediately deposit the money.

'And pray, Mr Landlord,' said Mrs Maple, 'let us know what it was that this body wanted, when she desired to speak with you?'

'She asked me to send and enquire at the Post-office if there were any letter directed for L.S., to be left till called for; and when she heard that there was none, I thought, verily, that she would have swooned.'

Elinor now warmly united with Harleigh, in begging that Mrs Maple would let her servants take charge of the young woman from London to Lewes, when, through the charity of the Admiral, she should arrive in town. Mrs Maple pronounced an absolute negative; but when Elinor, not less absolutely, declared that, in that case, she would hire the traveller for her own maid; and the more readily because she was tired to death of Golding, her old one, Mrs Maple, though with the utmost ill will, was frightened into compliance; and Elinor said that she would herself carry the good news to the Incognita.

The landlord desired to know in what name the place was to be taken.

This, also, Elinor undertook to enquire, and, accompanied by Harleigh, went to the room of the stranger.

They found her standing pensively by the window; the breakfast, which had been ordered for her by the Admiral, untouched.

'I understand you wish to go to Brighthelmstone?' said Elinor.

The stranger courtsied.

'I believe I know every soul in that place. Whom do you want to see there?—Where are you to go?'

She looked embarrassed, and with much hesitation, answered, 'To ... the Post-office, Madam.'

'O! what, you are something to the post-master, are you?'

'No, Madam ... I ... I ... go to the Post-office only for a letter!'

'A letter? Well! an hundred or two miles is a good way to go for a letter!'

'I am not without hopes to find a friend. The letter I had expected here was only to contain directions for the meeting.'

'O! if your letter is to be personified, I have nothing more to say. A man, or a woman?—which is it?'

'A woman, Madam.'

'Well, if you merely wish to go to Brighthelmstone, I'll get you conveyed within nine miles of that place, if you will come to me, at Mrs Maple's, in Upper Brooke-street, when you get to town.'

Surprise and pleasure now beamed brightly in the eyes of the stranger, who said that she should rejoice to pass through London, where, also, she particularly desired to make some enquiries.

'But we have no means for carrying you thither, except by the stage; and one of our gentlemen offers to take a place in it for you.'

The stranger looked towards Harleigh, and confusion seemed added to her embarrassment.

Harleigh hastily spoke. 'It is the old officer, that truly benevolent veteran, who wishes to serve you, and whose services, from the nobleness of his character, confer still more honour than benefit.'

Again she courtsied, and with an air in which Harleigh observed, with respect, not displeasure, her satisfaction in changing the object of this obligation.

'Well, that's settled,' said Elinor; 'but now the landlord wants your name, for taking your place.'

'My place?—Is there no machine, Madam, that sets off immediately?'

'None sooner than to-morrow. What name am I to tell him?'

'None sooner than to-morrow?'

'No; and if you do not give in your name, and secure it, you may be detained till the next day.'

'How very unfortunate!' cried she, walking about the room.

'Well, but what is your name?'

A crimson of the deepest hue forced its way through her dark complexion: her very eyes reddened with blushes, as she faintly answered, 'I cannot tell my name!'

She turned suddenly away, with a look that seemed to expect resentment, and anticipate being abandoned.

Elinor, however, only laughed, but laughed 'in such a sort' as proclaimed triumph over Harleigh, and contempt for the stranger.

Harleigh drew Elinor apart, saying, 'Can this, really, appear to you so ridiculous?'

'And can you, really, Harleigh, be allured by so glaring an adventurer? a Wanderer, without even a name!'

'She is not, at least, without probity, since she prefers any risk, and any suspicion, to falsehood. How easily, otherwise, might she assume any appellation that she pleased!'

'You are certainly bewitched, Harleigh!'

'You are certainly mistaken, Elinor! yet I cannot desert her, till I am convinced that she does not merit to be protected.'

Elinor returned to the stranger. 'You do not chuse, then, to have your place secured?'

'O yes Madam!—if it is impossible for me to attend any lady to town.'

'And what name shall you like for the book-keeper? Or what initials?—What think you of L.S.?'

She started; and Harleigh, again taking Elinor aside, more gravely said, 'Elinor, I am glad I am not—at this moment—my brother!—for certainly I could not forbear quarrelling with you!'

'I heartily wish, then,' cried she, with quickness, 'that, at this moment!—you were your brother!'

Harleigh, now, addressing the stranger, in whose air and manner distress seemed palpably gaining ground, gently said, 'To save you any further trouble, I will take a place in my own name, and settle with the landlord, that, if I do not appear to claim it, it is to be made over to the person who produces this card. The book-keeper shall have such another for a check.'

He put into her hand a visiting ticket, on which was engraven Mr Harleigh, and, not waiting for her thanks, conducted Elinor back to the parlour, saying, 'Pardon me, Elinor, that I have stopt any further enquiries. It is not from a romantic admiration of mystery, but merely from an opinion that, as her wish of concealment is open and confessed, we ought not, through the medium of serving her, to entangle her into the snares of our curiosity.'

'Oh, you are decided to be always right, I know!' cried Elinor, laughing, though piqued; 'and that is the very reason I always hate you! However, you excite my curiosity to fathom her; so let her come to me in town, and I'll take her under my own care, if only to judge your discernment, by finding out how she merits your quixotism.'

Harleigh then returned to the young woman, and hesitatingly said, 'Pardon my intrusion, but—permit me, as you have so unfortunately lost your purse-'

'If my place, Sir,' hastily interrupted the stranger, 'is taken, I can require nothing else.'

'Yet—you have the day to pass here; and you will with difficulty exist merely upon air, even where so delightedly you inhale it; and Miss Joddrel, I fear, has forgotten to bring you the little offering of your veteran friend; therefore—'

'If he has the infinite goodness to intend me any, sir, permit, at least, that he may be my only pecuniary creditor! I shall want no addition of that sort, to remember, gratefully and for ever! to whom it is I owe the deepest obligation of my life!'

Is this a house-maid? thought Harleigh; and again he rejoiced in the perseverance with which he had supported her; and, too much respecting her refusal to dispute it, expressed his good wishes for her welfare, and took leave; yet would not set out upon his journey till he had again sought to interest the old officer in her favour.

The guinea was still upon the tea-table; but the Admiral, who, in the fear of double dealing, had conceived some ideas to the disadvantage of the Incognita, no sooner heard that she had declined receiving any succour except from himself, than, immediately softened, he said that he would take care to see her well treated.

Harleigh then drove after the carriage of Mrs Maple and Elinor, who were already on their way to London.


CHAPTER III

The Admiral immediately repaired to the stranger. 'Young woman,' he cried, 'I hope you don't take it into your mind, that I was more disposed to serve you while I thought you of foreign culture, than now I know you to be of our own growth? If I came forwarder then, it was only because I was afraid that those who have had less occasion than I have had, to get the upper hand of their prejudices, would keep backwarder.'

The stranger bowed her thanks.

'But as to me,' he continued, 'I have had the experience of what it is to be in a strange land; and, moreover, a prisoner: in which time I came to an agreement with myself—a person over whom I keep a pretty tight hand! because why? If I don't the devil will! So I came, I say, to an agreement with myself, to remember all the ill-usage I then met with, as a memento to forbear exciting in others, those black passions which sundry unhandsome tricks excited, in those days, in myself.'

Observing her breakfast to be utterly neglected, he demanded, with an air of some displeasure, whether she had no longing to taste the food of her mother country again?

The fulness of her mind, she answered, had deprived her of appetite.

'Poor girl! poor woman!' cried he, compassionately, 'for I hardly know which to call you, those cap-flounces pon the cheeks making a young woman look no better than an old one. However, be you which you may, I can't consent to see you starve in a land of plenty; which would be a base ingratitude to our Creator, who, in dispensing the most to the upper class; grants us the pleasure of dispensing the overplus, ourselves, to the under class; which I take to be the true reason of Providence for ordering that difference between the rich and the poor; as, most like, we shall all find, when we come to give in our accounts in t'other world.'

He then enquired what it was she intended to do; adding, 'I don't mean as to your secrets, because they are what I have no right to meddle with; though I disapprove your having any, they being of little service, except to keep foul deeds from the light; for what is fair loves to be above board. Besides, as everything is sure to come out, sooner or later, it only breeds suspicion and trouble for nothing, to procrastinate telling to-day with your own free will, what you may be certain will be known to-morrow, or next day, with or without it. Don't be discomposed, however, for I don't say this by way of a sift, nor yet for a reproach; I merely drop it as a piece of advice.'

'And I should be happy, Sir, to endeavour to deserve it, by frankly explaining my situation, but that the least mistake, the smallest imprudence, might betray me to insupportable wretchedness.'

'Why then, if that's the case, you are very right to hold your tongue. If the law never makes a person condemn himself, much less ought a little civility. There are dangers enough in the world without running risks out of mere compliment.'

Then putting his guinea before her, upon the table, he charged her to keep it unbroken till she set out, assuring her that he should himself order whatever she could require for her dinner, supper, and lodging, and settle for the whole with the landlord; as well as with the book-keeper for her journey to London.

The stranger seemed almost overpowered with gratitude; but interrupting what she attempted to say, 'No thankings,' he cried, 'young woman! it's a bad sign when a good turn surprises a person. I have not escaped from such hard fare with my body, to leave my soul behind me; though, God knows, I may forget it all fast enough. There's no great fear of mortal man's being too good.'

Then, wishing her farewell, he was quitting the room, but, thoughtfully turning back, 'Before we part,' he said, 'it will be but Christian-like to give you a hint for your serious profit. In whatever guise you may have demeaned yourself, up to this present date, which is a solution I don't mean to meddle with, I hope you'll always conduct yourself in a becoming manner, for the rest of your days, in remembrance of your great good fortune, in landing safely upon this happy shore.'

He was going, but the Incognita stopt him, and again the dark hue of her skin, was inadequate to disguise the deep blushes that were burning upon her cheeks, as she replied, 'I see, Sir, through all your benevolence, that you believe me to be one of those unhappy persons, whose misfortunes have been the effect of their crimes: I have no way to prove my innocence; and assertion may but make it seem more doubtful; yet—'

'You are right! you are right!' interrupted he; 'I am no abettor of assertions. They are but a sort of cheap coinage, to make right and wrong pass current together.'

'I find I have been too quick,' she answered, 'in thinking myself happy! to receive bounty under so dreadful a suspicion, proves me to be in a desolate state indeed!'

'Young woman,' said the Admiral, in a tone approaching to severity, 'don't complain! We must all bear what we have earned. I can't but see what you are, though it's what I won't own to the rest of the crew, who think a flaw in the character excuse plenty for letting a poor weak female starve alive; for which, to my seeming, they deserve to want a crust of bread themselves. But I hope I know better than that where the main fault is apt to lie; for I am not ignorant how apt our sex is to misbehave to yours; especially in slighting you, if you don't slight them; a thing not to be defended, either to God or man. But for all that, young woman, I must make free to remark, that the devil himself never yet put it into a man's head, nor into the world's neither, to abandon, or leave, as you call it, desolate, a woman who has kept tight to her own duty, and taken a modest care of herself.'

The eyes of the stranger were now no longer bright from their mere natural lustre, nor from the beams of quick surprize, or of sudden vivacity; 'twas with trembling emotion that they shone, and with indignation that they sparkled. She took up the guinea, from which her sight seemed averted with horror, and said, 'Pardon me, Sir, but I must beg you to receive this again.'

'Why, what now? do you think, because I make no scruple to give you an item that I don't fancy being imposed upon; do you think, I say, because of that, I have so little Christian charity, as not to know that you may be a very good sort of woman in the main, for all some flaunty coxcomb may have played the scoundrel, and left you to the wide world, after teaching you to go so awry, that he knows the world will forsake you too? a thing for which, however, he'll pay well in time; as I make no doubt but the devil takes his own notes of all such actions.'

She now cast the guinea upon the table. 'I would rather, Sir,' she cried, 'beg alms of every passenger that I may meet, than owe succour to a species of pity that dishonours me!'

The Admiral looked at her with earnestness. 'I don't well know,' he said, 'what class to put you in; but if you are really a virtuous woman, to be sure I ought to ask your pardon for that little hint I let drop; and, moreover, if I asked it upon my knees, I can't say I should think it would be over-much, for affronting a virtuous woman, without cause. And, indeed, if I were free to confess the truth, I must own there's something about you, which I don't over-much know what to call, but that is so agreeable, that it goes against me to think ill of you.'

'Ah, Sir! think well of me, then!—let your benevolence be as liberal as it is kind, and try, for once, to judge favourably of a stranger upon trust!'

'Well, I will! I will, then! if you have the complaisance to wish for my good opinion, I will!' cried he, nodding, while his eyes glistened; 'though it's not my general method, I can tell you, young woman, to go the direct opposite road to my understanding. But, out of the way as things may look, you seem to me, in the main, to be an innocent person; so pray, Ma'am, don't refuse to accept this little token of my good will.'

The countenance of the stranger exhibited strong indecision. He enjoined her, however, to keep the guinea, and, after struggling vainly to speak, she sighed, and seemed distressed, but complied.

He nodded again, saying, 'Be of good cheer, my dear. Nothing comes of being faint-hearted. I give you my promise I'll see you in town. And, if I find that you turn out to be good; or, moreover, if you turn good, after having unluckily been t'other thing, I'll stand your friend. You may depend upon it.'

With a look of mingled kindness and concern, he then left the room.

And here, shocked, yet relieved, and happy, however forlorn, she remained, till a waiter brought her a fowl, a tart, and a pint of white wine, according to commands issued by the Admiral. She then heard that the whole of the boat-party had set off for London, except Mrs Ireton, the sick lady, who did not think herself sufficiently recovered to travel till the next day, and who had enquired for some genteel young lady to attend her to town; but she was so difficult, the waiter said, to please, that she had rejected half-a-dozen candidates who had been presented to her successively. She seemed very rich, he added, for she ordered things at a great rate, though she found fault with them as fast as they were carried to her; but what had put her the most out of humour of all, was that the young gentleman, her son, had set off without her, in a quarrel: which was not, however, so much to be wondered at, for the maids of the two other ladies said that the gentlewoman was of so aggravating a humour, that nobody could live with her; which had provoked her own woman to leave her short in France, and hire herself to a French lady.

The little repast of the stranger was scarcely over, when the waiter brought her word that the sick lady desired to see her up stairs.

Extremely surprised, she demanded for what purpose.

He answered, that a seventh young person whom he had taken into the lady's room, with an offer to serve her, upon being sharply treated, had as sharply replied; which had so affronted her, that she had ordered that no one else should be brought into her presence; though in two minutes more, she had rung the bell, said she was too ill to be left alone, and bid him fetch her the woman who came over from France.

The stranger, at first, refused to obey this imperious summons; but the wish of placing herself under female protection during her journey, presently conquered her repugnance, and she accompanied the messenger back.

Mrs Ireton was reclining upon an easy chair, still somewhat disordered from her voyage, though by no means as much in need of assistance for her shattered frame, as of amusement for her restless mind.

'So!' she cried, 'you are here still? Pray, if I may ask so confidential a question, what acquaintance may you have found in this inn?—The waiters?—or the grooms?'

'I was told, Madam, that you had some commands for me.'

'O, you are in haste, are you? you want to be shewing off those patches and bandages, perhaps? You won't forget a veil, I hope, to preserve your white skin? Not but 'twould be pity to make any sort of change in your dress, 'tis so prodigiously tasty!'

The stranger, offended, was now moving off, but, calling her back, 'Did not the waiter,' Mrs Ireton demanded, 'give you to understand that I sent for you?'

'Yes, Madam; and therefore—'

'Well, and what do you suppose it was for? To let you open and shut the door, just to give me all the cold wind of the passages? You suppose it was for that, do you? You surmize that I have a passion for the tooth-ache? You conclude that I delight in sneezing?—coughing?—and a stuft-up nose?'

'I am sorry, Madam, '

'Or perhaps you think me so robust, that it would be kind to give me a little indisposition, to prevent my growing too boisterous? You may deem my strength and health to be overbearing? and be so good as to intend making me more delicate? You may be of opinion that it would render me more interesting?'

'Indeed, Madam,'—

'Or, you may fancy that a friendly catarrh might be useful, in furnishing me with employment, from ordering water-gruel, and balm-tea, and barley-water, and filling up my leisure in devising successive slops?'

The difficulty of being heard made the stranger now cease to attempt speaking; and Mrs Ireton, after sundry similar interrogatories, angrily said, 'So you really don't think fit to initiate me into your motives for coming to me, without troubling yourself to learn mine for admitting you into my presence?'

'On the contrary, Ma'am, I desire—'

'O! I am mistaken, am I? It's on the contrary, is it? You are vastly kind to set me right; vastly kind, indeed! Perhaps you purpose to give me a few lessons of behaviour?'

'I am so wholly at a loss, Madam, why I have been summoned, that I can divine no reason why I should stay. I beg, therefore, to take my leave.'

Again she was retreating; but Mrs Ireton, struck by her courage, began to conceive that the mystery of her birth and business, might possibly terminate in a discovery of her belonging to a less abject class than her appearance announced; and therefore, though firmly persuaded that what might be diminished in poverty, would be augmented in disgrace, her desire was so inflamed to develop the secret, that, softening her tone, she asked the young person to take a chair, and then entered into discourse with some degree of civility.

Yet with all this restraint, inflicted upon a nature that, to the privilege of uttering whatever it suggested, claimed that of hearing only what it liked, she could gather no further intelligence, than that the stranger had received private information of the purposed sailing of the vessel, in which they all came over: but her birth, her name, her connexions, her actual situation, and her object in making the voyage, resisted enquiry, eluded insinuation, and baffled conjecture. Nevertheless, her manners were so strikingly elevated above her attire, that, notwithstanding the disdain with which, in the height of her curiosity, Mrs Ireton surveyed her mean apparel, and shrunk from her dusky skin, she gave up her plan of seeking for any other person to wait upon her, during her journey to town, and told the Incognita that, if she could make her dress a little less shocking, she might relinquish her place in the stage-coach, to occupy one in a post-chaise.

To avoid new and untried risks, in travelling wholly alone, the stranger acceded to this proposal; and immediately, by the assistance of the maid of the inn, appropriated the guinea of the Admiral to purchasing decent clothing, though of the cheapest and coarsest texture.

The next morning they set off together for London.


CHAPTER IV

The good understanding with which the eagerness of curiosity on one side, and the subjection of caution on the other, made the travellers begin their journey, was of too frail a nature to be of long endurance. 'Tis only what is natural that flows without some stimulus; what is factitious prospers but while freshly supplied with such materials as gave it existence. Mrs Ireton, when she found that neither questions, insinuations, nor petty artifices to surprise confessions, succeeded in drawing any forth, cast off a character of softness that so little paid the violence which its assumption did her humour; while the stranger, fatigued by finding that not one particle of benevolence, was mixed with the avidity for amusement which had given her a place in the chaise, ceased all efforts to please, and bestowed no further attentions, than such as were indispensably due to the mistress of the vehicle in which she travelled.

At a little distance from Rochester, the chaise broke down. No one was hurt; but Mrs Ireton deemed the mere alarm an evil of the first magnitude; remarking that this event might have brought on her death; and remarking it with the resentment of one who had never yet considered herself as amenable to the payment of that general, though dread debt to nature. She sent on a man and horse for another carriage, and was forced to accept the arm of the stranger, to support her till it arrived. But so deeply was she impressed with her own ideas of the hardships that she endured, that she put up at the first inn, went to bed, sent for an apothecary, and held it to be an indispensable tribute to the delicacy of her constitution, to take it for granted that she could not be removed for some days, without the most imminent hazard to her life.

Having now no other resource, she hung for comfort, as well as for assistance, upon her fellow-traveller, to whom she gave the interesting post of being the repository of all her complaints, whether against nature, for constructing her frame with such exquisite daintiness, or against fate, for its total insensibility to the tenderness which that frame required. And though, from recently quitting objects of sorrow, and scenes of woe, in the dreadful apparel of awful reality, the Incognita had no superfluous pity in store for the distresses of offended self-importance, she yet felt relief from experiencing milder usage, and spared no assiduity that might purchase its continuance.

It was some days before Mrs Ireton thought that she might venture to travel, without appearing too robust. And, in this period, one only circumstance called forth, with any acrimony, the ill humour of her disposition. This was a manifest alteration in the complexion of her attendant, which, from a regular and equally dark hue, appeared, on the second morning, to be smeared and streaked; and, on the third, to be of a dusky white. This failed not to produce sundry inquisitive comments; but they never succeeded in obtaining any explanatory replies. When, however, on the fourth day, the shutters of the chamber, which, to give it a more sickly character, had hitherto been closed, were suffered to admit the sun-beams of a cheerful winter's morning, Mrs Ireton was directed, by their rays, to a full and marvellous view, of a skin changed from a tint nearly black, to the brightest, whitest, and most dazzling fairness. The band upon the forehead, and the patch upon the cheek, were all that remained of the original appearance.

The first stare at this unexpected metamorphosis, was of unmingled amazement; but it was soon succeeded by an expression of something between mockery and anger, evinced, without ceremony or reserve, by the following speech: 'Upon my word, Ma'am, you are a very complete figure! Beyond what I could have conjectured! I own that! I can't but own that. I was quite too stupid to surmize so miraculous a change. And pray, Ma'am, if I may take the liberty to enquire, who are you?'

The stranger looked down.

'Nay, I ought not to ask, I confess. It's very indelicate, I own; very rude, I acknowledge; but, I should imagine, it can hardly be the first time that you have been so good as to pardon a little rudeness. I don't know, I may be mistaken, to be sure, but I should imagine so.'

The Incognita now raised her eyes. A sense of ill treatment seemed to endue her with courage; but her displeasure, which, though not uttered, was not disguised, no sooner reached the observation of Mrs Ireton, than she conceived it to be an insolence to justify redoubling her own.

'You are affronted, I hope, Ma'am? Nay, you have reason enough, I acknowledge; I can't but acknowledge that! to see me impressed with so little awe by your wonderful powers; for 'twas but an hour or two since, that you were the blackest, dirtiest, raggedest wretch I ever beheld; and now—you are turned into an amazing beauty! Your cheeks are all bedaubed with rouge, and you are quite a belle! and wondering, I suppose, that I don't beseech you to sit on the sofa by my side! And, to be sure, it's very ill bred of me: I can't deny that; only as it is one of the rudenesses that I conceive you to have had the goodness to submit to before, I hope you'll forgive it.'

The young woman begged leave to retire, till she should be called for the journey.

'O! what, you have some other metamorphosis to prepare, perhaps? Those bandages and patches are to be converted into something else? And pray, if it will not be too great a liberty to enquire, what are they to exhibit? The order of Maria Theresa? or of the Empress of all the Russias? If I did not fear being impertinent, I should be tempted to ask how many coats of white and red you were obliged to lay on, before you could cover over all that black.'

The stranger, offended and tired, without deigning to make any answer, walked back to the chamber which she had just quitted.

The astonished Mrs Ireton was in speechless rage at this unbidden retreat; yet anger was so inherently a part of her composition, that the sight she saw with the most lively sensation was whatever authorized its vent. She speedily, therefore, dispatched a messenger, to say that she was taken dangerously ill, and to desire that the young woman would return.

The Incognita, helpless for seeking any more genial mode of travelling, obeyed the call, but had scarcely entered the apartment, when Mrs Ireton, starting, and forgetting her new illness, exclaimed, in a powerful voice, 'Why, what is become of your black patch?'

The young woman, hastily putting her hand to her cheek, blushed extremely, while she answered, 'Bless me, it must have dropt off!—I will run and look for it.'

Mrs Ireton peremptorily forbade her to move; and, staring at her with a mixture of curiosity and harshness, ordered her to draw away her hand. She resisted for some time, but, overpowered by authoritative commands, was reduced, at length, to submit; and Mrs Ireton then perceived, that neither wound, scar, nor injury of any sort, had occasioned the patch to have been worn.

The excess of her surprize at this discovery, led her to apprehend some serious imposition. She fearfully, therefore, rose, to ring the bell, still fixing her eyes upon the face of the young woman, who, in her confusion, accidentally touching the bandage which crossed her forehead, displaced it, and shewed that feature, also, as free from any cause for having been bound up, as the cheek.

It was now rather consternation than amazement with which Mrs Ireton was seized, till the augmenting disorder, and increasing colour of her new attendant, changed all fear of any trick into personal pique at having been duped; and she protested that if such beggar-stratagems were played upon her any more, she would turn over the impostor to the master of the inn.

The paleness of terror with which this menace overspread the complexion of the stranger, forced a certain, however unwilling conviction upon the mind of Mrs Ireton, that rouge, at least, was not amongst the artifices of which she had to complain. But, though relieved from her own alarm, by the alarm which she inspired, she was rather irritated than appeased in finding something less to detect, and, scoffingly perusing her face, 'You are a surprising person, indeed!' she cried, 'as surprising a person as ever I had the honour to see! So you had disfigured yourself in that horrid manner, only to extort money from us upon false pretences? Very ingenious, indeed! mighty ingenious, I confess! Why that new skin must have cost you more than your new gown. Pray which did you get the best bargain?'

The stranger did not dare risk any sort of reply.

'O, you don't chuse to tell me? But how could I be so indiscreet as to ask such a thing? Will it be impertinent, too, if I enquire whether you always travel with that collection of bandages and patches? and of black and white outsides? or whether you sometimes change them for wooden legs and broken arms?'

Not a word of answer was returned.

'So you won't tell me that, neither? Nay, you are in the right, I own. What business is it of mine to confine your genius to only one or two methods of maiming or defacing yourself? as if you did not find it more amusing to be one day lame, and another blind; and, to-day, it should seem, dumb? The round must be entertaining enough. Pray do you make it methodically? or just as the humour strikes you?'

A fixed silence still resisted all attack.

'O, I am diving too deeply into the secrets of your trade, am I? Nay, I ought to be contented, I own, with the specimens with which I have already been indulged. You have not been niggardly in varying them. You have been bruised and beaten; and dirty and clean; and ragged and whole; and wounded and healed; and a European and a Creole, in less than a week. I suppose, next, you will dwindle into a dwarf; and then, perhaps, find some surprising contrivance to shoot up into a giantess. There is nothing that can be too much to expect from so great an adept in metamorphoses.'

The pleasure of giving vent to spleen, disguised from Mrs Ireton, that by rendering its malignancy so obvious, she blunted its effect. She continued, therefore, her interrogatories a considerable time, before she discovered, that the stillness with which they were heard was produced by resolution, not awe. Almost intolerably offended when a suspicion of this truth occurred, she assumed a tone yet more imperious. 'So I am not worth an answer? You hold it beneath you to waste your breath upon me? And do you know whom it is you dare treat in this manner? Do you imagine that I am a fellow-adventurer?'

The hand of the young woman was now upon the lock of the door, but there, trembling, it stopt, withheld by a thousand terrors from following its first impulse; and the entrance of a waiter, with information that a chaise was at the door, interrupted any further discourse. The journey was resumed, and the rest of the way was only rendered supportable to the stranger, from the prospect that its conclusion would terminate all intercourse with one who, so wilfully and so wantonly, seemed to revel in her powers of mockery and derision.


CHAPTER V

Upon the entrance of the travellers into London, the curiosity of Mrs Ireton was more than ever inflamed, to find that the journey, with all its delays, was at an end, before she had been able to gratify that insatiable passion in a single point. Yet every observation that she could make tended to redouble its keenness. Neither ill humour nor haughtiness, now the patches and bandages were removed, could prevent her from perceiving that the stranger was young and beautiful; nor from remarking that her air and manner were strikingly distinguished from the common class. One method, however, still remained for diving into this mystery; it was clear that the young woman was in want, whatever else might be doubtful. Mrs Ireton, therefore, resolved to allow no recompense for her attendance, but in consideration of what she would communicate of her history.

At a large house in Grosvenor Square they stopt. Mrs Ireton turned exultingly to the stranger: but her glance met no gratification. The young woman, instead of admiring the house, and counting the number of steps that led to the vestibule, or of windows that commanded a view of the square, only cast her eyes upwards, as if penetrated with thankfulness that her journey was ended.

Surprised that stupidity should thus be joined with cunning, Mrs Ireton now intently watched the impression which, when her servants appeared, would be made by their rich liveries.

The stranger, however, without regarding them, followed their mistress into the hall, which that lady was passing through in stately silence, meaning to confound the proud vagrant more completely, by dismissing her from the best drawing-room; when the words, 'Permit me, Madam, to wish you good morning,' made her look round. She then saw that her late attendant, without waiting for any answer, was tranquilly preparing to be gone. Amazed and provoked, she deigned to call after her, and desired that she would come the next day to be paid.

'I am more than paid already, Madam,' the Incognita replied, 'if my little services may be accepted as cancelling my obligation for the journey.'

She had no difficulty, now, to leave the house without further interruption, so astonished was Mrs Ireton, at what she thought the effrontery of a speech, that seemed, in some measure, to level her with this adventurer; though, in her own despite, she was struck with the air of calm dignity with which it was uttered.

The Wanderer obtained a direction to the house of Mrs Maple, from a servant; and demanded another to Titchfield Street. To the latter she rapidly bent her steps; but, there arrived, her haste ended in disappointment and perplexity. She discovered the apartment in which, with her husband and child, the lady whom she sought had resided; but it was no longer inhabited; and she could not trace whether her friend had set off for Brighthelmstone, or had only changed her lodging. After a melancholy and fruitless search, she repaired, though with feet and a mind far less eager, to Upper Brooke Street, where she soon read the name of Mrs Maple upon the door of one of the capital houses. She enquired for Miss Joddrel, and begged that young lady might be told, that a person who came over in the same boat with her from France, requested the honour of admission.

To this message she presently heard the voice of Elinor, from the landing-place, answer, 'O, she's come at last! Bring her up Tomlinson, bring her up!'

'Yes, Ma'am; but I'll promise you she is none of the person you have been expecting.'

'How can you tell that Tomlinson? What sort of figure is she?'

'As pretty as can be.'

'As pretty as can be, is she? Go and ask her name.'

The man obeyed.

The stranger, disconcerted, answered, 'My name will not be known to Miss Joddrel, but if she will have the goodness to receive, I am sure she will recollect me.'

Elinor, who was listening, knew her voice, and, calling Tomlinson up stairs, and heartily laughing, said, 'You are the greatest fool in the whole world, Tomlinson! It is she! Bid her come to me directly.'

Tomlinson did as he was ordered, but grinned, with no small satisfaction, at sight of the surprise with which, when they reached the landing-place, his young mistress looked at the stranger.

'Why, Tomlinson,' she cried, 'who have you brought me hither?'

Tomlinson smirked, and the Incognita could not herself refrain from smiling, but with a countenance so little calculated to excite distrust, that Elinor, crying, 'Follow me,' led the way into her dressing room.

The young woman, then, with an air that strongly supplicated for indulgence, said, 'I am truly shocked at the strange appearance which I must make; but as I come now to throw myself upon your protection, I will briefly—though I can enter into no detail—state to you how I am circumstanced.'

'O charming! charming!' cried Elinor, clapping her hands, 'you are going, at last, to relate your adventures! Nay, no drawing back! I won't be disappointed! If you don't tell me every thing that ever you did in your life, and every thing that ever you said, and every thing that ever you thought, I shall renounce you!'

'Alas!' answered the Incognita, 'I am in so forlorn a situation, that I must not wonder if you conclude me to be some outcast of society, abandoned by my friends from meriting their desertion, a poor destitute Wanderer, in search of any species of subsistence!'

'Don't be cast down, however,' cried Elinor, 'for I will help you on your way. And yet you have exactly spoken Aunt Maple's opinion of you.'

'And I have no right, I acknowledge, to repine, at least, none for resentment: yet, believe me, Madam, such is not the case! and if, as you have given me leave to hope, you will have the benevolence to permit me to travel in your party, or in whatever way you please, to Brighthelmstone, I may there meet with a friend, under whose protection I may acquire courage to give a more intelligible account of myself.'

A rap at the street door made Elinor ring the bell, and order, that when Mr Harleigh came, he should be shewn immediately up stairs.

Harleigh, presently appearing, looked round the apartment, with striking eagerness, yet evident disappointment; and, slightly bowing to the scarcely noticed, yet marked courtsie of the stranger, said, 'Tomlinson told me that our fellow-traveller was at last arrived?'

Elinor, taking the young woman apart, whispered a hasty injunction that she would not discover herself. Then, addressing Harleigh, 'I believe,' she said, 'you dream of nothing but that dismal Incognita. However, do not fancy you have all the mysterious charmers to yourself. I have one of my own, now; and not such a dingy, dowdy heroine as yours!'

Harleigh turned with quickness to the stranger; but she looked down, and her complexion, and bloom, and changed apparel, made a momentary suspicion die away.

Elinor demanded what news he had gathered of their strayed voyager?

None, he answered; and uneasily added, that he feared she had either lost herself, or been misled, or betrayed, some other way.

'O, pray don't waste your anxiety!' cried Elinor; 'she is in perfect safety, I make no doubt.'

'I should be sorry,' he gravely replied, 'to think you in equal danger.'

'Should you?' cried she in a softened tone; 'should you, Harleigh, be sorry if any evil befel me?'

'But why,' he asked, 'has Tomlinson given me this misinformation?'

'And why, Mr Harleigh, because Tomlinson told you that a stranger was here, should you conclude it could be no other than your black fugitive?'

Again Harleigh turned to the traveller, and fixed his eyes upon her face: the patch, the bandage, the large cap, had hitherto completely hidden its general form; and the beautiful outline he now saw, with so entire a contrast of complexion to what he remembered, again checked, or rather dissolved his rising surmizes.

Elinor begged him to be seated, and to quiet his perturbed spirit.

He took a chair, but, in passing by the young woman, her sex, her beauty, her modest air, gave him a sensation that repelled his using it, and he leant upon its back, looking expressively at Elinor; but Elinor either marked not the hint, or mocked it. 'So you have really,' she said, 'taken the pains to go to that eternal inn again, to enquire after this maimed and defaced Dulcinea? What in the world can have inspired you with such an interest for this wandering Creole?

"Tis not her face does love create,
For there no graces revel.'—

The bell of Mrs Maple now ringing, Elinor made a sign to the Incognita not to avow herself, and flew down stairs to caution Tomlinson to silence.

The chair which Harleigh had rejected for himself, he then offered to the fair unknown. She declined it, but in a voice that made him start, and wish to hear her speak again. His offer then became a request, and she thanked him in a tone that vibrated certainty upon his ears, that it could be no other than the voice of his fellow-voyager.

He now looked at her with an earnest gaze, that seemed nearly to draw his eyes from their sockets. The embarrassment that he occasioned her brought him to his recollection, and, apologising for his behaviour, he added; 'A person—a lady—who accompanied us, not long since, from abroad, had a voice so exactly resembling yours—that I find it rather impossible than difficult not to believe that I hear the same. Permit me to ask—have you any very near relation returned lately from France?'

She blushed, but without replying.

'I fancy,' he cried, 'I must have encountered two sisters?—yet you have some reason, I own, to be angry at such a supposition—such a comparison—'

He paused, and a smile, which she could not repress, forced her to speak; 'By no means!' she cried; 'I know well how good you have been to the person to whom you allude, and I beg you will allow me—in her name—to return you the most grateful acknowledgements.'

Harleigh, now, yet more curiously examining her, said, 'It would not have been easy to have forborne taking an interest in her fate. She was in evident distress, yet never suffered herself to forget that she had escaped from some yet greater. Her mind seemed fraught with strength and native dignity. There was something singular, indescribable, in her manner of supporting the most harassing circumstances. It was impossible not to admire her.'

The blush of the stranger now grew deeper, but she remained silent, till Elinor, re-entering, cried, 'Well, Harleigh, what say you to my new demoiselle? And where would you have looked for your heart, if such had seemed your Dulcinea?'

'I should, perhaps, have been but the safer!' answered he, laughing.

'Pho! you would not make me believe any thing so out of nature, as that, when you were in such a tindery fit as to be kindled by that dowdy, you could have resisted being blown into flames at once by a creature such as this?'

'Man is a perverse animal, Elinor; that which he regards as pointed for his destruction, frequently proves harmless. We are all—boys and libertines alone excepted—upon our guard against beauty; for, as every sense is up in arms to second its assault, our pride takes the alarm, and rises to oppose it. Our real danger is where we see no risk.'

'You enchant me, Harleigh! I am never so delighted as when I hear beauty set at nought—for I always suspect, Harleigh, that you do not think me handsome?'

'If I think you better than handsome, Elinor—'

'Pho! you know there is no such better in nature; at least not in such nature as forms taste in the mind of man; which I certainly do not consider as the purest of its works; though you all hold it, yourselves, to be the noblest. Nevertheless, imagination is all-powerful; if, therefore, you have taken the twist to believe in such sublimity, you may, perhaps, be seriously persuaded, that your heart would have been more stubborn to this dainty new Wanderer than to your own walnut-skinned gypsey.'

'Walnut-skinned?'

'Even so, noble knight-errand, even so! This person whom you now behold, and whom, if we believe our eyes, never met them till within this half hour, if we give credit to our ears, scrambled over with us in that crazy boat from France.'

Harleigh was here summoned to Miss Maple, and Elinor returned to her interrogatories; but the stranger only reverted to her hopes, that she might still depend upon the promised conveyance to Brighthelmstone?

'Tell me, at least, what it was you flung into the sea?'

'Ah, Madam, that would tell everything!'

'You are a most provoking little devil,' cried Elinor, impatiently, 'and I am half tempted to have nothing more to say to you. Give me, however, some account how you managed matters with that sweet tender dove Mrs Ireton.'

The recital that ensued of the disasters, difficulties, and choler of that lady, proved so entertaining to Elinor, that she soon not only renewed her engagement of taking her unknown guest free to Lewes, but joined the warmest assurances of protection. 'Not that we must attempt,' she cried, 'to get rid of the spite of Aunt Maple, for if we do, alter so completely the basis of her composition, that she won't know how to stand upright.'

'But now,' she continued, 'where are you to dine? Aunt Maple is too fusty to let you sit at our table.'

The stranger earnestly solicited permission to eat alone: Elinor consented; assigned her a chamber, and gave orders to Mrs Golding, her own maid, to take care of the traveller.

The repast below stairs was no sooner finished, than Elinor flew back to summon the Incognita to descend for exhibition. 'I have told them all,' she said, 'that you are arrived, though I have revealed nothing of your metamorphosis; and there is a sister of mine, a conceited little thing, who is just engaged to be married, and who is wild to see you; and it is a rule, you know, to deny nothing to a bride elect; probably, poor wretch, because everyone knows what a fair way she is in to be soon denied everything! That quiz, Harleigh, would not stay; and that nothingly Ireton has nearly shrugged his shoulders out of joint, at the very idea of so great a bore as seeing you again. Come, nevertheless; I die to enjoy Aunt Maple's astonishment at your new phiz.'

The stranger sought to evade this request as a pleasantry; but finding that it was insisted upon seriously, protested that she had neither courage nor spirits for being produced as an object of sport.

Elinor now again felt a strong temptation to draw back from her promise; but while, between anger and generosity, she hung suspended, a message arrived from Mrs Maple, to order that the woman from France should be sent to the kitchen.

Elinor, changing the object of her displeasure, now warmly repeated her resolution to support the stranger; and, hastening to the dining-parlour, declared to her aunt, and to the party, that the woman from France should not be treated with indignity; that she was evidently a person who had been too well brought up to be consigned to domestics; and that she herself admired, and would abet her spirit, in refusing to be stared at like a wild beast.

CHAPTER VI

The affairs of Mrs Maple kept her a week longer in London; but the impatience of the Wanderer to reach Brighthelmstone, was compelled to yield to an utter inability of getting thither unaided. During this period, she gathered, from various circumstances, that Elinor had been upon the point of marriage with the younger brother of Harleigh, a handsome and flourishing lawyer; but that repeated colds, ill treated, or neglected, had menaced her with a consumption, and she had been advised to try a change of climate. Mrs Maple accompanied her to the south of France, where she had resided till her health was completely re-established. Harleigh, then, in compliment to his brother, who was confined by his profession to the capital, crossed the Channel to attend the two ladies home. They had already arrived at —— on their return, when an order of Robespierre cast them into prison, whence enormous bribes, successful stratagems, and humane, though concealed assistance from some compassionate inhabitants of the town, enabled them, in common with the Admiral, the Iretons, and Riley, to effect their escape to a prepared boat, in which, through the friendly darkness of night, they reached the harbour of their country and their wishes.

The stranger learnt also from Elinor, by whom secresy or discretion were as carelessly set aside, as by herself they were fearfully practised, that young Ireton, urged by a rich old uncle, and an entailed estate, to an early marriage, after addressing and jilting half the women of England, Scotland, and Ireland, had run through France, Switzerland, and Italy, upon the same errand; yet was returned home heart-whole, and hand-unshackled; but that, she added, was not the extraordinary part of the business, male coquets being just as common, and only more impertinent than female; all that was worth remarking, was his conduct for the last few days. Some accounts which he had to settle with her aunt, had obliged him to call at their house, the morning after their arrival in London. He then saw Selina, Elinor's younger sister, a wild little girl, only fourteen years of age, who was wholly unformed, but with whom he had become so desperately enamoured, that, when Mrs Maple, knowing his character, and alarmed by his assiduities, cautioned him not to make a fool of her young niece, he abruptly demanded her in marriage. As he was very rich, Mrs Maple had, of course, Elinor added, given her consent, desiring only that he would wait till Selina reached her fifteenth birth-day; and the little girl, when told of the plan, had considered it as a frolic, and danced with delight.

During this interval, the time of the stranger was spent in the tranquil employment of needle-work, for which she was liberally supplied with cast-off materials, to relieve her necessities, from the wardrobe of Elinor, through whose powerful influence she was permitted to reside entirely up stairs. Here she saw only her protectress, into whose apartment Mrs Maple did not deign, and no one else dared, to intrude unbidden. The spirit of contradiction, which was termed by Elinor the love of independence, fixed her design of supporting the stranger, to whom she delighted to do every good office which Mrs Maple deemed superfluous, and whom she exulted in thus exclusively possessing, as a hidden curiosity. But when she found that no enquiry produced any communication, and that nothing fresh offered for new defiance to Mrs Maple, a total indifference to the whole business took place of its first energy, and the young woman, towards the end of the week, fell into such neglect that it was never mentioned, and hardly even remembered, that she was an inhabitant of the house.

When the morning, most anxiously desired by herself, for the journey to Lewes, arrived, she heard the family engaged in preparations to set off, yet received no intimation how she was to make one of the party. With great discomfort, though with tolerable patience, she awaited some tidings, till the sound of carriages driving up to the street door, alarmed her with apprehensions of being deserted, and, hastily running down stairs, she was drawn by the voice of Elinor to the door of the breakfast-parlour; but the sound of other voices took from her the courage to open it, though the baggage collected around her shewed the journey so near, that she deemed it unsafe to return to her chamber.

In a few minutes, Harleigh, loaded with large drawings, crossed the hall, and, observing her distress, enquired into its cause.

She wished to speak to Miss Joddrel.

He entered the parlour, and sent out Elinor, who, exclaiming, 'O, it's you, is it? Mercy on me! I had quite forgotten you!—' ran back, crying, 'Aunt, here's your old friend, the grim French voyager! Shall she come in?'

'Come in? What for, Miss Joddrel? Because Mr Harleigh was so kind as to make a hoy of my boat, does it follow that you are to make a booth of my parlour?'

'She is at the door!' said Harleigh, in a low voice.

'Then she is at her proper place; where else should such a sort of body be?'

Harleigh took up a book.

'O, but do let her come in, Aunt, do let her come in!' cried the young Selina. 'I was so provoked at not seeing her the other day, that I could have cried with pleasure! and sister Elinor has kept her shut up ever since, and refused me the least little peep at her.'

The opposition of Mrs Maple only the more strongly excited the curiosity of Selina, who, encouraged by the clamorous approbation of Elinor, flew to the door.

There, stopping short, she called out, 'La! here's nothing but a young woman!—La! Aunt, I'm afraid she's run away!'

'And if she is, Niece, we shall not break our hearts, I hoped not but, if she's decamped, it's high time I should enquire whether all is safe in the house.'

'Decamped?' cried Elinor, 'Why she's at the door! Don't you know her, Aunt? Don't you see her, Ireton?'

The stranger, abashed, would have retreated. Harleigh, raising his eyes from his book, shook his head at Elinor, who, laughing and regardless, seized the hand of the young person, and dragged her into the parlour.

'Who is this?' said Mrs Maple.

'Who, Aunt? Why your memory is shorter than ever! Don't you recollect our dingy French companion, that you took such a mighty fancy to?'

Mrs Maple turned away with angry contempt; and the housekeeper, who had been summoned, appearing, orders were given for a strict examination whether the swarthy traveller, who followed them from France, were gone.

The stranger, changing colour, approached Elinor, and with an air that claimed her protection, said, 'Will you not, Madam, have the goodness to explain who I am?'

'How can I,' cried Elinor, laughing, 'when I don't know it myself?'

Every one stared; Harleigh turned round; the young woman blushed, but was silent.

'If here is another of your Incognitas, Miss Joddrel,' said Mrs Maple, 'I must beg the favour that you'll desire her to march off at once. I don't chuse to be beset by such sort of gentry quite so frequently. Pray, young woman, what is it you want here?'

'Protection, Madam, and compassion!' replied the stranger, in a tone of supplication.

'I protest,' said Mrs Maple, 'she has just the same sort of voice that that black girl had! and the same sort of cant! And pray, young woman, what's your name?'

'That's right, Mrs Maple, that's right!' cried Ireton; 'make her tell her name!'

'To be sure I shall!' said Mrs Maple, seating herself on a sofa, and taking out her snuff-box. 'I have a great right to know the name of a person that comes, in this manner, into my parlour. Why do you not answer, young woman?'

The stranger, looking at Elinor, clasped her hands in act of entreaty for pity.

'Very fine, truly!' said Mrs Maple: 'So here's just the second edition of the history of that frenchified swindler!'

'No, no, Aunt; it's only the sequel to the first part, for it's the same person, I assure you. Did not you come over with us from France, Mademoiselle? In the same boat? and with the same surly pilot?'

The stranger silently assented.

Mrs Maple, now, doubly enraged, interrogated her upon the motives of her having been so disfigured, with the sternness and sharpness of addressing a convicted cheat.

The stranger, compelled to speak, said, with an air of extreme embarrassment, 'I am conscious, Madam, how dreadfully all appearances are against me! Yet I have no means, with any prudence, to enter into an explanation: I dare not, therefore, solicit your good opinion, though my distress is so urgent, that I am forced to sue for your assistance, I ought, perhaps, to say your charity!'

'I don't want,' said Mrs Maple, 'to hear all that sort of stuff over again. Let me only know who you are, and I shall myself be the best judge what should be done for you. What is it, then, once for all, that you call yourself? No prevarications! Tell me your name, or go about your business.'

'Yes, your name! your name!' repeated Elinor.

'Your name! your name!' echoed Selina.

'Your name! your name!' re-echoed Ireton.

The spirits and courage of the stranger seemed now to forsake her; and, with a faultering voice, she answered, 'Alas! I hardly know it myself!'

Elinor laughed; Selina tittered; Ireton stared; the leaves of the book held by Harleigh were turned over with a speed that shewed how little their contents engaged him; and Mrs Maple, indignantly swelling, exclaimed, 'Not know your own name? Why I hope you don't come into my house from the Foundling Hospital?'

Harleigh, throwing down his book, walked hastily to Mrs Maple, and said, in a low voice, 'Yet, if that should be the case, would she be less an object of compassion? of consideration?'

'What your notions may be upon such sort of heinous subjects, Mr Harleigh,' Mrs Maple answered, with a look of high superiority, 'I do not know; but as for mine, I think encouraging things of that kind, has a very immoral tendency.'

Harleigh bowed, not as acquiescent in her opinion, but as declining to argue it, and was leaving the room, when Elinor, catching him by the arm, called out, 'Why, Harleigh! what are you so sour for? Are you, also, angry, to see a clean face, and a clean gown? I'll make the demoiselle put on her plasters and patches again, if that will please you better.'

This forced him to smile and to stay; and Elinor then ended the inquisition, by proposing that the stranger should go to Lewes in the chaise with Golding, her own maid, and Fenn, Mrs Maple's housekeeper.

Mrs Maple protested that she would not allow any such indulgence to an unknown pauper; and Mrs Fenn declared, that there were so many hats, caps, and things of consequence to take care of, that it would be impossible to make room for a mouse.

Elinor, ever alert to carry a disputed point, felt her generosity doubly excited to support the stranger; and, after some further, but overpowered opposition from Mrs Maple, the hats, caps, and things of consequence were forced to submit to inferior accommodation, and the young woman obtained her request, to set off for Sussex, with the housekeeper and Elinor's maid.


CHAPTER VII

The house of Mrs Maple was just without the town of Lewes, and the Wanderer, upon her arrival there, learnt that Brighthelmstone was still eight miles farther. She earnestly desired to go on immediately; but how undertake such a journey on foot, so late, and in the dark month of December, when the night appears to commence at four o'clock in the afternoon? Her travelling companions both left her in the court-yard, and she was fain, uninvited, to follow them to the apartment of the housekeeper; where she was beginning an apology upon the necessity that urged her intrusion, when Selina came skipping into the room.

The stranger, conceiving some hope of assistance from her extreme youth, and air of good humour, besought her interest with Mrs Maple for permission to remain in the house till the next day. Selina carried the request with alacrity, and, almost instantly returning, gave orders to the housekeeper to prepare a bed for her fellow-traveller, in the little room upon the stairs.

The gratitude excited by this support was so pleasant to the young patronness, that she accompanied her protégée to the destined little apartment, superintended all the regulations for her accommodation and refreshments, and took so warm a fancy to her, that she made her a visit every other half-hour in the course of the evening; during which she related, with earnest injunctions to secrecy, all the little incidents of her little life, finishing her narration by intimating, in a rapturous whisper, that she should very soon have a house of her own, in which her aunt Maple would have no sort of authority. 'And then,' added she, nodding, 'perhaps I may ask you to come and see me!'

No one else appeared; and the stranger might tranquilly have passed the night, but from internal disturbance how she should reach Brighthelmstone the following morning, without carriage, friends, money, or knowledge of the road thither.

Before the tardy light invited her to rise the next day, her new young friend came flying into the room. 'I could not sleep,' she cried, 'all last night, for the thought of a play that I am to have a very pretty dress for; and that we have fixed upon acting amongst ourselves; and so I got up on purpose to tell you of it, for fear you should be gone.'

She then read through every word of her own part, without a syllable of any other.

They were both soon afterwards sent for into the parlour by Elinor, who was waiting breakfast for Mrs. Maple, with Harleigh and Ireton. 'My dear demoiselle,' she cried, 'how fares it? We were all so engrossed last night, about a comedy that we have been settling to massacre, that I protest I quite forgot you.'

'I ought only, Madam,' answered the stranger, with a sigh, 'to wonder, and to be grateful that you have ever thought of me.'

'Why what's the matter with you now? Why are you so solemn? Is your noble courage cast down? What are you projecting? What's your plan?'

'When I have been to Brighthelmstone, Madame, when I have seen who—or what may await me there—'

Mrs. Maple, now appearing, angrily demanded who had invited her into the parlour? telling her to repair to the kitchen, and make known what she wanted through some of the servants.

The blood mounted into the cheeks of the Incognita, but she answered only by a distant courtsie, and turning to Elinor and Selina, besought them to accept her acknowledgements for their goodness, and retired.

Selina and Elinor, following her into the ante-room, asked how she meant to travel?

She had one way only in her power; she must walk.

'Walk?' exclaimed Harleigh, joining them, 'in such a season? And by such roads?'

'Walk?' cried Ireton, advancing also, 'eight miles? In December?'

'And why not, gentlemen?' called out Mrs Maple, 'How would you have such a body as that go, if she must not walk? What else has she got her feet for?'

'Are you sure,' said Ireton, 'that you know the way?'

'I was never in this part of the world till now.'

'Ha! Ha! pleasant enough! And what are you to do about money? Did you ever find that purse of yours that you—lost, I think, at Dover?'

'Never!'

'Better and better!' cried Ireton, laughing again, yet feeling for his own purse, and sauntering towards the hall.

Harleigh was already out of sight.

'Pour soul!' said Selina, 'I am sure, for one, I'll help her.'

'Let us make a subscription,' said Elinor, producing half a guinea, and looking round to Mrs Maple.

Selina joined the same sum, full of glee to give, for the first time, as much as her sister.

Mrs Maple clamorously ordered them to shut the parlour door.

With shame, yet joy, the stranger accepted the two half guineas, intimated her hopes that she should soon repay them, repeated her thanks, and took leave.

The sisters would still have detained her, but Mrs Maple peremptorily insisted upon breakfasting without further delay.

The Incognita was proceeding to the housekeeper's room, for a packet of the gifts of Elinor, but she was stopt in the hall by Ireton, who was loitering about, playing with his purse, and jerking and catching it from hand to hand.

'Here, my dear,' he cried, 'look at this, and take what you will from it.'

She coldly thanked him, and, saying that the young ladies had amply supplied her, would have moved on: but he prevented her, repeating his offer, and adding, while with uncontrolled freedom he stared at her, 'How the deuce, with such a pretty face as that, could you ever think of making yourself look such a fright?'

She told him that she was in haste.

'But what was the whim of it?'

She desired him to make way, every moment of day-light being precious to her.

'Hang day-light!' cried he, 'I never liked it; and if you will but wait a few minutes—'

Selina, here, running to call him to breakfast, he finished in a whisper, 'I'll convey you in my own chaise wherever you like to go;' and then, forced to put up his purse, he gallantly handed his fair bride-elect back to the parlour.

The stranger, entering the housekeeper's room, met Harleigh, who seriously remonstrated against her walking project, offering his servant to procure her a post-chaise. The sigh of her negative expressed its melancholy economy, though she owned a wish that she could find some meaner vehicle that would be safe.

Harleigh then disappeared; but, a few minutes afterwards, when she was setting out from the garden-gate, she again met him, and he told her that he was going to order a parcel from a stationer's at Brighthelmstone; and that a sort of chaise-cart, belonging to a farmer just by, would be sent for it, almost immediately. 'I do not recommend,' added he, smiling, 'such a machine for its elegance; and, if you would permit me to offer you one more eligible—'

A grave motion of the head repressed him from finishing his phrase, and he acquainted her that he had just been to the farm, to bespeak a sober driver, with whom he had already settled for his morning's work.

This implied assurance, that he had no plan of following the machine, induced her to agree to the proposition; and, when the little carriage was in sight, he expressed his good wishes that she might find the letter, or the friend, that she desired, and returned to the breakfast parlour.

The length of the way, joined to the dirt of the roads, made her truly sensible of his consideration, in affording her this safe conveyance.

When she arrived at the Post-office, the words, 'Oh, you are come at last!' struck her ear, from the street; but not conceiving herself to be addressed, they failed to catch her attention, till she saw, waiting to give her his hand, while exclaiming, 'What the deuce can have made you so long in coming?' young Ireton.

Far less pleased than surprised, she disengaged herself from him with quickness, and enquired for the post-master.

He was not within.

She was extremely disturbed, and at a loss where to wait, or what to do.

'Why did not you stay for my chaise?' said Ireton. 'When I found that you were gone, I mounted my steed, and came over by a short cut, to see what was become of you; and here you have kept me cooling my heels all this devil of a time. That booby of a driver must have had a taste for being out-crawled by a snail.'

Without answering him, she asked whether there were any clerk at hand, to whom she could apply?

Oh, yes! and she was immediately shewn into an office, and followed, without any ceremony, by Ireton, though she replied not a word to any thing that he said.

A young man here received her, of whom, in a fearful voice, she demanded whether he had any letter directed for L.S., to be left till called for.

'You must make her tell you her name, Sir!' cried Ireton, with an air of importance. 'I give you notice not to let her have her letter, without a receipt, signed by her own hand. She came over with Mrs Maple of Lewes, and a party of us, and won't say who she is. 'T has a very ugly look, Sir!'

The eye of the stranger accused him, but vainly, of cruelty.

The clerk, who listened with great curiosity, soon produced a foreign letter, with the address demanded.

While eagerly advancing to receive it, she anxiously enquired, whether there were no inland letter with the same direction?

None, she was answered.

Ireton then, clapping his hand upon the shoulder of the clerk, positively declared, that he would lodge an information against him, if he delivered any letter, under such circumstances, without a signed receipt.

An almost fainting distress was now visible in the face of the Incognita, as the clerk, surprised and perplexed, said, 'Have you any objection, Ma'am, to giving me your name?'

She stammered, hesitated, and grew paler, while Ireton smiled triumphantly, when the party was suddenly joined by Harleigh.

Ireton ceased his clamour, and hung back, ashamed.

Harleigh, approaching the stranger, with an apology for his intrusion, was struck with her disordered look, and enquired whether she were ill?

'Ah, Sir!' she cried, reviving with hope at his sight, and walking towards the window, whither, wondering, he followed, 'assist me in mercy!—you know, already, that some powerful motive deters me from naming myself—'

'Have I been making any indiscreet enquiry?' cried he, gently, yet in a tone of surprise.

'You? O no! You have been all generosity and consideration!'

Harleigh, much gratified, besought her to explain herself with openness.

'They insist upon my telling my name—or they detain my letter!'

'Is that all?' said he, and, going to the clerk, he demanded the letter, for which he gave his own address and receipt, with his word of honour that he was authorised to require it by the person to whom it was written.

He then delivered it into her hand.

The joy of its possession, joined to the relief from such persecution, filled her with a delight which, though beaming from all her features, she had not yet found words to express, when Ireton, whom Harleigh had not remarked, burst into a significant, though affected laugh.

'Why, Harleigh! why, what the deuce can have brought you hither?' cried he. Harleigh wished to retort the question; but would not hazard a raillery that might embarrass the stranger, who now, with modest grace, courtsied to him; while she passed Ireton without notice, and left the room.

Each wished to follow her, but each was restrained by the other. Ireton, who continued laughing maliciously, owned that his journey to Brighthelmstone had been solely to prevail with the clerk to demand the name of the stranger, before he gave up the letter; but Harleigh protested that he had merely ridden over to offer his mediation for her return to Lewes, if she should miss the friend, or letter, of which she came in search.

Ireton laughed still more; and hoped that, from such abundant charity, he would attribute his own ride, also, to motives of as pure benevolence. He then begged he might not interfere with the following up of so charitable a purpose: but Harleigh assured him that he had neither right, pretension, nor design to proceed any farther.

'If that's the case,' cried Ireton, 'since charity is the order of the day, I'll see what is become of her myself.'

He ran out of the room.

Harleigh, following, soon joined him, and they saw the Incognita enter a milliner's shop. They then separated; Harleigh pleading business for not returning immediately to Lewes; while Ireton, mounting his horse, with an accusing shake of the head, rode off.

Harleigh strolled to the milliner's, and, enquiring for some gloves, perceived, through the glass-door of a small parlour, the stranger reading her letter.

He begged that the milliner would be so good as to tell the lady in the inner room, that Mr Harleigh requested to speak to her.

A message thus open could neither startle nor embarrass her, and he was instantly admitted.

He found her pale and agitated. Her letter, which was in her hand, she hastily folded, but looked at nothing else, while she waited an explanation of his visit.

'I could not,' he said, 'go back to Lewes without knowing whether your expectations are answered in coming hither; or whether you will permit me to tell the Miss Joddrels that they may still have the pleasure to be of some use to you.'

She appeared to be unable to speak.

'I fear to seem importunate,' he continued, 'yet I have no intention, believe me, to ask any officious questions. I respect what you have said of the nature of your situation, too much to desire any information beyond what may tend to alleviate its uneasiness.'

She held her hands before her eyes, to hide her fresh gushing tears, but they trickled fast through her fingers, as she answered, 'My situation is now deplorable indeed!—I have no letter, no direction from the person whom I had hoped to meet; and whose abode, whose address, I know not how to discover! I must not apply to any of my original friends: unknown, and in circumstances the most strange, if not suspicious, can I hope to make myself any new ones?—Can I even subsist, when, though thus involved in mystery, I am as indigent as I am friendless, yet dare not say who, nor what I am, and hardly even know it myself!'

Touched with compassion, he drew nearer to her, meaning, from an almost unconscious impulse of kindness, to take her hand; but feeling, with equal quickness, the impropriety of allowing his pity such a manifestation, he retreated to his first place, and, in accents of gentle, but respectful commiseration, expressed his concern for her distress.

Somewhat soothed, yet heavily sighing, 'To fail finding,' she said, 'either the friend, or her direction, that I expected, overwhelms me with difficulty and perplexity. And even this letter from abroad, though most welcome, has grievously disappointed me! I am promised, however, another, which may bring me, perhaps, happier tidings. I must wait for it patiently; but the person from whom it comes little imagines my destitute state! The unfortunate loss of my purse makes it, by this delay of all succour, almost desperate!'

The hand of Harleigh was involuntarily in his pocket, but before he could either draw out his purse, or speak, she tremulously added, colouring, and holding back, 'I am ashamed to have mentioned a circumstance, which seems to call for a species of assistance, that it is impossible I should accept.'

Harleigh bowed, acquiescent.

Her eyes thanked him for sparing her any contest, and she then gratefully acceded to his proposal, of soliciting for her the renewed aid and countenance of the Miss Joddrels, from whom some little notice might be highly advantageous, in securing her decent treatment, during the few days, perhaps more, that she might be kept waiting at Brighthelmstone for another letter.

He gently exhorted her to re-animate her courage, and hoped to convince her, by the next morning, that he had not intruded upon her retirement from motives of idle and useless curiosity.

As soon as he was gone, she treated with Miss Matson, the milliner, to whom Harleigh had considerately named her as a young person known to Mrs Maple, for a small room in her house during a few days; and then, somewhat revived, she endeavoured, by recollecting the evils which she had escaped, to look forward, with better hopes of alleviation, to those which might yet remain to be encountered.


CHAPTER VIII

The next morning, the Wanderer had the happy surprise of seeing Elinor burst into her chamber. 'We are all on fire,' she cried, 'at our house, so I am come hither to cool myself. Aunt Maple and I have fought a noble battle; but I have won the day.'

She then related, that Harleigh had brought them an account of her disappointments, her letter, her design to wait for another, and her being at the milliner's. 'Aunt Maple,' she continued, 'treated the whole as imposition; but I make it a rule never to let her pitiful system prevail in the house. And so, to cut the matter short, for I hate a long story, I gave her to understand, that, if she would not let you return to Lewes, and stay with us till your letter arrives, I should go to Brighthelmstone myself, and stay with you. This properly frightened her; for she knew I would keep my word.'

'And would you, Madam?' said the stranger, smiling.

'Why not? Do you think I would not do a thing only because no one else would do it? I am never so happy as in ranging without a guide. However, we came to a compromise this morning; and she consents to permit your return, provided I don't let you enter her chaise, and engage for keeping you out of every body's way.'

The stranger, evidently hurt and offended, declined admission upon such terms. Her obligations, she said, were already sufficiently heavy, and she would struggle to avoid adding to their weight, and to supply her own few wants herself, till some new resource might open to her assistance.

Elinor, surprised, hastily demanded whether she meant to live alone, that she might only be aided, and only be visited by Mr Harleigh.

The stranger looked all astonishment.

'Nay, that will certainly be the most pleasant method; so I don't affect to wonder at it; nevertheless—'

She hesitated, but her face was tinted with a glow of disturbance, and her voice announced strong rising emotion, as she presently added, 'If you think of forming any attachment with that man—' She stopt abruptly.

The heightened amazement of the stranger kept her for a few instants speechless; but the troubled brow of Elinor soon made her with firmness and spirit answer, 'Attachment? I protest to you, Madam, except at those periods when his benevolence or urbanity have excited my gratitude, my own difficulties have absorbed my every thought!'

'I heartily congratulate your apathy!' said Elinor, her features instantly dilating into a smile; 'for he is so completely a non-descript, that he would else incontestably set you upon hunting out for some new Rosamund's Pond. That is all I mean.'

She then, but with gaiety and good humour, enquired whether or not the stranger would return to Lewes.

Nothing, to the stranger, could be less attractive at this moment; yet the fear of such another misinterpretation and rebuff, and the unspeakable dread of losing, in her helpless situation, all female countenance, conquered her repugnance.

Elinor then said that she would hurry home, and send off the same elegant machine from the farm, which, she found, had been made use of in her service the preceding day.

Far from exhilarated was the young person whom she left, who, thus treated, could scarcely brook the permission to return, which before she would have solicited. Small are the circumstances which reverse all our wishes! and one hour still less resembles another in our feelings, than in our actions.

Upon arriving again at the house of Mrs Maple, she was met by Selina, who expressed the greatest pleasure at her return, and conducted her to the little room which she had before occupied; eagerly announcing that she had already learnt half her part, which she glibly repeated, crying, 'How lucky it is that you are come back; for now I have got somebody to say it to!'

Mrs Maple, she added, had refused her consent to the whole scheme, till Elinor threatened to carry it into execution in Farmer Gooch's barn, and to invite all the county.

She then entered into sundry details of family secrets, the principal of which was, that she often thought that she should be married before her sister Elinor, though Sister Elinor was twenty-two years old, and she herself was only fourteen: but Sister Elinor had had a violent quarrel with Mr Dennis Harleigh, whom she had been engaged to marry before she went abroad, about the French Revolution, which Sister Elinor said was the finest thing in the world, but which Mr Dennis said was the very worst. But, for all that, he loved her so, that he had made his brother fetch her home, and wanted the marriage to take place directly: and Aunt Maple wished it too, of all things, because Sister Elinor was so hard to manage; for, now she was of age, she did everything that she liked; and she protested that she would not give her consent, unless Mr Dennis promised to change his opinion upon the French Revolution; so they quarrelled again the day before they left town; and Aunt Maple, quite frightened, invited Mr Harleigh, the elder brother, to come and spend a week or two at Lewes, to try to bring matters round again.

These anecdotes were interrupted by the appearance of Elinor, of whom the Incognita entreated, and obtained, permission to reside, as in town, wholly in her own room.

'I wish you could hear,' said Elinor, 'how we all settle your history in the parlour. No two of us have the same idea of whom or what you are.' She then entered upon the subject of the play, which was to be the Provoked Husband, in compliment to Miss Arbe, a young lady of celebrated talents, who, having frequently played the part of Lady Townly, with amazing applause, at private theatres, had offered her services for that character, but would study no other. This, Elinor complained, was singularly provoking, as Harleigh, who alone of the whole set was worth acting with, must necessarily be Lord Townly. However, since she could not try her own theatrical skill, by the magnetizing powers of reciprocated exertions, she determined, in relinquishing what was brilliant, to adopt at least what was diverting; for which reason she had taken the part of Lady Wronghead. Selina was to be Miss Jenny; Ireton, 'Squire Richard; and she had pitched upon Mr Scope and Miss Bydel, two famous, formal quizzes, residing in Lewes, to compliment them with the fogrum parts of Manly and Lady Grace; characters which always put the audience to sleep; but that, as they were both good sort of souls, who were never awake themselves, they would not find out. The other parts she had chiefly arranged for the pleasure of giving a lesson of democracy to Aunt Maple; for she had appointed Sir Francis Wronghead to Mr Stubbs, an old steward belonging to Lord Rockton; Count Basset to young Gooch, a farmer's son; Myrtylla to Golding, her own maid, and John Moody to Tomlinson, the footman.

The air of attention with which the stranger listened, whether she answered or not, renewed again in Elinor the pleasure which she had first found in talking to her; and thus, between the two sisters, she had almost constantly a companion till near midnight.

To be left, then, alone was not to be left to unbroken slumbers. She had no dependence, nor hope, but in an expected second letter, yet had devised no means to secure its immediate reception, even if its quick arrival corresponded with her wishes. As soon, therefore, as she heard the family stirring the next morning, she descended, with an intention of going to the housekeeper's room, to make some arrangement for that purpose.

Ireton, who caught a glimpse of her upon the stairs, met and stopt her. 'My dear,' he cried, 'don't think me such a prig as to do you any mischief; but take a hint! Don't see quite so much of a certain young lady, whom I don't wish should know the world quite so soon! You understand me, my dear?'

Inexpressibly offended, she was contemptuously shrinking from him, when they were joined by Harleigh, who asked, with an air of respect that was evidently meant to give a lesson to Ireton, whether she would permit him to call at the post-office, to order that her letters should be forwarded to Lewes.

This offer was irresistible, and, with looks of the brightest gratitude, she was uttering her acknowledgements, when the voice of Elinor, from a distance, sounding tremulous and agitated, checked her, and she hastily retreated.

But her room-door was only shut to be almost instantly thrown open by Elinor herself, who, entering with a large parcel in her hands, while her face shewed pain and disorder, said, 'See how I have been labouring to assist and to serve you, at the very moment of your insidious duplicity!'

Thunderstruck by the harshness of an attack nearly as incomprehensible as it was vehement, the stranger fixed her eyes upon her accuser with a look that said, Are you mad?

The silent, yet speaking expression was caught by Elinor, who, struck with sudden shame, frankly begged her pardon; and, after a little reflexion, coolly added, 'You must never mind what I say, nor what I do; for I sport all sort of things, and in all sort of manners. But it is merely to keep off stagnation: I dread nothing like a lethargy. But pray what were you all about just now?'

The Incognita related her intended purpose; its interruption; the offer of Mr Harleigh; and its acceptance.

Elinor looked perturbed again, and said, 'You seem mighty fond, methinks, of employing Mr Harleigh for your Mercury!'

'He is so good as to employ himself. I could never think of taking such a liberty.'

Elinor put up her lip; but told her to make what use she could of the parcel, and, with an abrupt 'Good morning,' went down to breakfast.

The stranger, amazed and confounded, remained for some time absorbed by conjectures upon this scene.

The parcel contained cast-off clothes of almost every description; but, much as she required such aid, the manner in which it was offered determined her upon its rejection.

In a few hours, the maid who brought her meals, was desired by Mr Harleigh to inform her, that he had executed her commission at the post-office.

This assurance revived her, and enabled her to pass the day in tolerable tranquillity, though perfectly alone, and without any species of employment to diversify her ruminations, or help to wear away the tediousness of expectation.

When the next day, however, and the next, passed without her seeing any of the family, she felt disconcerted and disturbed. To be abandoned by Elinor, and even by Selina, made her situation appear worse than forlorn; and her offended spirit deemed the succour thus afforded her, inadequate to compensate for the endurance of universal disesteem and avoidance. She determined, therefore, to quit the inhospitable mansion, persuaded that no efforts could be too difficult, no means too laborious, that might rescue her from an abode which she could no longer inhabit, without seeming to herself to be degraded.

But the idea of this project had a facility of which its execution did not partake. She had no money, save what she had received from the two sisters; even that, by a night and day spent at the milliner's, was much diminished. She could not quit the neighbourhood of Brighthelmstone, while still in expectation of a letter; and if, while awaiting it in any other house, the compassion, or the philanthropy of Harleigh should urge him to see her, might not Elinor conclude that she had only retreated to receive his visits alone?

Apprehensions such as these frightened her into forbearance: but in teaching her prudence, they did not endow her with contentment. Her hours lingered in depression and uncertainty; her time was not employed but consumed; her faculties were not enjoyed, but wasted.

Yet, upon more mature reflexion, she enquired by what right she expected kinder treatment. Unknown, unnamed, without any sort of recommendation, she applied for succour, and it was granted her: if she met with the humanity of being listened to, and the charity of being assisted, must she quarrel with her benefactors, because they gave not implicit credit to the word of a lonely

Wanderer for her own character? or think herself ill used that their donations and their aid were not delicate as well as useful?

This sober style of reasoning soon chased away resentment, and, with quieter nerves, she awaited some termination to her suspence and solitude.

Meantime, most of the other inhabitants of the house, were engaged by studying their parts for the intended representation, which so completely occupied some by choice, and others by complaisance, or necessity, that no visit or excursion was made abroad, till several days after their arrival at Lewes. Mrs Maple then, with her whole party, accepted an invitation to dine and spend the evening with the family of their principal actress, Miss Arbe; but a sudden indisposition with which that lady was seized after dinner, forced them home again early in the evening. Their return being unexpected, the servants were all out, or out of the way, but, entering by a door leading from the garden, which they found open, they were struck with the sound of music. They stopped, and distinctly heard a harp; they listened, and found that it was played with uncommon ability.

"Tis my harp!' cried Selina, 'I am sure of that!'

'Your harp?' said Mrs Maple; 'why who can be playing it?'

'Hist! dear ladies,' said Harleigh; "tis some exquisite performer.'

'It must be Lady Kendover, then,' said Mrs Maple, 'for nobody else comes to our house that plays the harp.'

A new movement was now begun; it was slow and pathetic, and played with so much taste and expression, though mixed with bursts of rapid execution, that the whole auditory was equally charmed and surprized; and every one, Mrs Maple herself not excepted, with uplifted finger seemed to beseech attention from the rest.

An Arpeggio succeeded, followed by an air, which produced, alternately, tones sweet, yet penetrating, of touching pathos or impassioned animation; and announced a performer whom nature had gifted with her finest feelings, to second, or rather to meet the soul-pervading refinements of skilful art.

When the voice ceased, the harp was still heard; but some sounds made by an involuntary, though restrained tribute of general approbation, apparently found their way to the drawing-room, where it was played; for suddenly it stopped, the instrument seemed hastily to be put away, and some one was precipitately in motion.

Everybody then hastened up stairs; but before they could reach the landing-place, a female figure, which they all instantly recognized for that of the unknown young woman, glided out of the drawing-room, and, with the quick motion of fear, ran up another flight of stairs.

'Amazing!' cried Mrs Maple, stopping short; 'could any body have credited assurance such as this? That bold young stroller has been obtruding herself into my drawing-room, to hear Lady Kendover play!'

Harleigh, who had contrived to be the first to enter the apartment, now returned to the door, and, with a smile of the most animated pleasure, said, 'No one is here!—Not a creature!'

His tone and air spoke more than his words, and, to the quick conceptions of Elinor, pronounced: This divine singer, whom you were all ready to worship, is no other than the lonely Wanderer whom you were all ready to condemn!

Mrs Maple now, violently ringing the bell, ordered one of her servants to summon the woman who came from abroad.

The stranger obeyed, with the confused look of a person who expected a reprimand, to which she had not courage to reply.

'Be so good as to tell me,' said Mrs Maple, 'what you have been into my drawing-room for? and whether you know who it is, that has taken the liberty to play upon my niece's harp?'

The Incognita begged a thousand pardons, but said that having learnt, from the house-maid, that the family was gone out for the day, she had ventured to descend, to take a little air and exercise in the garden.

'And what has that to do with my niece's harp?—And my drawing-room?'

'The door, Madam, was open. It was long since I had seen an instrument—I thought no one would hear me—'

'Why you don't pretend that it was you who played?'

The young woman renewed her apology.

'You?—You play upon a harp?—And pray who was it that sung?'

The stranger looked down.

'Well, this is surprising indeed!—And pray where might such a body as you learn these things?—And what use can such a body want them for? Be so good as to tell me that; and who you are?'

The stranger, in the utmost disturbance, painfully answered, 'I am truly ashamed, Madam, so often to press for your forbearance, but my silence is impelled by necessity! I am but too well aware how incomprehensible this must seem, but my situation is perilous—I cannot reveal it! I can only implore your compassion!—'

She retired hastily.

No one pursued nor tried to stop her. All, except Harleigh, remained nearly stupified by what had passed, for no one else had ever considered her but as a needy travelling adventurer. To him, her language, her air, and her manner, pervading every disadvantage of apparel, poverty, and subjection, had announced her, from the first, to have received the education, and to have lived the life of a gentlewoman; yet to him, also, it was as new, though not as wonderful, as to the rest, to find in her all the delicately acquired skill, joined to the happy natural talents, which constitute a refined artist.

Elinor seemed absorbed in mortification, not sooner to have divined what Harleigh had so immediately discovered; Selina, triumphant, felt enchanted with an idea that the stranger must be a disguised princess; Mrs Maple, by a thousand crabbed grimaces, shewed her chagrin, that the frenchified stroller should not rather have been detected as a positive vagabond, then proved, by her possession of cultivated talents, to have been well brought up; and Ireton, who had thought her a mere female fortune-hunter, was utterly overset, till he comforted himself by observing, that many mere adventurers, from fortuitous circumstances, obtain accomplishments that may vie, in brilliancy, with those acquired by regular education and study.

Doubts, however, remained with all: they were varied, but not removed. The mystery that hung about her was rather thickened than cleared, and the less she appeared like an ordinary person, the more restless became conjecture, to dive into some probable motive, for the immoveable obstinacy of her concealment.

The pause was first broken by Elinor, who, addressing Harleigh, said, 'Tell me honestly, now, what, all together, you really and truly think of this extraordinary demoiselle?'

'I think her,' answered he, with readiness, 'an elegant and well bred young woman, under some extraordinary and inexplicable difficulties: for there is a modesty in her air which art, though it might attain, could not support; and a dignity in her conduct in refusing all succour but yours, that make it impossible for me to have any doubt upon the fairness of her character.'

'And how do you know that she refuses all succour but mine? Have you offered her yours?'

'She will not let me go so far. If she perceive such an intention, she draws back, with a look that would make the very mentioning it insolent.'

Elinor ran up stairs.

She found the stranger disturbed and alarmed, though she was easily revived upon seeing Elinor courteous, almost respectful; for, powerfully struck by a discovery, so completely accidental, of talents so superior, and satisfied by the assurance just received from Harleigh, that his pecuniary aid had never been accepted, she grew ashamed of the angry flippancy with which she had last quitted the room, and of the resolute neglect with which she had since kept aloof. She now apologized for having stayed away, professed a design to be frequent in her future visits, and presented, with generous importunity, the trifles which she blushed to have offered so abruptly.

Addressed thus nearly upon equal terms, the stranger gracefully accepted the donation, and, from the relief produced by this unexpected good treatment, her own manners acquired an ease, and her language a flow, that made her strikingly appear to be what Harleigh had called her, a well bred and elegant young woman; and the desire of Elinor to converse with her no longer hung, now, upon the mere stimulus of curiosity; it became flattering, exhilarating, and cordial.

The stranger, in return, upon nearer inspection, found in Elinor a solid goodness of heart, that compensated for the occasional roughness, and habitual strangeness of her manners. Her society was gay and original; and, to great quickness of parts, and liberality of feeling, she joined a frankness of character the most unbounded. But she was alarming and sarcastic, aiming rather to strike than to please, to startle than to conquer. Upon chosen and favourite subjects she was impressive, nay eloquent; upon all others she was careless, flighty, and indifferent, and constantly in search of matter for ridicule: yet, though severe, almost to ferocity, where she conceived herself to be offended, or injured, she became kind, gentle, and generously conceding, when convinced of any errour.

Selina, when her sister retired, tripped fleetly into the chamber, whisperingly revealing, that it was Mr Ireton who had persuaded her to relinquish her visits; but that she would now make them as often as ever.

Thus supported and encouraged, the stranger, again desiring to stay in the house, earnestly wished to soften the ill will of Mrs Maple; and having heard, from Selina, that the play occupied all hands, she begged Mrs Fenn to accept her services at needle-work.

Mrs Fenn conveyed the proposal to her mistress, who haughtily protested that she would have nothing done under her roof, by she did not know who; though she tacitly suffered Mrs Fenn to try the skill of the proposer with some cambric handkerchiefs.

These she soon returned, executed with such admirable neatness, that Mrs Fenn immediately found her other similar employment; which she presented to her with the air of conferring the most weighty of obligations.

And such, in the event, it proved; for she now continued to receive daily more business of the same sort, without any hint relative to her departure; and heard, through Selina, that Mrs Maple herself had remarked, that this was the first singer and player she had ever known, who had not been spoilt by those idle habits for a good huswife.

The Incognita now thankfully rejoiced in the blessing bestowed upon her, by that part of her education, which gave to her the useful and appropriate female accomplishment of needle-work.


CHAPTER IX

Mrs Maple was of opinion, that every woman ought to live with a needle and thread in her hand; the stranger, therefore, had now ample occupation; but as labour, in common with all other evils, is relative, she submitted cheerfully to any manual toil, that could rescue her from the mental burthen of exciting ill will and reproach.

Two days afterwards, Elinor came to summon her to the drawing-room. They were all assembled, she said, to a rehearsal, and in the utmost confusion for want of a prompter, not a soul, except Miss Arbe, knowing a word, or a cue, of any part but his own; and Miss Arbe, who took upon her to regulate everything, protested that she could not consent to go on any longer in so slovenly a manner.

In this dilemma it had occurred to Elinor to have recourse to the stranger; but the stranger desired to be excused: Mrs Maple seemed now to be softened in her favour; and it would be both imprudent and improper to risk provoking fresh irritation, by coming forward in an enterprise that was a known subject of dissention.

Elinor, when she had formed a wish, never listened to an objection. 'What an old fashioned style you prose in!' she cried; 'who could believe you came so lately from France? But example has no more force without sympathy, than precept had without opinion! However, I'll get you a licence from Aunt Maple in a minute.'

She went down stairs, and, returning almost immediately, cried, 'Aunt Maple is quite contented. I told her I was going to send for Mr Creek, a horrible little pettifogging wretch, who lives in this neighbourhood, and whom she particularly detests, to be our prompter; and this so woefully tormented her, that she proposed you herself. I have ample business upon my hands, between my companions of the buskin, and this pragmatical old aunt; for Harleigh himself refused to act against her approbation, till I threatened to make over Lord Townly to Sir Lyell Sycamore, a smart beau at Brighthelmstone, that all the mammas and aunts are afraid of. And then poor aunty was fain, herself, to request Harleigh to take the part. I could manage matters no other way.'

Personal remonstrances were vain, and the stranger was forced down stairs to the theatrical group.

All that was known of her situation having been sketched by Elinor, and detailed by Selina, the mixt party there assembled, was prepared to survey her with a curiosity which she found extremely abashing. She requested to have the book of the play; but Elinor, engaged in arranging the entrances and exits, did not heed her. Harleigh, however, comprehending the relief which any occupation for the eyes and hands might afford her, presented it to her himself.

It preserved her not, nevertheless, from a volley of questions, with which she was instantly assailed from various quarters. 'I find Ma'am, you are lately come from abroad,' said Mr Scope, a gentleman self-dubbed a deep politician, and who, in the most sententious manner, uttered the most trivial observations: 'I have no very high notion, I own, of the morals of those foreigners at this period. A man's wife and daughters belong to any man who has a taste to them, as I am informed. Nothing is very strict. Mr Robertspierre, as I am told, is not very exact in his dealings.'

'But I should like to know,' cried Gooch, the young farmer, 'whether it be true, of a reality, that they've got such numbers and numbers, and millions and millions of red-coats there, all made into generals, in the twinkling, as one may say, of an eye?'

'Money must be a vast scarce commodity there,' said Mr Stubbs, the steward: 'did you ever happen to hear, Ma'am, how they go to work to get in their rents?'

Before the stranger could attempt any reply to these several addresses, Miss Arbe, who was the principal person of the party, seating herself in the chair of honour, desired her to advance, saying, 'I understand you sing and play amazingly well. Pray who were your masters?'

While the Incognita hesitated, Miss Bydel, a collateral and uneducated successor to a large and unexpected fortune, said, 'Pray, first of all, young woman, what took you over to foreign parts? I should like to know that.'

Elinor, now, being ready, cut short all further investigation by beginning the rehearsal.

During the first scenes, the voice of the Incognita was hardly audible. The constraint of her forced attendance, and the insurmountable awkwardness of her situation, made all exertion difficult, and her tones were so languid, and her pronunciation was so inarticulate, that Elinor began seriously to believe that she must still have recourse to Mr Creek. But Harleigh, who reflected how much the faculties depend upon the mind's being disengaged, saw that she was too little at her ease to be yet judged.

Everyone else, absorbed in his part and himself, in the hope of being best, or the shame of being worst; in the fear of being out, or the confusion of not understanding what next was to be done, was regardless of all else but his own fancied reputation of the hour.

Harleigh, however, as the play proceeded, and the inaccuracy of the performers demanded greater aid, found the patience of his judgment recompensed, and its appreciation of her talents just. Her voice, from seeming feeble and monotonous, became clear and penetrating: it was varied, with the nicest discrimination, for the expression of every character, changing its modulation from tones of softest sensibility, to those of archest humour; and from reasoning severity, to those of uncultured rusticity.

When the rehearsal was over, Miss Bydel, who had no other idea of the use of speech than that of asking questions, said, 'I should be glad, before you go, to say a few words to you, young woman, myself.'

The stranger stood still.

'In the first place, tell me, if you please, what's your name?'

The Incognita coloured at this abrupt demand, but remained silent.

'Nay,' said Miss Bydel, 'your name, at least, can be no such great secret, for you must be called something or other.'

Ireton, who had hitherto appeared decided not to take any notice of her, now exclaimed, with a laugh, 'I will tell you what her name is, Miss Bydel; 'tis L.S.'

The stranger dropt her eyes, but Miss Bydel, not comprehending that Ireton meant two initial letters, said. 'Elless? Well I see no reason why anybody should be ashamed to own their name is Elless.'

Selina, tittering, would have cleared up the mistake; but Ireton, laughing yet more heartily, made her a sign to let it pass.

Miss Bydel continued: 'I don't want to ask any of your secrets, as I say, Mrs Elless, for I understand you don't like to tell them; but it will be discovering no great matter, to let me know whether your friends are abroad, or in England? and what way you were maintained before you got your passage over in Mrs Maple's boat.'

'Don't let that young person go,' cried Miss Arbe, who had now finished the labours of her theatrical presidency, 'till I have heard her play and sing. If she is so clever, as you describe her, she shall perform between the acts.'

The stranger declared her utter inability to comply with such a request.

'When I believed myself unheard,' she cried, 'musick, I imagined, might make me, for a few moments, forget my distresses: but an expected performance—a prepared exhibition!—pardon me!—I have neither spirits nor powers for such an attempt!'

Her voice spoke grief, her look, apprehension; yet her manner so completely announced decision, that, unopposed even by a word, she re-mounted the stairs to her chamber.

She was, there, surprised by the sight of a sealed packet upon her table, directed, 'For L.S. at her leisure.'

She opened it, and found ten bank notes, of ten pounds each.

A momentary hope which she had indulged, that this letter, by some accidental conveyance, had reached her from abroad, was now changed into the most unpleasant perplexity: such a donation could not come from any of the females of the family; Mrs Maple was miserly, and her enemy; and the Miss Joddrels knew, by experience, that she would not refuse their open assistance: Mr Harleigh, therefore, or Mr Ireton, must have conveyed this to her room.

If it were Mr Ireton, she concluded he meant to ensnare her distress into an unguarded acceptance, for some latent purpose of mischief; if it were Mr Harleigh, his whole behaviour inclined her to believe, that he was capable of such an action from motives of pure benevolence: but she could by no means accept pecuniary aid from either, and determined to keep the packet always ready for delivery, when she could discover to whom it belonged.

She was surprised, soon afterwards, by the sight of Selina. 'I would not let Mr Ireton hinder me from coming to you this once,' she cried, 'do what he could; for we are all in such a fidget, that there's only you, I really believe, can help us. Poor Miss Arbe, while she was teaching us all what we have to do, put her part into her muff, and her favourite little dog, that she doats upon, not knowing it was there, poor thing, poked his nose into the muff to warm himself; and when Miss Arbe came to take her part, she found he had sucked it, and gnawed it, and nibbled it, all to tatters! And she says she can't write it out again if she was to have a diamond a word for it; and as to us, we have all of us got such immensities to do for ourselves, that you are the only person; for I dare say you know how to write. So will you, now, Ellis? for they have all settled, below, that your real name is Ellis.'

The stranger answered that she should gladly be useful in any way that could be proposed. The book, therefore, was brought to her, with writing implements, and she dedicated herself so diligently to copying, that the following morning, when Miss Arbe was expected, the part was prepared.

Miss Arbe, however, came not; a note arrived in her stead, stating that she had been so exceedingly fatigued the preceding day, in giving so many directions, that she begged they would let somebody read her part, and rehearse without her; and she hoped that she should find them more advanced when she joined them on Monday.

The stranger was now summoned not only as prompter, but to read the part of Lady Townly. She could not refuse, but her compliance was without any sort of exertion, from a desire to avoid, not promote similar calls for exhibition.

Elinor remarked to Harleigh, how inadequate were her talents to such a character. Harleigh acquiesced in the remark; yet his good opinion, in another point of view, was as much heightened, as in this it was lowered: he saw the part which she had copied for Miss Arbe; and the beautiful clearness of the hand-writing, and the correctness of the punctuation and orthography, convinced him that her education had been as successfully cultivated for intellectual improvement, as for elegant accomplishments.

Elinor herself, now, would only call the stranger Miss Ellis, a name which, she said, she verily believed that Miss Bydel, with all her stupidity, had hit upon, and which therefore, henceforth, should be adopted.

CHAPTER X

The Incognita continued to devote herself to needle-work till the morning of the next rehearsal. She was then again called to the double task of prompting, and of reading the part of Lady Townly, Miss Arbe having, unceremoniously, announced, that as she had already performed that character three several times, and to the most brilliant audiences, though at private theatres, any further practice for herself would be a work of supererogation; and if the company, she added, would but be so good as to remember her directions, she need only attend personally at the final rehearsal.

The whole party was much offended by this insinuation of its inferiority, as well as by so contemptuous an indifference to the prosperity of the enterprize. Nor was this the only difficulty caused by the breach of attendance in Miss Arbe. The entertainment was to conclude with a cotillon, of which Ireton had brought the newest steps and method from France, but which, through this unexpected failure, the sett was incomplete for practising. Elinor was persuaded, that in keeping the whole group thus imperfect, both in the play and in the dance, it was the design of Miss Arbe to expose them all to ridicule, that her own fine acting and fine steps might be contrasted to the greater advantage. To obviate, as much as possible, this suspected malice, the stranger was now requested to stand up with them; for as she was so lately come from abroad, they concluded that she might know something of the matter.

They were not mistaken: the steps, the figure, the time, all were familiar to her; and she taught the young Selina, dropt hints to Elinor, endeavoured to set Miss Bydel right, and gave a general, though unpremeditated lesson to everyone, by the measured grace and lightness of her motions, which, little as her attire was adapted to such a purpose, were equally striking for elegance and for modesty.

Harleigh, however, alone perceived her excellence: the rest had so much to learn, or were so anxious to shine, that if occasionally they remarked her, it was rather to be diverted by seeing any one dance so ill equipped, than to be struck with the elevated carriage which no such disadvantage could conceal.

Early on the morning preceding the intended representation, the stranger was summoned to the destined theatre, where, while she was aiding the general preparations, of dresses, decorations, and scenery, previous to the last grand rehearsal, which, in order to try the effect of the illuminations, was fixed to take place in the evening, Mrs Maple, with derision marked in every feature of her face, stalked into the room, to announce to her niece, with unbridled satisfaction, that all her fine vagaries would now end in nothing, as Miss Arbe, at last, had the good sense to refuse affording them her countenance.

Elinor, though too much enraged to inquire what this meant, soon, perforce, learnt, that an old gentleman, a cousin of Miss Arbe's, had ridden over with an apology, importing, that the most momentous reasons, yet such as could not be divulged, obliged his relation to decline the pleasure of belonging to their dramatic party.

The offence given by this abrupt renunciation was so general, though Elinor, alone, allowed it free utterance, that Mr Giles Arbe, the bearer of these evil tidings, conceived it to be more advisable to own the plump truth, he said, at once, than to see them all so affronted without knowing what for; though he begged them not to mention it, his cousin having peremptorily charged him not to speak out: but the fact was, that she had repented her engagement ever since the first rehearsal; for though she should always be ready to act with the Miss Joddrels, who were nieces to a baronet, and Mr Harleigh, who was nephew to a peer, and Mr Ireton, who was heir to a large entailed estate; she was yet apprehensive that it might let her down, in the opinion of the noble theatrical society to which she belonged, if she were seen exhibiting with such common persons as farmers and domestics; whom, however, for all his cousin's nicety, Mr Giles said he thought to be full as good men as any other; and, sometimes, considerably better.

Mrs Maple was elevated into the highest triumph by this explanation. 'I told you how it would be!' she cried. 'Young ladies acting with mere mob! I am truly rejoiced that Miss Arbe has given you the slip.'

Elinor heard this with a resentment, that determined her, more vehemently than ever, not to abandon her project; she proudly, therefore, returned thanks, by Mr Giles, for the restoration of the part, which she had resigned in mere complaisance, as there was nothing in the world she so much desired as to act it herself, even though it must be now learnt in the course of a day; and she begged leave, as a mark that she was not offended at the desertion, to borrow the dress of the character, which she knew to be ready, and with which she would adorn herself the following night, at the performance.

This last clause, she was well aware, would prove the most provoking that she could devise, to Miss Arbe, who was renowned for being finically tenacious of her attire; but Elinor would neither add a word to her message, nor suffer one to be taken from it; and when Mr Giles Arbe, frightened at the ill success of his confidence, would have offered some apology, she drove him from the house, directing a trusty person in the neighbourhood, to accompany him back, with positive orders not to return without the dress.

She then told the stranger to study the part of Lady Wronghead, to fill up the chasm.

The stranger began some earnest excuses, but they were lost in the louder exclamations of Mrs Maple, whose disappointment in finding the scheme still supported, was aggravated into rage, by the unexpected proposition of admitting the stranger into the set.

'What, Miss Joddrel!' she cried, 'is it not enough that you have made us a by-word in the neighbourhood, by wanting to act with farmers and servants? Must you also bring a foundling girl into your sett? an illegitimate stroller, who does not so much as know her own name?'

The stranger, deeply reddening, gravely answered, 'Far from wishing to enter into any plan of amusement, I could not have given my consent to it, even if solicited.'

'Nobody asks what you could have done, I hope!' Mrs Maple began, when Elinor, pushing the stranger into a large light closet, and throwing the part after her, shut the door, charging her not to lose a moment, in getting ready for the final rehearsal that very evening.

The Incognita, fixed not to look at the manuscript, now heard, perforce, a violent quarrel between the aunt and the niece, the former protesting that she would never agree to such a disgrace, as suffering a poor straggling pauper to mix herself publicly with their society; and the latter threatening, that, if forced to grant such a triumph to Miss Arbe, as that of tamely relinquishing the undertaking, she would leave the country and settle at once in France, and in the house of Robespierre himself.

Harleigh, who, in a hasty and dashing, but masterly manner, was colouring some scenery; had hitherto been silent; but now, advancing, he proposed, as a compromise, that the performance should be deferred for a week, in which time Miss Sycamore, a young lady at Brighthelmstone, whom they all knew, would learn, he doubted not, the part, and supply, with pleasure, the vacant place.

To this Mrs Maple, finding no hope remained that she could abolish the whole project, was sullenly assenting, when Elinor reproachfully exclaimed, 'What, Don Quixote! is your spirit of chivalry thus cooled? and are you, too, for rejecting, with all this scorn, the fellow-voyager you were so strenuous to support?'

'Scorn?' repeated Harleigh, 'No! I regard her, rather, with reverence. 'Tis she herself that has declined the part, and with a dignity that does her honour. All she suffers to be discerned of her, announces distinguished merit; and yet, highly as I have conceived of her character, she is unknown to us; except by her distresses; and these, though they call loudly for our sympathy and assistance, and, through the propriety of her conduct, lay claim to our respect, may be thought insufficient by the world, to justify Mrs Maple, who has two young ladies so immediately under her care, for engaging a perfect stranger, in a scheme which has no reference to humanity, or good offices.'

'Ah ha, Mr Harleigh!' cried Ireton, shaking his head, 'you are afraid of what she may turn out! You think no better of her, at last, than I do.'

'I think, on the contrary, so well of her,' answered Harleigh, 'that I am sincerely sorry to see her thus haughtily distanced. I often wish these ladies would as generously, as I doubt not that they might safely, invite her into their private society. Kindness such as that might produce a confidence, which revolts from public and abrupt enquiry; and which, I would nearly engage my life, would prove her innocence and worth, and vindicate every trust.'

He then begged them to consider, that, should their curiosity and suspicions work upon her spirits, till she were urged to reveal, prematurely, the secret of her situation, they would themselves be the first to condemn her for folly and imprudence, if breaking up the mystery of her silence should affect either her happiness or her safety.

Mrs Maple would have been inconsolable at a defence against which she had nothing positive to object, had she not reaped some comfort from finding that even Harleigh opposed including the stranger in the acting circle.

The delay of the performance, and an application to Miss Sycamore, seemed now settled, when Mrs Fenn, the housekeeper, who was also aiding in the room, lamented the trouble to be renewed for the supper-preparations, as neither the fish, nor the pastry, nor sundry other articles, could keep.

This was a complaint to which Mrs Maple was by no means deaf. The invitations, also, were made; the drawing-room was given up for the theatre; another apartment was appropriated for a green-room; and there was not any chance that the house could be restored to order, nor the maids to their usual occupations, till this business were finally over.

Her rancour now suddenly relented, with regard to the stranger, and, to the astonishment of every one, she stopt Harleigh from riding over to Brighthelmstone, to apply to Miss Sycamore, by concedingly saying, that, since Mr Harleigh had really so good an opinion of the young woman who came from France, she must confess that she had herself, of late, taken a much better notion of her, by finding that she was so excellent a needle-woman; and, therefore, she did not see why they should send for so finical a person as Miss Sycamore, who was full of airs and extravagance, to begin all over again, and disappoint so much company, when they had a body in the house who might do one of the parts, so as to pass amongst the rest, without being found out for what she was.

Harleigh expressed his doubts whether the young person herself, who was obviously in very unpleasant circumstances, might chuse to be brought forward in so public an amusement.

The gentleness of Mrs Maple was now converted into choler; and she desired to know, whether a poor wretch such as that, who had her meat, drink, and lodging for nothing, should be allowed to chuse any thing for herself one way or another.

Elinor, dropping, though not quite distinctly, some sarcastical reflections upon the persistence of Harleigh in preferring Miss Sycamore to his Dulcinea, retired to her room to study the part of Lady Townly; saying that she should leave them full powers, to wrangle amongst themselves, for that of Lady Wronghead.

Harleigh, who had not seen the stranger turned into the closet, now entered it, in search of a pencil. Not a little was then his surprize to find her sketching, upon the back of a letter, a view of the hills, downs, cottages, and cattle, which formed the prospect from the window.

It was beautifully executed, and undoubtedly from nature. Harleigh, with mingled astonishment and admiration, clasped his hands, and energetically exclaimed, 'Accomplished creature! who ... and what are you?'

Confused, she blushed, and folded up her little drawing. He seemed almost equally embarrassed himself, at the expression and the question which had escaped him. Mrs Maple, following, paradingly told the stranger, that, as she had hemmed the last cambric-handkerchiefs so neatly, she might act, upon this particular occasion, with the Miss Joddrels; only first premising, that she must not own to a living soul her being such a poor forlorn creature; as the only way to avoid disgrace to themselves, amongst their acquaintance, for admitting her, would be to say that she was a young lady of family, who came over with them from France.

To the last clause, the stranger calmly answered that she could offer no objection, in a manner which, to the attentive Harleigh, clearly indicated that it was true; but that, with respect to performing, she was in a situation too melancholy, if not disastrous, to be capable of making any such attempt.

Mrs Maple was so angry at this presumption, that she replied, 'Do as you are ordered, or leave my house directly!' and then walked, in high wrath, away.

The stranger appeared confounded: she felt an almost resistless impulse to depart immediately; but something stronger than resentment told her to stay: it was distress! She paused a moment, and then, with a sigh, took up the part, and, without looking at Harleigh, who was too much shocked to offer any palliation for this grossness, walked pensively to her chamber.

She was soon joined by Elinor, who, in extreme ill humour, complained that that odious Lady Townly was so intolerably prolix, that there was no getting her endless babbling by heart, at such short notice: and that, but for the triumph which it would afford to Miss Arbe, to find out their embarrassment, and the spite that it would gratify in Aunt Maple, the whole business should be thrown up at once. Sooner, however, than be conquered, either by such impertinence, or such malignity, she would abandon Lady Townly to the prompter, whom Miss Arbe might have the surprise and amusement to dizen out in her fine attire.

Then, declaring that she hated and would not act with Miss Sycamore, who was a creature of insolence and conceit, she flung the part of Lady Townly to the Incognita, saying, that she must abide herself by that of Lady Wronghead; a name which she well merited to keep for the rest of her life, from her inconceivable mismanagement of the whole affair.

The stranger earnestly entreated exemption from the undertaking, and solicited the intercession of Elinor with Mrs Maple, to soften the hard sentence denounced against her refusal. To act such a character as that of Lady Townly, she should have thought formidable, if not impossible, even in her gayest moments: but now, in a situation the most helpless, and with every reason to wish for obscurity, the exertion would be the most cruel that could be exacted.

Elinor, however, listened only to herself: Miss Arbe must be mortified; Mrs Maple must be thwarted; and Miss Sycamore must be omitted: these three things, she declared, were indispensable, and could only be accomplished by defying all obstacles, and performing the comedy upon the appointed day.

The stranger now saw no alternative between obsequiously submitting, or immediately relinquishing her asylum.

How might she find another? she knew not where even to seek her friend, and no letter was arrived from abroad.

There was no resource! She decided upon studying the part.

This was not difficult: she had read it at three rehearsals, and had carefully copied it; but she acquired it mechanically because unwillingly, and while she got the words by rote, scarcely took their meaning into consideration.

When called down, at night, to the grand final rehearsal, she gave equal surprise to Harleigh, from finding her already perfect in so long a part, and from hearing her repeat it with a tameness almost lifeless.

At the scene of the reconciliation, in the last act, he took her hand, and slightly kissed the glove. Ireton called out, 'Embrace! embrace!—the peace-making is always decided, at the theatre, by an embrace. You must throw your arms lovingly over one another's shoulders.'

Harleigh did not advance, but he looked at the stranger, and the blush upon her cheeks shewed her wholly unaccustomed even to the mention of any personal liberty; Ireton, however, still insisting, he laughingly excused himself, by declaring, that he must do by Lord Townly as he would do by himself; and he never meant, should he marry, to be tender to his wife before company.

Mrs Maple now, extremely anxious for her own credit, told all the servants, that she had just discovered, that the stranger who came from France, was a young lady of consequence, and she desired that they would make a report to that effect throughout the neighbourhood; and, in the new play-bills which were now written, she suffered to see inserted, Lady Townly by Miss Ellis.

Harleigh was the first to address the stranger by this name, previously taking an opportunity, with an air of friendly regard, to advise that she would adopt it, till she thought right to declare her own. She thanked him gratefully for his counsel, confessing, that she had long felt the absurdity of seeming nameless; and adding, 'but I had made no preparation for what I so little expected, as the length of time in which I have been kept in this almost unheard of situation! and the hourly hope of seeing it end, made me decide to spare myself, at least by silence, from deceit.'

The look of Harleigh shewed his approbation of her motive, while his words strengthened her conviction, that it must now give way to the necessity of some denomination. 'Be it Ellis, then,' said she, smiling, 'though evasion may, perhaps, be yet meaner than falsehood! Nevertheless, I am rather more contented to make use of this name, which accident has bestowed upon me, than positively to invent one for myself.'

Ellis, therefore, which appellation, now, will be substituted for that of the Incognita, seeing no possibility of escaping this exhibition, comforted herself, that, however repugnant it might be to her inclinations and her sense of propriety, it gave her, at least, some chance, during the remainder of her stay at Lewes, of being treated with less indignity.


CHAPTER XI

The hope of meeting with more consideration in the family, inspirited Ellis with a wish, hitherto unfelt, of contributing to the purposed entertainment. The part which she had been obliged to undertake, was too prominent to be placed in the back ground; and the whole performance must be flat, if not ridiculous, unless Lady Townly were a principal person. She read over, therefore, repeated, and studied the character, with an attention more alive to its meaning, style, and diversities; and the desire which animated all that she attempted, of doing with her best means whatever unavoidably must be done, determined her to let no effort in her power be wanting, to enliven the representation.

The lateness of this resolution, made her application for its accomplishment so completely fill up her time, that not a moment remained for those fears of self-deficiency, with which diffidence and timidity enervate the faculties, and often, in sensitive minds, rob them of the powers of exertion.

When the hour of exhibition approached, and she was summoned to the apartment destined for the green-room, universal astonishment was produced by her appearance. It was not from her dress; they had seen, and already knew it to be fanciful and fashionable; nor was it the heightened beauty which her decorations displayed; this, as she was truly lovely, was an effect that they expected: but it was from the ease with which she wore her ornaments, the grace with which she set them off, the elegance of her deportment, and an air of dignified modesty, that spoke her not only accustomed to such attire, but also to the good breeding and refined manners, which announce the habits of life to have been formed in the superior classes of society.

Selina, as she opened the door, exultingly called out, 'Look! look! only look at Ellis! did you ever see anything in the world so beautiful?'

Ireton, to whom dress, far more than feature or complexion, presented attraction, exclaimed, 'By my soul, she's as handsome as an angel!'

Elinor, thus excited, came forward; but seemed struck speechless.

They now all flocked around her; and Mrs Maple, staring, cried, 'Why who did you get to put your things on for you?' when suddenly recollecting the new account which she had herself given, and caused to be spread of this young person, she forced a laugh, and added, 'Bless me, Miss Ellis, if I had not quite forgotten whom I was speaking to! Why should not Miss Ellis know how to dress herself as well as any other young lady?'

'Why, indeed,' said Miss Bydel, 'it makes a prodigious change, a young lady's turning out a young lady, instead of a common young woman. I've seen a good many of the Ellis's. Pray, Ma'am, does your part of the family come from Yorkshire? or Devonshire? for I should like to know.'

'And, if there were any gentlemen of your family, with you, Ma'am, in foreign parts,' said Mr Scope, 'I should be glad to have their opinion of this Convention, now set up in France: for as to ladies, though they are certainly very pleasing, they are but indifferent judges in the political line, not having, ordinarily, heads of that sort. I speak without offence, inferiority of understanding being no defect in a female.'

'Well, I thought from the first,' said young Gooch, 'and I said it to sisters, that the young lady was a young lady, by her travelling, and that. But pray, Ma'am, did you ever look on, to see that Mr Robert Speer mow down his hundreds, like to grass in a hay-field? We should not much like it if they were to do so in England. But the French have no spirit. They are but a poor set; except their generals, or the like of that. And, for them, they'll fight you like so many lions. They are afraid of nobody.'

'By what I hear, Ma'am,' said Mr Stubbs, 'a gentleman, in that country, may have rents due to the value of thousands, and hardly receive a frog, as one may say, an acre.'

While thus her fellow-performers surrounded the Incognita, Harleigh, alone, held back, absorbed in contemplating the fine form, which a remarkably light and pretty robe, now first displayed; and the beautiful features, and animated complexion, which were set off to their utmost lustre, by the waving feathers, and artificial flowers, which were woven into her soft, glossy, luxuriant brown hair. But though he forbore offering her any compliments, he no sooner observed that she was seized with a sudden panic, upon a servant's announcing, that the expected audience, consisting of some of the principal families of Sussex, was arrived, than he addressed, and endeavoured to encourage her.

'I am aware, Sir,' she said, 'that it may seem rather like vanity than diffidence, for one situated as I am to feel any alarm; for as I can have raised no expectations, what have I to fear from giving any disappointment? Nevertheless, now the time is come, the attempt grows formidable. It must seem so strange—so wond'rous strange, to those who know not how little my choice has been consulted—'

She was interrupted, for all was ready; and Harleigh was summoned to open the piece, by the famous question, 'Why did I marry?'

The fright which now had found its way into the mind of the new Lady Townly, augmented every moment till she appeared; and it was then so great, as nearly to make her forget her part, and occasion what, hesitatingly, she was able to utter, to be hardly audible, even to her fellow-performers. The applause excited by her beauty, figure, and dress, only added to her embarrassment. She with difficulty kept to her post, and finished her first scene with complete self-discontent. Elinor, who watched her throughout it, lost all admiration of her exterior attractions, from contempt of her feeble performance.

But her second scene exhibited her in another point of view; her self-displeasure worked her up to exertions that brought forth the happiest effects; and her evident success produced ease, by inspiring courage. From this time, her performance acquired a wholly new character: it seemed the essence of gay intelligence, of well bred animation, and of lively variety. The grace of her motions made not only every step but every turn of her head remarkable. Her voice modulated into all the changes that vivacity, carelesness, pride, pleasure, indifference, or alarm demanded. Every feature of her face spoke her discrimination of every word; while the spirit which gave a charm to the whole, was chastened by a taste the most correct; and while though modest she was never awkward; though frightened, never ungraceful.

A performance such as this, in a person young, beautiful, and wholly new, created a surprize so powerful, and a delight so unexpected, that the play seemed soon to have no other object than Lady Townly, and the audience to think that no other were worth hearing or beholding; for though the politeness exacted by a private representation, secured to everyone an apparent attention, all seemed vapid and without merit in which she was not concerned; while all wore an air of interest in which she bore the smallest part; and she soon never spoke, looked, nor moved, but to excite pleasure, admiration, and applause, amounting to rapture.

Whether this excellence were the result of practice and instruction, or a sudden emanation of general genius, accidentally directed to a particular point, was disputed by the critics amongst the audience; and disputed, as usual, with the greater vehemence, from the impossibility of obtaining documents to decide, or direct opinion. But that which was regarded as the highest refinement of her acting, was a certain air of inquietude, which was discernible through the utmost gaiety of her exertions, and which, with the occasional absence and sadness, that had their source in her own disturbance, was attributed to deep research into the latent subjects of uneasiness belonging to the situation of Lady Townly. This, however, was nature, which would not be repressed; not art, that strove to be displayed.

But no pleasure excited by her various powers, approached to the pleasure which they bestowed upon Harleigh, who could look at, could listen to her alone. To himself, he lost all power of doing justice; wrapt up in the contemplation of an object thus singular, thus excelling, thus mysterious, all ambition to personally shining was forgotten. He could not fail to speak his part with sense and feeling; he could not help appearing fashioned to represent a man of rank and understanding; but that address which gives life and meaning to every phrase; that ingenuity, which beguiles the audience into an illusion, which, for the current moment, inspires the sympathy due to reality; that skill which brings forth on the very instant, all the effect which, to the closet reader, an author can hope to produce from reflection; these, the attributes of good acting, and for which his taste, his spirit, and his judgment all fitted him, were now, from slackened self-attention, beyond his reach, though within his powers. At a public theatre, such an actress might have proved a spur to have urged the exertions of competition; in this private one, where success, except to vanity, was unimportant, her merit was, to Harleigh, an absorbent that occupied, exclusively, all his faculties.

In the last act, where Lady Townly becomes serious, penitent, and pathetic, the new actress appeared to yet greater advantage: the state of her mind accorded with distress, and her fine speaking eyes, her softly touching voice, her dejected air, and penetrating countenance, made quicker passage to the feelings of her auditors, even than the words of the author. All were moved, tears were shed from almost every eye, and Harleigh, affected and enchanted, at the moment of the peace-making, took her hand with so much eagerness, and pressed it to his lips with so much pleasure, that the rouge, put on for the occasion, was paler than the blushes which burnt through it on her cheeks. He saw this, and, checking his admiration, relinquished with respect the hand which he had taken nearly with rapture.

When the play was over, and the loudest applause had marked its successful representation, the company arose to pay their compliments to Mrs Maple. Lady Townly, then, followed by every eyes, was escaping from bearing her share in the bursts of general approbation; when a youth of the most engaging appearance, and evidently of high fashion, sprang over the forms, to impede her retreat; and to pour forth the highest encomiums upon her performance, in well-bred, though enthusiastic language, with all the eager vivacity of early youth, which looks upon moderation as insipidity, and measured commendation as want of feeling.

Though confused by being detained, Ellis could not be angry, for there was no impertinence in his fervour, no familiarity in his panegyric; and though his speech was rapid, his manners were gentle. His eulogy was free from any presumption of being uttered for her gratification; it seemed simply the uncontrollable ebullition of ingenuous gratitude.

Surprised still more than all around her, at the pleasure which she found she had communicated, some share of it now stole insensibly into her own bosom; and this was by no means lessened, by seeing her youthful new admirer soon followed by a lady still younger than himself, who called out, 'Do you think, brother, to monopolize Miss Ellis?' And, with equal delight, and nearly equal ardour, she joined in the acknowledgements made by her brother, for the entertainment which they had received; and both united in declaring that they should never endure to see or hear any other Lady Townly.

There was a charm, for there seemed a sincerity in this youthful tribute of admiration, that was highly gratifying to the new actress; and Harleigh thought he read in her countenance, the soothing relief experienced by a delicate mind, from meeting with politeness and courtesie, after a long endurance of indignity or neglect.

Almost everybody among the audience, one by one, joined this little set, all eager to take a nearer view of the lovely Lady Townly, and availing themselves of the opportunity afforded by this season of compliment, for examining more narrowly whom it was that they addressed.

Mrs Maple, meanwhile, suffered the utmost perplexity: far from foreseeing an admiration which thus bore down all before it, she had conceived that, the piece once finished, the actress would vanish, and be thought of no more: nor was she without hope, in her utter disdain of the stranger, that the part thus given merely by necessity, would be so ill represented, as to disgust her niece from any such frolics in future. But when, on the contrary, she found that there was but one voice in favour of this unknown performer; when not all her own pride, nor all her prejudice, could make her blind to that performer's truly elevated carriage and appearance; when every auditor flocked to her, with 'Who is this charming Miss Ellis?'—'Present us to this incomparable Miss Ellis;' she felt covered with shame and regret; though compelled, for her own credit, to continue repeating, that she was a young lady of family who had passed over with her from the Continent.

Provoked, however, she now followed the crowd, meaning to give a hint to the Incognita to retire; but she had the mortification of hearing her gallant new enthusiast pressing for her hand, in a cotillon, which they were preparing to dance; and though the stranger gently, yet steadily, was declining his proposition, Mrs Maple was so much frightened and irritated that such a choice should be in her power, that she called out impatiently, 'My Lord, we must have some refreshments before the dance. Do pray, Lady Aurora Granville, beg Lord Melbury to come this way, and take something.'

The young lord and lady, with civil but cold thanks, that spoke their dislike of this interference, both desired to be excused; but great was their concern, and universal, throughout the apartment, was the consternation, upon observing Miss Ellis change colour, and sink upon a chair, almost fainting. Harleigh, who had strongly marked the grace and dignity with which she had received so much praise, now cast a glance of the keenest indignation at Mrs Maple, attributing to her rude interruption of the little civilities so evidently softening to the stranger, this sudden indisposition;

but Mrs Maple either saw it not, or did not understand it, and seized, with speed, the opportunity of saying, that Miss Ellis was exhausted by so much acting, and of desiring that some of the maids might help her to her chamber.

Elinor stood suspended, looking not at her, but at Harleigh. Everyone else came forward with inquiry, fans, or sweet-scented vials; but Ellis, a little reviving, accepted the salts of Lady Aurora Granville, and, leaning against her waist, which her arm involuntarily encircled, breathed hard and shed a torrent of tears.

'Why don't the maids come?' cried Mrs Maple. 'Selina, my dear, do call them. Lady Aurora, I am quite ashamed. Miss Ellis, what are you thinking of, to lean so against Her Ladyship? Pray, Mr Ireton, call the maids for me.'

'Call no one, I beg!' cried Lady Aurora: 'Why should I not have the pleasure of assisting Miss Ellis?' And, bending down, she tried better to accommodate herself to the ease and relief of her new acquaintance, who appeared the more deeply sensible of her kindness, from the ungenerous displeasure which it evidently excited in Mrs Maple. And when, in some degree recovered, she rose to go, she returned her thanks to Lady Aurora with so touching a softness, with tearful eyes, and in a voice so plaintive, that Lady Aurora, affected by her manner, and charmed by her merit, desired still to support her, and, entreating that she would hold by her arm, begged permission of Mrs Maple to accompany Miss Ellis to her chamber.

Mrs Maple recollecting, with the utmost confusion, the small and ordinary room allotted for Ellis, so unlike what she would have bestowed upon such a young lady as she now described for her fellow-voyager, found no resource against exposing it to Lady Aurora, but that of detaining the object of her compassionate admiration; she stammered, therefore, out, that as Miss Ellis seemed so much better, there could be no reason why she should not stay below, and see the dance.

Ellis gladly courtsied her consent; and the watchful Harleigh, in the alacrity of her acceptance, rejoiced to see a revival to the sentiments of pleasure, which the acrimonious grossness of Mrs Maple had interrupted.

Lord Melbury now took the hand of Selina, and Harleigh that of Lady Aurora. Elinor would not dance, but, seating herself, fixed her eyes upon Harleigh, whose own were almost perpetually wandering to watch those of his dramatic consort.

Since the first scene, in which the stranger had so ill entered into the spirit of Lady Townly's character, Elinor had ceased to deem her worthy of observation; and, giving herself up wholly to her own part, had not witnessed the gradations of the improvements of Ellis, her rising excellence, nor her final perfection. In her own representation of Lady Wronghead, she piqued herself upon producing new effects, and had the triumph, by her cleverness and eccentricities, her grotesque attitudes and attire, and an unexpected and burlesque manner of acting, to bring the part into a consequence of which it had never appeared susceptible. Happy in the surprise and diversion she occasioned, and constantly occupied how to augment it, she only learnt the high success of Lady Townly, by the bursts of applause, and the unbounded admiration and astonishment, which broke forth from nearly every mouth, the instant that the audience and the performers were united. Amazed, she turned to Harleigh, to examine the merits of such praise; but Harleigh, no longer silent, cautious, or cold, was himself one of the 'admiring throng,' and so openly, and with an air of so much pleasure, that she could not catch his attention for any critical discussion.

After two country dances, and two cotillons, the short ball was broken up, and Lady Aurora hastened to seat herself by Miss Ellis, and Lord Melbury to stand before and to converse with her, followed by all the youthful part of the company, to whom she seemed the sovereign of a little court which came to pay her homage. Harleigh grew every instant more enchanted; for as she discoursed with her two fervent new admirers, her countenance brightened into an animation so radiant, her eyes became so lustrous, and smiles of so much sweetness and pleasure embellished every feature, that he almost fancied he saw her now for the first time, though her welfare, or her distresses, had for more than a month chiefly occupied his mind. Who art thou? thought he, as incessantly he contemplated her; where hast thou thus been formed? And for what art thou designed?

Supper being now announced, Mrs Maple commissioned Harleigh to lead Lady Aurora down stairs, adding, with a forced smile of civility, that Miss Ellis must consult her health in retiring.

'Yes, Ma'am; and Miss Ellis knows,' cried Lady Aurora, offering her arm, 'who is to be her chevalier.'

Again embarrassed, Mrs Maple saw no resource against exposing her shabby chamber, but that of admitting its occupier to the supper table. She hastily, therefore, asked whether Miss Ellis thought herself well enough to sit up a little longer; adding, 'For my part, I think it will do you good.'

'The greatest!' cried Ellis, with a look of delight; and, to the speechless consternation of Mrs Maple, Lord Melbury, calling her the Queen of the night, took her hand, to conduct her to the supper-room. Ellis would have declined this distinction, but that the vivacity of her ardent new friend, precipitated her to the staircase, ere she was aware that she was the first to lead the way thither. Gaily, then, he would have placed her in the seat of honour, as Lady President of the evening; but, more now upon her guard, she insisted upon standing till the visitors should be arranged, as she was herself a resident in the house.

Lord Melbury, however, quitted her not, and would talk to no one else; and finding that his seat was destined to be next to that of Mrs Maple, who called him to her side, he said, that he never supped, and would therefore wait upon the ladies; and, drawing a chair behind that of Ellis, he devoted himself to conversing with her, upon her part, upon the whole play, and upon dramatic works, French and English, in general, with the eagerness with which such subjects warm the imagination of youth, and with a pleasure which made him monopolize her attention.

Harleigh listened to every word to which Ellis listened, or to which she answered; and scarcely knew whether most to admire her good sense, her intelligent quickness, her elegant language, or the meaning eyes, and varied smiles which spoke before she spoke, and shewed her entire conception of all to which she attended.

No one now could address her; she was completely engrossed by the young nobleman, who allowed her not time to turn from him a moment.

Such honours shewn to a pauper, a stroller, a vagabond; and all in the present instance, from her own unfortunate contrivance, Mrs Maple considered as a personal disgrace; a sensation which was three-fold encreased when the party broke up, and Lady Aurora, taking the chair of her brother, rallied him upon the envy which his situation had excited; while, in the most engaging manner, she hoped, during her sojourn at Brighthelmstone, to have frequently the good fortune of taking her revenge. Then, joining in their conversation, she became so pleased, so interested, so happy, that twice Mrs Howel, the lady under whose care she had been brought to Lewes, reminded Her Ladyship that the horses were waiting in the cold, before she could prevail upon herself to depart. And, even then, that lady was forced to take her gently by the arm, to prevent her from renewing the conversation which she most unwillingly finished. 'Pardon me, dear Madam,' said Lady Aurora; 'I am quite ashamed; but I hope, while I am so happy as to be with you, that you will yourself conceive a fellow feeling, how difficult it is to tear one's self away from Miss Ellis.'

'What honour Your Ladyship does me!' cried Ellis, her eyes glistening: 'and Oh!—how happy you have made me!'—

'How kind you are to say so!' returned Lady Aurora, taking her hand.

She felt a tear drop upon her own from the bent-down eyes of Ellis.

Startled, and astonished, she hoped that Miss Ellis was not again indisposed?

Smilingly, yet in a voice that denoted extreme agitation, 'Lady Aurora alone,' she answered, 'can be surprised that so much goodness—so unlooked for—so unexpected—should be touching!'

'O Mrs Maple,' cried Lady Aurora, in taking leave of that lady, 'what a sweet creature is this Miss Ellis!'

'Such talents and a sensibility so attractive,' said Lord Melbury, 'never met before!'

Ellis heard them, and with a pleasure that seemed exquisite, yet that died away the moment that they disappeared. All then crowded round her, who had hitherto abstained; but she drooped; tears flowed fast down her cheeks; she courtsied the acknowledgements which she could not pronounce to her complimenters and enquirers, and mounted to her chamber.

Mrs Maple concluded her already so spoiled, by the praises of Lord Melbury and Lady Aurora Granville, that she held herself superior to all other; and the company in general imbibed the same notion. Many disdain, or affect to disdain, the notice of people of rank for themselves, but all are jealous of it for others.

Not such was the opinion of Harleigh; her pleasure in their society seemed to him no more than renovation to feelings of happier days. Who, who, thought he again, can'st thou be? And why, thus evidently accustomed to grace society, why art thou thus strangely alone—thus friendless—thus desolate—thus mysterious?


CHAPTER XII

Selina, regarding herself as a free agent, since Ireton professed a respect for Ellis that made him ashamed of his former doubts, flew, the next morning, to the chamber of that young person, to talk over the play, Lord Melbury, and Lady Aurora Granville: but found her protégée absorbed in deep thought, and neither able nor willing to converse.

When the family assembled to breakfast, Mrs Maple declared that she had not closed her eyes the whole night, from the vexation of having admitted such an unknown Wanderer to sup at her table, and to mix with people of rank.

Elinor was wholly silent.

They were not yet separated, when Lady Aurora Granville and Mrs Howel called to renew their thanks for the entertainment of the preceding evening.

'But Miss Ellis?' said Lady Aurora, looking around her, disappointed; 'I hope she is not more indisposed?'

'By no means. She is quite well again,' answered Mrs Maple, in haste to destroy a disposition to pity, which she thought conferred undue honour upon the stranger.

'But shall we not have the pleasure to see her?'

'She ... generally ... breakfasts in her own room,' answered Mrs Maple, with much hesitation.

'May I, then,' said Lady Aurora, going to the bell, 'beg that somebody will let her know how happy I should be to enquire after her health?'

'Your Ladyship is too good,' cried Mrs Maple, in great confusion, and preventing her from ringing; 'but Miss Ellis—I don't know why—is so fond of keeping her chamber, that there is no getting her out of it ... some how. '

'Perhaps, then, she will permit me to go up stairs to her?'

'O no, not for the world! besides ... I believe she has walked out.'

Lady Aurora now applied to Selina, who was scampering away upon a commission of search; when Mrs Maple, following her, privately insisted that she should bring back intelligence that Miss Ellis was taken suddenly ill.

Selina was forced to comply, and Lady Aurora with serious concern, to return to Brighthelmstone ungratified.

Mrs Maple was so much disconcerted by this incident, and so nettled at her own perplexed situation, that nothing saved Ellis from an abrupt dismission, but the representations of Mrs Fenn, that some fine work, which the young woman had just begun, would not look of a piece if finished by another hand.

The next morning, the breakfast party was scarcely assembled, when Lord Melbury entered the parlour. He had ridden over, he said, to enquire after the health of Miss Ellis, in the name of his sister, who would do herself the pleasure to call upon her, as soon as she should be sufficiently recovered to receive a visit.

Elinor was struck with the glow of satisfaction which illumined the face of Harleigh, at this reiterated distinction. A glow of a far different sort flushed that of Mrs Maple, who, after various ineffectual evasions, was constrained to say that she hoped Miss Ellis would be well enough to appear on the morrow. And, to complete her provocation, she was reduced, when Lord Melbury was gone, to propose, herself, that Selina should lend the girl a gown, and what else she might require, for being seen, once again, without involving them all in shame.

Ellis, informed by Selina of these particulars, shed a torrent of grateful tears at the interest which she had thus unexpectedly excited; then, reviving into a vivacity which seemed to renew all the pleasure that she had experienced on the night of the play, she diligently employed herself in appropriating the attire which Selina supplied for the occasion.

Mrs Maple, now, had no consolation but that the stay of Lady Aurora in the neighbourhood would be short, as that young lady and her brother were only at Brighthelmstone upon a visit to the Honourable Mrs Howel; who, having a capital mansion upon the Steyne, resided there the greatest part of the year.

Mrs Howel accompanied her young guest to Lewes the following morning. Miss Ellis was enquired for without delay, and as Mrs Maple would suffer no one to view her chamber, she was summoned into the drawing-room.

She entered it with a blush of bright pleasure upon her cheeks; yet with eyes that were glistening, and a bosom that seemed struggling with sighs. Lady Aurora hastened to meet her, uttering such kind expressions of concern for her indisposition, that Ellis, with charmed sensibility, involuntarily advanced to embrace her; but rapidly, and with timid shame, drew back, her eyes cast down, and her feelings repressed. Lady Aurora, perceiving the design, and its check, instantly held out her hand, and smilingly saying, 'Would you cheat me of this kindness?' led her to a seat next to her own upon a sofa.

The eyes of the stranger were not now the only ones that glistened. Harleigh could not see her thus benignly treated, or rather, as he conceived, thus restored to the treatment to which she had been accustomed, and which he believed her to merit, without feeling tears moisten his own.

With marked civility, though not with the youthful enthusiasm of Lady Aurora, Mrs Howel, also, made her compliments to Miss Ellis. Lord Melbury arrived soon afterwards, and, the first ceremonies over, devoted his whole attention to the same person.

O powerful prejudice! thought Harleigh; what is judgment, and where is perception in your hands? The ladies of this house, having first seen this charming Incognita in tattered garments, forlorn, desolate, and distressed; governed by the prepossession thus excited of her inferiority, even, to this moment, either neglect or treat her harshly; not moved by the varied excellencies that should create gentler ideas, nor open to the interesting attractions that might give them more pleasure than they could bestow! While these visitors, hearing that she is a young lady of family, and meeting her upon terms of equality, find, at once, that she is endowed with talents and accomplishments for the highest admiration, and with a sweetness of manners, and powers of conversation, irresistibly fascinating.

The visit lasted almost the whole morning, during which he observed, with extreme satisfaction, not only that the dejection of Ellis wore away, but that a delight in the intercourse seemed reciprocating between herself and her young friends, that gave new beauty to her countenance, and new spirit to her existence.

When the visitors rose to be gone, 'I cannot tell you, Miss Ellis,' said Lady Aurora, 'how happy I shall be to cultivate your acquaintance. Will you give me leave to call upon you for half an hour tomorrow?'

Ellis, with trembling pleasure, cast a fearful glance at Mrs Maple, who hastily turned her head another way. Ellis then gratefully acceded to the proposal.

'Miss Ellis, I hope,' said Mrs Howel, in taking leave, 'will permit me, also, to have some share of her society, when I have the honour to receive her at Brighthelmstone.'

Ellis, touched, enchanted, could attempt no reply beyond a courtesy, and stole, with a full heart, and eyes overflowing, to her chamber, the instant that they left the house.

Mrs Maple was now in a dilemma which she would have deemed terrible beyond all comparison, but from what she experienced the following minute, when the butler put upon the table a handful of cards, left by the groom of Mrs Howel, amongst which Mrs Maple perceived the name of Miss Ellis, mingled with her own, and that of the Miss Joddrels, in an invitation to a small dancing-party on the ensuing Thursday.

'This exceeds all!' she cried: 'If I don't get rid of this wretch, she will bring me into universal disgrace! she shall not stay another day in my house.'

'Has she, Madam, for a single moment,' said Harleigh, with quickness, 'given you cause to repent your kind assistance, or reason to harbour any suspicion that you have not bestowed it worthily?'

'Why, you go beyond Elinor herself, now, Mr Harleigh! for even she, you see, does not ask me to keep her any longer.'

'Miss Joddrel,' answered Harleigh, turning with an air of gentleness to the mute Elinor, 'is aware how little a single woman is allowed to act publicly for herself, without risk of censure.'

'Censure?' interrupted Elinor, disdainfully, 'you know I despise it!'

He affected not to hear her, and continued, 'Miss Joddrel leaves, therefore, Madam, to your established situation in life, the protection of a young person whom circumstances have touchingly cast upon your compassion, and who seems as innocent as she is indigent, and as formed, nay elegant in her manners, as she is obscure and secret in her name and history. I make not any doubt but Miss Joddrel would be foremost to sustain her from the dangers of lonely penury, to which she seems exposed if deserted, were my brother already—' He approached Elinor, lowering his voice; she rose to quit the room, with a look of deep resentment; but could not first escape hearing him finish his speech with 'as happy as I hope soon to see him!'

'Ah, Mr Harleigh,' said Mrs Maple, 'when shall we bring that to bear?'

'She never pronounces a positive rejection,' answered Harleigh, 'yet I make no progress in my peace-offerings.'

He would then have entered more fully upon that subject, in the hope of escaping from the other: Mrs Maple, however, never forgot her anger but for her interest; and Selina was forced to be the messenger of dismission.

She found Ellis so revived, that to destroy her rising tranquillity would have been a task nearly impossible, had Selina possessed as much consideration as good humour. But she was one amongst the many in whom reflection never precedes speech, and therefore, though sincerely sorry, she denounced, without hesitating, the sentence of Mrs Maple.

Ellis was struck with the deepest dismay, to be robbed thus of all refuge, at the very moment when she flattered herself that new friends, perhaps a new asylum, were opening to her. Whither could she now wander? and how hope that others, to whom she was still less known, would escape the blasting contagion, and believe that distress might be guiltless though mysterious? A few shillings were all that she possessed; and she saw no prospect of any recruit. Elinor had not once spoken to her since the play; and the childish character, even more than the extreme youth of Selina, made it seem improper, in so discarded a state, to accept any succour from her clandestinely. Nevertheless, the awaited letter was not yet arrived; the expected friend had not yet appeared. How, then, quit the neighbourhood of Brighthelmstone, where alone any hope of receiving either still lingered? The only idea that occurred to her, was that of throwing herself upon the compassion of her new acquaintances, faithfully detailing to them her real situation at Mrs Maple's, and appealing to their generosity to forbear, for the present, all enquiry into its original cause.

This determined, she anxiously desired, before her departure, to restore, if she could discover their owner, the anonymous bank-notes, which she was resolute not to use; and, hearing the step of Harleigh passing her door in descending the stairs, she hastened after him, with the little packet in her hand.

Turning round as he reached the hall, and observing, with pleased surprise, her intention to speak to him, he stopt.

'You have been so good to me, Sir,' she said, 'so humane and so considerate, by every possible occasion, that I think I may venture to beg yet one more favour of you, before I leave Lewes.'

Her dejected tone extremely affected him, and he waited her explanation with looks that were powerfully expressive of his interest in her welfare.

'Some one, with great, but mistaken kindness,' she continued, 'has imagined my necessities stronger than my ...' She stopt, as if at a loss for a word, and then, with a smile, added, 'my pride, others, perhaps, will say; but to me it appears only a sense of right. If, however, my lengthened suspense forces me to require more assistance of this sort than I already owe to the Miss Joddrels, and to the benevolent Admiral, I shall have recourse to the most laborious personal exertions, rather than spread any further the list of my pecuniary creditors.'

Harleigh did not, or seemed not to understand her, yet would not resist taking the little packet, which she put into his hands, saying, 'I have some fear that this comes from Mr Ireton; I shall hold myself inexpressibly obliged to you, Sir, if you will have the goodness to clear up that doubt for me; and, should it prove a fact, to return it to him with my thanks, but the most positive assurance that its acceptance is totally impossible.'

Harleigh looked disturbed, yet promised to obey.

'And if,' cried she, 'you should not find Mr Ireton to be my creditor, you may possibly discover him in a person to whom I owe far other services, and unmingled esteem. And should that be the case, say to him, I beg, Sir, that even from him I must decline an obligation of this sort, though my debts to him of every other, are nearly as innumerable as their remembrance will be indelible.'

She then hastened away, leaving Harleigh impressed with such palpable concern, that she could no longer doubt that the packet was already deposited with its right owner.

He passed into the garden, and she was going back, when, at the entrance of the breakfast-parlour, she perceived Elinor, who seemed sternly occupied in observing them.

Ellis courtsied, and stood still. Elinor moved not, and was gloomily silent.

Struck with her mien, her stillness, and her manner, Ellis, in a fearful voice, enquired after her health; but received a look so indignant, yet wild, that, affrighted and astonished, she retreated to her chamber.

As she turned round upon entering it, to shut herself in, immediately before her stood Elinor.

She looked yet paler, and seemed in a sort of stupor. Ellis respectfully held open the door, but she did not advance: the fury, however, of her aspect was abated, and Ellis, in a voice condolingly soft, asked whether she might hope that Miss Joddrel would, once more, condescend to sit with her before her departure.

At these words Elinor seemed to shake herself, and presently, though in a hollow tone, pronounced, 'Are you then going?'

Ellis plaintively answered Yes!

'And ... with whom?' cried Elinor, raising her eyes with a glance of fire.

'With no one, Madam. I go alone.'

This answer was uttered with a firmness that annulled all suspicion of deceit.

Elinor appeared again to breathe.

'And whither?' she demanded, 'whither is it you go?'

'I know not, alas!—but I mean to make an attempt at Howel Place.'

The countenance of Elinor now lost its rigidity, and with a cry almost of extacy, she exclaimed, 'Upon Lord Melbury?—your new admirer? O go to him!—hasten to him!—dear, charming Ellis, away to him at once!—'

Ellis, half smiling, answered, 'No, Madam; I go to Lady Aurora Granville.'

Elinor, without replying, left the room; but, quick in action as in idea, returned, almost instantly, loaded with a packet of clothes.

'Here, most beautiful Ophelia!' she cried, 'look over this trumpery. You know how skilfully you can arrange it. You must not appear to disadvantage before dear little Lord Melbury.'

Ellis now, nearly offended, drew back.

'O, I know I ought to be excommunicated for giving such a hint,' cried Elinor, whose spirits were rather exalted than recovered; 'though every body sees how the poor boy is bewitched with you: but you delicate sentimentalists are never yourselves to suspect any danger, till the men are so crazy 'twould be murder to resist them; and then, you know, acceptance is an act of mere charity.'

Ellis laughed at her raillery, yet declined her wardrobe, saying that she had resolved upon frankly stating to Lady Aurora, all that she was able to make known of her situation.

'Well, that's more romantic,' returned Elinor, 'and so 'twill be more touching; especially to the little peer; for as you won't say who you are, he can do no less than, like Selina, conclude you to be a princess in disguise; and that, as you know, will bring the match so properly forward, that parents, and uncles, and guardians, and all those supernumeraries of the creation, will learn the business only just in time to drown themselves.'

Ellis heard this with a calmness that shewed her superior to offering any vindication of her conduct; and Elinor more gently added, 'Now don't construe all this into either a sneer or a reprimand. If you imagine me an enemy to what the old court call unequal connexions, you do me egregious injustice. I detest all aristocracy: I care for nothing upon earth but nature; and I hold no one thing in the world worth living for but liberty! and liberty, you know, has but two occupations, plucking up and pulling down. To me, therefore, 'tis equally diverting, to see a beggar swell into a duchess, or a duchess dwindle into a beggar.'

Ellis tried to smile, but felt shocked many ways; and Elinor, gay, now, as a lark, left her to get ready for Howel Place.

While thus employed, a soft tap called her to the door, where she perceived Harleigh.

'I will detain you,' he said, 'but a moment. I can find no owner for your little packet; you must suffer it, therefore, still to encumber you; and should any accident, or any transient convenience, make its contents even momentarily useful to you, do not let any idea of its having ever belonged to Mr Ireton impede its employment: I have examined that point thoroughly, and I can positively assure you, that he has not the least knowledge even of its existence.'

As she held back from taking it, he put it upon a step before the door, and descended the stairs without giving her time to answer.

She did not dare either to follow or to call him, lest Elinor should again appear; but she felt convinced that the bank-notes were his own, and became less uneasy at a short delay, though equally determined upon restitution.

She was depositing them in her work-bag, when Selina came jumping into the room. 'O Ellis,' she cried, 'I have the best news in the world for you! Aunt Maple fell into the greatest passion you ever saw, at hearing you were going to Howel Place. "What!" says she, "shall I let her disgrace me for ever, by making known what a poor Wanderer I have taken into my house, and permitted to eat at my table? It would be a thing to ruin me in the opinion of the whole world." So then, after the greatest fuss that ever you knew in your life, she said you should not be turned away till Lady Aurora was gone.'

Ellis, however, hurt by this recital, rejoiced in the reprieve.

The difficulties, nevertheless, of Mrs Maple did not end here; the next morning she received a note from Mrs Howel, with intelligence that Lady Aurora Granville was prevented from making her intended excursion, by a very violent cold; and to entreat that Mrs Maple would use her interest with Miss Ellis, to soften Her Ladyship's disappointment, by spending the day at Howel Place; for which purpose Mrs Howel begged leave to send her carriage, at an early hour, to Lewes.

Mrs Maple read this with a choler indescribable. She would have sent word that Ellis was ill, but she foresaw an endless embarrassment from inquiring visits; and, after the most fretful, but fruitless lamentations, passionately declared that she would have nothing more to do with the business, and retired to her room; telling Elinor that she might answer Mrs Howel as she pleased, only charging her to take upon herself all responsibility of consequences.

Elinor, enchanted, fixed upon two o'clock for the arrival of the carriage; and Ellis, who heard the tidings with even exquisite joy, spent the intermediate time in preparations, for which she no longer declined the assisting offers of Elinor, who, wild with renovated spirits, exhorted her, now in raillery, now in earnest, but always with agitated vehemence, to make no scruple of going off with Lord Melbury to Gretna Green.

When the chaise arrived, Mrs Maple restless and curious, suddenly descended; but was filled with double envy and malevolence, at sight of the look of pleasure which Ellis wore; but which gave to Harleigh a satisfaction that counter-balanced his regret at her quitting the house.

'I have only one thing to mention to you, Mrs Ellis,' said Mrs Maple, with a gloomy scowl; 'I insist upon it that you don't say one syllable to Mrs Howel, nor to Lady Aurora, about your meanness, and low condition, and that ragged state that we found you in, patched, and blacked, and made up for an object to excite pity. Mind that! for if you go to Howel Place only to make out that I have been telling a parcel of stories, I shall be sure to discover it, and you shall repent it as long as you live.'

Ellis seemed tempted to leave the room without condescending to make any reply; but she checked herself, and desired to understand more clearly what Mrs Maple demanded.

'That there may be only one tale told between us, and that you will be steady to stand to what I have said, of your being a young lady of good family, who came over with me from France.'

Ellis, without hesitation, consented; and Harleigh handed her to the chaise, Mrs Maple herself not knowing how to object to that civility, as the servants of Mrs Howel were waiting to attend their lady's guest. 'How happy, how relieved,' cried he, in conducting her out, 'will you feel in obtaining at last, a little reprieve from the narrow prejudice which urges this cruel treatment!'

'You must not encourage me to resentment,' cried she, smiling, 'but rather bid me, as I bid myself, when I feel it rising, subdue it by recollecting my strange—indefinable situation in this family!'


CHAPTER XIII

The presage of Harleigh proved as just as it was pleasant: the heart of Ellis bounded with delight as she drove off from the house; and the hope of transferring to Lady Aurora the obligation for succour which she was now compelled to owe to Mrs Maple, seemed almost lifting her from earth to heaven.

Her fondest wishes were exceeded by her reception. Mrs Howel came forward to meet her, and to beg permission not to order the carriage for her return, till late at night. She was then conducted to the apartment of Lady Aurora, by Lord Melbury, who assured her that his sister would have rejoiced in a far severer indisposition, which had procured her such a gratification. Lady Aurora welcomed her with an air of so much goodness, and with looks so soft, so pleased, so partial, that Ellis, in taking her held-out hand, overpowered by so sudden a transition from indignity to kindness, and agitated by the apprehensions that were attached to the hopes which it inspired, burst into tears, and, in defiance of her utmost struggles for serenity, wept even with violence.

Lady Aurora, shocked and alarmed, asked for her salts; and Lord Melbury flew for a glass of water; but Ellis, declining both, and reviving without either, wiped, though she could not dry her eyes and smiled, while they still glistened, with such grateful sensibility, yet beaming happiness, that both the brother and the sister soon saw, that, greatly as she was affected, nothing was wanting to her restoration. 'It is not sorrow,' she cried, when able to speak; "tis your goodness, your kindness, which thus touch me!'

'Can you ever have met with anything else?' said Lord Melbury, warmly; 'if you can—by what monsters you must have been beset!'

'No, my Lord, no,' cried she: 'I am far from meaning to complain; but you must not suppose the world made up of Lady Aurora Granvilles!'

Lady Aurora was much moved. It seemed evident to her that her new favourite was not happy; and she had conceived such high ideas of her perfections, that she was ready to weep herself, at the bare suggestion that they were not recompensed by felicity.

The rest of the morning passed in gentle, but interesting conversation, between the two young females; or in animated theatrical discussions, strictures, and declamation, with the young peer.

At dinner they joined Mrs Howel, who was charmed to see her young guests thus delighted, and could not refuse her consent to a petition of Lady Aurora, that she would invite Miss Ellis to assist her again, the next day, to nurse her cold with the same prudence.

The expressive eyes of Ellis spoke enchantment. They parted, therefore, only for the night; but just before the carriage was driven from the door, the coachman discovered that an accident had happened to one of the wheels, which could not be rectified till the next morning.

After some deliberation, Mrs Howel, at Lady Aurora's earnest desire, sent over a groom with a note to Mrs Maple, informing her of the circumstance, and begging that she would not expect Miss Ellis till the following evening.

The tears of Ellis, at happiness so unlooked for, were again ready to flow, and with difficulty restrained. She wrote a few words to Elinor, entreating her kind assistance, in searching a packet of some things necessary for this new plan; and Elinor took care to provide her with materials for remaining a month, rather than a day.

A chamber was now prepared for Ellis, in which nothing was omitted that could afford either comfort or elegance; yet, from the fulness of her mind, she could not, even for a moment, close her eyes, when she retired.

Some drawback, however, to her happiness was experienced the next morning, when she found Mrs Howel fearful that the cold of Lady Aurora menaced terminating in a violent cough. Dr P—— was immediately called in, and his principal prescription was, that Her Ladyship should avoid hot rooms, dancing, company, and talking. Mrs Howel, easily made anxious for Lady Aurora, not only from personal attachment, but from the responsibility of having her in charge, besought Her Ladyship to give up the play for that night, an assembly for the following, and to permit that the intended ball of Thursday should be postponed, till Her Ladyship should be perfectly recovered.

Lady Aurora, with a grace that accompanied all her actions, unhesitatingly complied; but enquired whether it would not be possible to persuade Miss Ellis to remain with them during this confinement? Mrs Howel repeated the request. The delight of Ellis was too deep for utterance. Joy of this tender sort always flung her into tears; and Lady Aurora, who saw that her heart was as oppressed as it was gentle, besought Mrs Howel to write their desire to Lewes.

Mrs Maple, however enraged and perplexed, had no choice how to act, without betraying the imposition which she had herself practised, and therefore offered no opposition.

Ellis now enjoyed a happiness, before which all her difficulties and disappointments seemed to sink forgotten, or but to be remembered as evils overpayed; so forcible was the effect upon her mind, of the contrast of her immediate situation with that so recently quitted. Mrs Howel was all politeness to her; Lord Melbury appeared to have no study, but whether to shew her most admiration or respect; and Lady Aurora behaved to her with a sweetness that went straight to her heart.

It was now that they first became acquainted with her uncommon musical talents. Lady Aurora had a piano forte in her room; and Mrs Howel said, that if Miss Ellis could play Her Ladyship an air or two, it might help to amuse, yet keep her silent. Ellis instantly went to the instrument, and there performed, in so fine a style, a composition of Haydn, that Mrs Howel, who, though by no means a scientific judge of music, was sufficiently in the habit of going to concerts, to have acquired the skill of discriminating excellence from mediocrity, was struck with wonder, and congratulated both her young guest and herself, in so seasonable an acquisition of so accomplished a visitor.

Lord Melbury, who was himself a tolerable proficient upon the violoncello, was enraptured at this discovery; and Lady Aurora, whose whole soul was music, felt almost dissolved with tender pleasure.

Nor ended here either their surprise or their satisfaction; they soon learnt that she played also upon the harp; Lord Melbury instantly went forth in search of one; and it was then, as this was the instrument which she had most particularly studied, that Ellis completed her conquest of their admiration; for with the harp she was prevailed upon to sing; and the sweetness of her voice, the delicacy of its tones, her taste and expression, in which her soul seemed to harmonize with her accents, had an effect so delightful upon her auditors, that Mrs Howel could scarcely find phrases for the compliments which she thought merited; Lord Melbury burst into the most rapturous applause; and Lady Aurora was enchanted, was fascinated: she caught the sweet sounds with almost extatic attention, hung on them with the most melting tenderness, entreated to hear the same air again and again, and felt a gratitude for the delight which she received, that was hardly inferior to that which her approbation bestowed.

Eager to improve these favourable sensations, Ellis, to vary the amusements of Lady Aurora, in this interval of retirement, proposed reading. And here again her powers gave the utmost pleasure; whether she took a French author, or an English one; the accomplished Boileau, or the penetrating Pope; the tenderly-refined Racine, or the all-pervading Shakespeare; her tones, her intelligence, her skilful modulations, gave force and meaning to every word, and proved alike her understanding and her feeling.

Brilliant, however, as were her talents, all the success which they obtained was short of that produced by her manners and conversation: in the former there was a gentleness, in the latter a spirit, that excited an interest for her in the whole house; but, while generally engaging to all by her general merit, to Lady Aurora she had peculiar attractions, from the excess of sensibility with which she received even the smallest attentions. She seemed impressed with a gratitude that struggled for words, without the power of obtaining such as could satisfy it. Pleasure shone lustrous in her fine eyes, every time that they met those of Lady Aurora; but if that young lady took her hand, or spoke to her with more than usual softness, tears, which she vainly strove to hide, rolled fast down her cheeks, but which, though momentarily overpowering, were no sooner dispersed, than every feature became re-animated with glowing vivacity.

Yet, that some latent sorrow hung upon her mind, Lady Aurora soon felt convinced; and that some solicitude or suspense oppressed her spirits, was equally evident: she was constantly watchful for the post, and always startled at sight of a letter. Lady Aurora was too delicate to endeavour to develope the secret cause of this uneasiness; but the good breeding which repressed the manifestation of curiosity, made the interest thus excited sink so much the deeper into her mind; and, in a short time, her every feeling, and almost every thought, were absorbed in tender commiseration for unknown distresses, which she firmly believed to be undeserved; and which, however nobly supported, seemed too poignant for constant suppression.

Lady Aurora, who had just reached her sixteenth year, was now budding into life, with equal loveliness of mind and person. She was fair, but pale, with elegant features, a face perfectly oval, and soft expressive blue eyes, of which the 'liquid lustre' spoke a heart that was the seat of sensibility; yet not of that weak romantic cast, formed by early and futile love-sick reading, either in novels or poems; but of compassionate feeling for woes which she did not suffer; and of anxious solicitude to lessen distress by kind offices, and affliction by tender sympathy.

With a character thus innately virtuous, joined to a disposition the most amiably affectionate, so attractive a young creature as the Incognita could not fail to be in unison. Without half her powers of pleasing, the most perfect good will of Lady Aurora would have been won, by the mere surmize that she was not happy: but when, to an idea so affecting to her gentle mind, were added the quick intelligence, the graceful manners, the touching sense of kindness, and the rare accomplishments of Ellis, so warm an interest was kindled in the generous bosom of Lady Aurora, that the desire to serve and to give comfort to her new favourite, became, in a short time, indispensable to her own peace.

Mrs Howel, the lady with whom she was at present a guest, possessed none of the endearing qualities which could catch the affections of a mind of so delicate a texture as that of Lady Aurora. She was well bred, well born, and not ill educated; but her heart was cold, her manners were stiff, her opinions were austere, and her resolutions were immoveable. Yet this character, with the general esteem in which, for unimpeachable conduct, she was held by the world, was the inducement which led her cousin, Lord Denmeath, the uncle and guardian of Lady Aurora, to fix upon her as a proper person for taking his ward into public; the tender and facile nature of that young lady, demanding, he thought, all the guard which the firmness of Mrs Howel could afford.

Lord Melbury was two years the senior of Lady Aurora: unassuming from his rank, and unspoiled by early independence, he was open, generous, kind-hearted and sincere; and though, from the ardour of juvenile freedom, and the credulity of youth, he was easily led astray, an instinctive love of right, and the acute self-reproaches which followed his least deviations, were conscious, and rarely erring guarantees, that his riper years would be happy in the wisdom of goodness.

In a house such as this, loved and compassionated by Lady Aurora, admired by Lord Melbury, and esteemed by Mrs Howel, what felicity was enjoyed by its new guest! Her suspenses and difficulties, though never forgotten, were rather gratefully than patiently endured; and she felt as if she could scarcely desire their termination, if it should part her from such heart-soothing society.

Smoothly thus glided the hours, till nearly a fortnight elapsed, Lady Aurora, though recovered, saying that she preferred this gentle social life, to the gayer or more splendid scenes offered to her abroad:

yet neither with gaiety nor splendour had she quarrelled; it was Ellis whom she could not bear to quit; Ellis, whose attractions and sweetness charmed her heart, and whose secret disturbance occupied all her thoughts.

The admiration of Lord Melbury was wrought still higher; yet the constant respect attending it, satisfied Mrs Howel, who would else have been alarmed, that his chief delight was derived from seeing that his sister, whom he adored, had a companion so peculiarly to her taste. Severely, however, Mrs Howel watched and investigated every look, every speech, every turn of the head of Ellis, with regard to this young nobleman; well aware that, as he was younger than herself, though her beauty was in its prime, his safety might depend, more rationally, upon her own views, or her own honour, than upon his prudence or indifference: but all that she observed tended to raise Ellis yet more highly in her esteem. The behaviour of that young person was open, pleasing, good-humoured and unaffected. It was evident that she wished to be thought well of by Lord Melbury; but it appeared to be equally evident that she honourably deserved his good opinion. Her desire to give him pleasure was unmixt with any species of coquetry: it was as wide from the dangerous toil of tender languor, as from the fascinating snares of alluring playfulness. The whole of her demeanour had a decorum, and of her conduct a correctness, as striking to the taste of Mrs Howel, as her conversation, her accomplishments, and her sentiments were to that of the youthful brother and sister. Mrs Howel often begged Lady Aurora to remark, that this was the only young lady whom she had ever invited to her house upon so short an acquaintance; nor should she, even to oblige Her Ladyship, have made this exception to her established rules, but that she knew Mrs Maple to be scrupulosity itself, with respect to the female friends whose intimacy she sanctioned with her nieces. It was well known, indeed, she observed, that Mrs Maple was forced to be the more exact in these points on account of the extraordinary liberties taken by the eldest Miss Joddrel, who, being now entirely independent, frequently flung off the authority of her aunt, and did things so strange, and saw people so singular, that she continually distressed Mrs Maple. Miss Ellis, therefore, having been brought back to her native land, by one so nice in these matters, must certainly be a young lady of good family; though there seemed reason to apprehend, that she was an orphan, and that she possessed little or no portion, by her never naming her friends nor her situation, notwithstanding they were subjects to which Mrs Howel often tried to lead.

CHAPTER XIV

Lady Aurora being now perfectly well, and the period of her visit at Brighthelmstone nearly expired, Mrs Howel could not dispense with repeating her dinner-invitation to Mrs Maple; and, three days previously to the return of Lady Aurora to her uncle, it was accepted.

The whole Lewes party felt the most eager curiosity to see Ellis in her new dwelling; but not trifling was the effort required by Mrs Maple to preserve any self-command, when she witnessed the high style in which that young person was treated throughout the house. Harleigh hastened to make his compliments to her, with an air of pleasure that spoke sympathising congratulation. Elinor was all eye, all scrutiny, but all silence. Ireton assumed, perforce, a tone of respect; and Selina, with such an example as Lady Aurora for her support, flew to embrace her protégée; and to relate, amongst sundry other little histories, that Mr Harleigh had been going back to town, only Aunt Maple had begged him to stay, till something could be brought about with regard to his brother Dennis, who was grown quite affronted at sister Elinor's long delays.

Mrs Maple, almost the whole dinner-time, had the mortification to hear, echoing from the sister to the brother, and re-echoed from Mrs Howel, the praises of Miss Ellis; how delightfully the retirement of Lady Aurora had passed in her society; the sweetness of her disposition, the variety of her powers, and her amiable activity in seeking to make them useful. Not daring to dissent, Mrs Maple, with forced smiles, gave a tacit concurrence; while the bright glow that animated the complexion, and every feature, of Harleigh, spoke that unequivocal approbation which comes warm from the heart.

Elinor, whose eyes constantly followed his, seemed sick during the whole repast, of which she scarcely at all partook. If Ellis offered to serve her, or enquired after her health, she darted at her an eye so piercing, that Ellis, shrinking and alarmed, determined to address her no more; though again, when any opportunity presented itself, for shewing some attention, the resolution was involuntarily set aside; but always with equal ill success, every attempt to soften, exciting looks the most terrific.

Lady Aurora surprised one of these glances, and saw its chilling effect. Astonished, at once, and grieved, she felt an impulse to rise, and to protect from such another shock her new and tenderly admired favourite. She now easily conceived why kindness was so touching to her; yet how any angry sensation could find its way in the breast of Miss Joddrel, or of any human being, against such sweetness and such excellence, her gentle mind, free from every feeling of envy, jealousy, or wrath, could form no conjecture. She sighed to withdraw her from a house where her merits were so ill appreciated; and could hardly persuade herself to speak to any one else at the table, from the eagerness with which she desired to dispel the gloom produced by Elinor's cloudy brow.

The looks of Elinor had struck Mrs Howel also; but not with similar compassion for their object; it was with alarm for herself. A sudden, though vague idea, seized her, to the disadvantage of Ellis. With all her accomplishments, all her elegance, was she, at last, but a dependent? Might she be smiled or frowned upon at will? And had she herself admitted into her house, upon equal terms, a person of such a description?

Doubt soon gives birth to suspicion, and suspicion is the mother of surmise. It was now strange that she should have been told nothing of the family and condition of Miss Ellis; there must be some reason for silence; and the reason could not be a good one.

Yet, was it possible that Mrs Maple could have been negligent upon such a subject? Mrs Maple who, far from being dangerously facile, in forming any connexion, was proud, was even censorious about every person that she knew or saw?

Mrs Howel now examined the behaviour of Mrs Maple herself to Ellis; and this scrutiny soon shewed her its entire constraint; the distance which she observed when not forced to notice her; the unwilling civility, where any attention was indispensable.

Something must certainly be wrong; and she determined, in the course of the evening, to find an opportunity for minutely, nay rigorously, questioning Mrs Maple. Ellis, meanwhile, fearing no one but Elinor, and watching no one but Lady Aurora, found sufficient occupation in the alternate panic and consolation thus occasioned; or if any chasm occurred, Lord Melbury with warm assiduities, and Harleigh with delicate attentions, were always at hand to fill it up.

When, early in the evening, that the horses might rest, the carriage of Mrs Maple arrived, the groom sent in a letter, which, he said, had just been brought to Lewes, according to order, by a messenger from the Brighthelmstone post-office. Ellis precipitately arose; but Mrs Maple held out her hand to take it; though, upon perceiving the direction, "For L.S., to be left at the post-office at Brighthelmstone till called for," fearing that Mrs Howel, who sat next to her, should perceive it also, she hastily said, 'It is not for me; let the man take it back again;' and, turning the seal upwards, redelivered it to the servant; anxious to avoid exhibiting an address, which might lead to a discovery that she now deemed personally ignominious.

Ellis, at this order, re-seated herself, not daring to make a public claim, but resolving to follow the footman out, and to desire to look at the direction of the letter. Elinor, however, stopping him, took it herself, and, after a slight glance, threw it upon a table, saying, 'Leave it for who will to own it.'

Ellis, changing colour, again arose; and would have seized it for examination, had not Ireton, who was nearer to the table, taken it up, and read, aloud, "For L.S." Again Ellis dropt upon her chair, distressed and perplexed, between eagerness to receive her letter, and shame and fear at acknowledging so mysterious a direction.

Her dread of the consequence of disobeying Mrs Maple, had made her, hitherto, defer relating her situation with regard to that lady; and she had always flattered herself, that the longer it was postponed, the greater would be her chance of inspiring such an interest as might cause an indulgent hearing.

Harleigh now took the letter himself, and, calmly saying that he would see it safely delivered, put it into his pocket.

Ellis, thus relieved from making an abrupt and unseasonable avowal, yet sure that her letter was in honourable custody, with difficulty refrained from thanking him. Lord Melbury and Mrs Howel thought there was something odd and unintelligible in the business, but forbore any enquiry; Lady Aurora, observing distress in her amiable Miss Ellis, felt it herself; but revived with her revival; and the rest of the company, though better informed, were compulsatorily silenced by the frowns of Mrs Maple.

Harleigh then, asking for a pen and some ink to write a letter, left the room. Ellis, tortured with impatience, and hoping to meet with him, soon followed. She was not mistaken: he had seated himself to write in an ante-room, which she must necessarily cross if she mounted to her chamber.

He softly arose, put the letter into her hand, bowed, and returned to his chair without speaking. She felt his delicacy as strongly as his kindness, but, breathless with eagerness, observed the silence of which he set the example, and, thanking him only by her looks, flew up stairs.

She was long absent, and, when she descended, it was with steps so slow, and with an air so altered, that Harleigh, who was still writing in the room through which she had to pass, saw instantly that her letter had brought disappointment and sorrow.

He had not, now, the same self-command as while he had hoped and thought that she was prosperous. He approached her, and, with a face of deep concern, enquired if there were any thing, of any sort, in which he could have the happiness to be of use to her? He stopt; but she felt his right to a curiosity which he did not avow, and immediately answered:

'My letter brings me no consolation! on the contrary, it tells me that I must depend wholly upon myself, and expect no kind of aid, nor even any intelligence again, perhaps for a considerable time!'

'Is that possible?' cried he, 'Does no one follow—or is no one to meet you?—Is there no one whose duty it is to guard and protect you? to draw you from a situation thus precarious, thus unfitting, and to which I am convinced you are wholly unaccustomed?'

'It is fatally true, at this moment,' answered Ellis, with a sigh, 'that no one can follow or support me; yet I am not deserted—I am simply unfortunate. Neither can any one here meet me: the few to whom I have any right to apply, know not of my arrival—and must not know it!—How I am to exist till I dare make some claim, I cannot yet devise: but, indeed, had it not been under this kind, protecting roof, that I have received such a letter—I think I must have sunk from my own dismay:—but Lady Aurora—' Her voice failed, and she stopt.

'Lady Aurora,' cried Harleigh, 'is an angel. Her quick appreciation of your worth, shews her understanding to be as good as her soul is pure. I can wish you no better protection. But pardon me, if I venture again to repeat my surprise—I had almost said my indignation—that those to whom you belong, can deem it right—safe—or decent, to commit you—young as you are, full of attractions, and evidently unused to struggle against the dangers of the world, and the hardships of life, to commit you to strangers—to chance!—'

'I know not how,' she cried, 'to leave you under so false an impression of those to whom I belong. They are not to blame. They are more unhappy than I am myself at my loneliness and its mystery: and for my poverty and my difficulties, they are far, far from suspecting them! They are ignorant of my loss at Dover, and they cannot suppose that I have missed the friend whom I came over to join.'

'Honour me,' cried he, 'with a commission, and I will engage to discover, at least, whether that friend be yet at Brighthelmstone.'

'And without naming for whom you seek her?' cried Ellis, her eyes brightening with sudden hope.

'Naming?' repeated he, with an arch smile.

She blushed, deeply, in recollecting herself; but, seized with a sudden dread of Elinor, drew back from her inadvertent acceptance; and, though warmly thanking him, declined his services; adding that, by waiting at Brighthelmstone, she must, ultimately, meet her friend, since all her letters and directions were for that spot.

Harleigh was palpably disappointed; and Ellis, hurt herself, opened her letter, to lessen, she told him, his wonder, perhaps censure, of her secresy, by reading to him its injunction. This was the sentence: 'Seek, then, unnamed and unknown, during this dread interval of separation, to reside with some worthy and happy family, whose social felicity may bring, at least, reflected happiness to your own breast.'

'That family,' she added, 'I flatter myself I have found here! for this house, from the uniform politeness of Mrs Howel, the ingenuous goodness of Lord Melbury, and the angelic sweetness of his sister, has been to me an earthly paradise.'

She then proceeded, without waiting to receive his thanks for this communication; which he seemed hardly to know how to offer, from the fulness of his thoughts, his varying conjectures, his conviction that her friends, like herself, were educated, feeling, and elegant; and his increased wonder at the whole of her position. Charming, charming creature! he cried, what can have cast thee into this forlorn condition? And by what means—and by whom—art thou to be rescued?

Not chusing immediately to follow, he seated himself again to his pen.

Somewhat recovered by this conversation, Ellis, now, was able to command an air of tolerable composure, for re-entering the drawing-room, where she resolved to seek Elinor at once, and endeavour to deprecate her displeasure, by openly repeating to her all that she had entrusted to Mr Harleigh.

As she approached the door, every voice seemed employed in eager talk; and, as she opened it, she observed earnest separate parties formed round the room; but the moment that she appeared, every one broke off abruptly from what he or she was saying, and a completely dead silence ensued.

Surprized by so sudden a pause, she seated herself on the first chair that was vacant, while she looked around her, to see whom she could most readily join. Mrs Howel and Mrs Maple had been, evidently, in the closest discourse, but now both fixed their eyes upon the ground, as if agreeing, at once, to say no more. Ireton was chatting, with lively volubility, to Lord Melbury, who attended to him with an air that seemed scared rather than curious; but neither of them now added another word. Elinor stood sullenly alone, leaning against the chimney-piece, with her eyes fastened upon the door, as if watching for its opening: but not all the previous resolution of Ellis, could inspire courage sufficient to address her, after viewing the increased sternness of her countenance. Selina was prattling busily to Lady Aurora; and Lady Aurora, who sat nearly behind her, and whom Ellis perceived the last, was listening in silence, and bathed in tears.

Terror and affliction seized upon Ellis at this sight. Her first impulse was to fly to Lady Aurora; but she felt discouraged, and even awed, by the strangeness of the general taciturnity, occasioned by her appearance. Her eyes next, anxiously, sought those of Lord Melbury, and instantly met them; but with a look of gravity so unusual, that her own were hastily withdrawn, and fixt, disappointed, upon the ground. Nor did he, as hitherto had been his constant custom, when he saw her disengaged, come to sit by her side. No one spoke; no one seemed to know how to begin a general or common conversation; no one could find a word to say.

What, cried she, to herself, can have happened? What can have been said or done, in this short absence, to make my sight thus petrifying? Have they told what they know of my circumstances? And has that been sufficient to deprive me of all consideration? to require even avoidance? And is Lord Melbury thus easily changed? And have I lost you—even you! Lady Aurora?

This last thought drew from her so deep a sigh, that, in the general silence which prevailed, it reached every ear. Lady Aurora started, and looked up; and, at the view of her evident dejection, hastily arose, and was crossing the room to join her; when Mrs Howel, rising too, came between them, and taking herself the hand which Lady Aurora had extended for that of Ellis, led Her Ladyship to a seat on a sofa, where, in the lowest voice, she apparently addressed to her some remonstrance.

Ellis, who had risen to meet the evident approach of Lady Aurora, now stood suspended, and with an air so embarrassed, so perturbed, that Lord Melbury, touched by irresistible compassion, came forward, and would have handed her to a chair near the fire; but her heart, after so sudden an appearance of general estrangement, was too full for this mark of instinctive, not intentional kindness, and courtsying the thanks which she could not utter, she precipitately left the room.

She met Harleigh preparing to enter it, but passed him with too quick a motion to be stopt, and hurried to her chamber.

There her disturbance, as potent from positive distress, as it was poignant from mental disappointment, would nearly have amounted to despair, but for the visibly intended support of Lady Aurora; and for the view of that kind hand, which, though Mrs Howel had impeded her receiving, she could not prevent her having seen stretched out for her comfort. The attention, too, of Lord Melbury, though its tardiness ill accorded with his hitherto warm demonstrations of respect and kindness, shewed that those feelings were not alienated, however they might be shaken.

These two ideas were all that now sustained her, till, in about an hour, she was followed by Selina, who came to express her concern, and to relate what had passed.

Ellis then heard, that the moment that she had left the room, Mrs Howel, almost categorically, though with many formal apologies, demanded some information of Mrs Maple, what account should be given to Lord Denmeath, of the family and condition in life, of the young lady introduced, by Mrs Maple, into the society of Lady Aurora Granville, as Her Ladyship proposed intimately keeping up the acquaintance. Mrs Maple had appeared to be thunderstruck, and tried every species of equivocation; but Mr Ireton whispered something to Lord Melbury, upon which a general curiosity was raised; and Mr Ireton's laughs kept up the enquiry, 'till, bit by bit,' continued Selina, 'all came out, and you never saw such a fuss in your life! But when Mrs Howel found that Aunt Maple did not take you in charge from your friends, because she did not know them; and when Mr Ireton told of your patches, and black skin, and ragged dress, Mrs Howel stared so at poor aunt, that I believe she thought that she had been out of her senses. And then, poor Lady Aurora fell a-crying, because Mrs Howel said that she must break off the connexion. But Lady Aurora said that you might be just as good as ever, and only disguised to make your escape; but Mrs Howel said, that, now you were got over, if there were not something bad, you would speak out. So then poor Lady Aurora cried again, and beckoned to me to come and tell her more particulars. Sister Elinor, all the time, never spoke one word. And this is what we were all doing when you came in.'

Ellis, who, with pale cheeks, but without comment, had listened to this recital, now faintly enquired what had passed after she had retired.

'Why, just then, in came Mr Harleigh, and Aunt Maple gave him a hundred reproaches, for beginning all the mischief, by his obstinacy in bringing you into the boat, against the will of every creature, except just the old Admiral, who knew nothing of the world, and could judge no better. He looked quite thunderstruck, not knowing a word of what had passed. However, he soon enough saw that all was found out; for Mrs Howel said, 'I hope, Sir, you will advise us, how to get rid of this person, without letting the servants know the indiscretion we have been drawn into, by treating her like one of ourselves.'

'Well? and Mr Harleigh's answer?—' cried the trembling Ellis.

'Miss Joddrel, Madam, he said, knows as well as myself, all the circumstances which have softened this mystery, and rendered this young lady interesting in its defiance. She has generously, therefore, held out her protection; of which the young lady has shown herself to be worthy, upon every occasion, since we have known her, by rectitude and dignity: yet she is, at this time, without friends, support, or asylum: in such a situation, thus young and helpless, and thus irreproachably conducting herself, who is the female—what is her age, what her rank, that ought not to assist and try to preserve so distressed a young person from evil? Lady Aurora, upon this, came forward, and said, "How happy you make me, Mr Harleigh, by thus reconciling me to my wishes!" And then she told Mrs Howel that, as the affair no longer appeared to be so desperate, she hoped that there could be no objection to her coming up stairs, to invite you down herself. But Mrs Howel would not consent.'

'Sweet! sweet Lady Aurora!' broke forth from Ellis; 'And Lord Melbury? what said he?'

'Nothing; for he and Mr Ireton left the room together, to go on with their whispers, I believe. And Elinor was just like a person dumb. But Lady Aurora and Mr Harleigh had a great deal of talk with one another, and they both seemed so pleased, that I could not help thinking, how droll it would be if their agreeing so about you should make them marry one another.'

'Then indeed would two beings meet,' said Ellis, 'who would render that state all that can be perfect upon earth; for with active benevolence like his, with purity and sweetness like hers, what could be wanting?—And then, indeed, I might find an asylum!'

A servant came, now, to inform Selina that the carriage was at the door, and that Mrs Maple was in haste.

What a change did this day produce for Ellis! What a blight to her hopes, what difficulties for her conduct, what agitation for her spirits!


CHAPTER XV

Ellis, who soon heard the carriage drive off for Lewes, waited in terrour to learn the result of this scene; almost equally fearful of losing the supporting kindness of Lady Aurora through timid acquiescence, as of preserving it through efforts to which her temper and gentle habits were repugnant.

In about half an hour, Mrs Howel's maid came to enquire whether Miss Ellis would have any thing brought up stairs for supper; Mrs Howel having broken up the usual evening party, in order to induce Lady Aurora, who was extremely fatigued, to go to rest.

Not to rest went Ellis, after such a message, though to that bed which had brought to her, of late, the repose of peace and contentment, and the alertness of hope and pleasure. A thousand schemes crossed her imagination, for averting the desertion which she saw preparing, and which her augmenting attachment to Lady Aurora, made her consider as a misfortune that would rob her of every consolation. But no plan occurred that satisfied her feeling without wounding her dignity: the first prompted a call upon the tender heart of Lady Aurora, by unlimited confidence; the second, a manifestation how ill she thought she merited the change of treatment that she experienced, by resentfully quitting the house: but this was no season for the smallest voluntary hazard. All chance of security hung upon the exertion of good sense, and the right use of reason, which imperiously demanded active courage with patient forbearance.

She remitted, therefore, forming any resolution, till she should learn that of Mrs Howel.

It was now the first week of February, and, before the break of day, a general movement in the house gave her cause to believe that the family was risen. She hastened to dress herself, unable to conjecture what she had to expect. The commotion continued; above and below the servants seemed employed, and in haste; and, in a little time, some accidental sounds reached her ears, from which she gathered that an immediate journey to London was preparing.

What could this mean? Was she thought so intruding, that by change of abode alone they could shake her off? or so dangerous, that flight, only, could preserve Lady Aurora from her snares? And was it thus, she was to be apprized that she must quit the house? Without a carriage, without money, and without a guide, was she to be turned over to the servants? and by them turned, perhaps, from the door?

Indignation now helped to sustain her; but it was succeeded by the extremest agitation, when she saw, from her window, Lord Melbury mounting his horse, upon which he presently rode off.

And is it thus, she cried, that all I thought so ingenuous in goodness, so open in benevolence, so sincere in partiality, subsides into neglect, perhaps forgetfulness?—And you, Lady Aurora, will you, also, give me up as lightly?

She wept. Indignation was gone: sorrow only remained; and she listened in sadness for every sound that might proclaim the departure which she dreaded.

At length, she heard a footstep advance slowly to her chamber, succeeded by a tapping at her door.

Her heart beat with hope. Was it Lady Aurora? had she still so much kindness, so much zeal?—She flew to meet her own idea—but saw only the lady of the house.

She sighed, cruelly disappointed; but the haughty distance of Mrs Howel's air restored her courage; for courage, where there is any nobleness of mind, always rises highest, when oppressive pride seeks to crush it by studied humiliation.

Mrs Howel fixed her eyes upon the face of Ellis, with an expression that said, Can you bear to encounter me after this discovery? Then, formally announcing that she had something important to communicate, she added, 'You will be so good as to shut the door,' and seated herself on an arm-chair, by the fire side; without taking any sort of notice that her guest was still standing.

Ellis could far better brook behaviour such as this from Mrs Maple, from whom she had never experienced any of a superior sort; but by Mrs Howel she had been invited upon equal terms, and, hitherto, had been treated not only with equality but distinction: hard, therefore, she found it to endure such a change; yet her resentment was soon governed by her candour, when it brought to her mind the accusation of appearances.

Mrs Howel then began an harangue palpably studied: 'You cannot, I think, young woman—for you must excuse my not addressing you by a name I now know you to have assumed;—you cannot, I think, be surprised to find that your stay in this house is at an end. To avoid, however, giving any publicity to your disgrace, at the desire of Mrs Maple, who thinks that its promulgation, in a town such as this, might expose her, as well as yourself, to impertinent lampoons, I shall take no notice of what has passed to any of my people; except to my housekeeper, to whom it is necessary I should make over some authority, which you will not, I imagine, dispute. For myself, I am going to town immediately with Lady Aurora. I have given out that it is upon sudden business, with proper directions that my domestics may treat you with civility. You will still breakfast, therefore, in the parlour; and, at your own time, you will ask for a chaise, which I have bespoken to carry you back to Lewes. To prevent any suspicion in the neighbourhood, I shall leave commands that a man and horse may attend you, in the same manner as when you came hither. No remark, therefore, will follow your not having my own carriage again, as I make use of it myself. Lord Melbury is set off already. We shall none of us return till I hear, from Mrs Maple, that you have left this part of the country; for, as I can neither receive you, nor notice you where I might happen to meet with you, such a difference of conduct, after this long visit, might excite animadversion. The sooner, therefore, you change your quarters, the better; for I coincide in the opinion of Mrs Maple, that it is wisest, for all our sakes, that this transaction should not be spread in the world. And now, young woman, all I ask of you in return for the consideration I shew you, is this; that you will solemnly engage to hold no species of intercourse with Lady Aurora Granville, or with Lord Melbury, either by speech, or writing, or message. If you observe this, I shall do you no hurt; if not, expect every punishment my resentment can inflict, and that of the noble family, involved in the indignity which you have made me suffer, by a surreptitious entrance into my house as a young lady of fashion.'

No sort of answer was offered by Ellis. She stood motionless, her eyes fixed, and her air seeming to announce her almost incredulous of what she heard.

'Do you give me,' said Mrs Howel, 'this promise? Will you bind yourself to it in writing?'

Ellis still was silent, and looked incapable of speaking.

'Young woman,' said Mrs Howel, with increased austerity, 'I am not to be trifled with. Will you bind yourself to this agreement, or will you not?'

'What agreement, Madam?' she now faintly asked.

'Not to seek, and even to refuse, any sort of intercourse with Lady Aurora Granville, or with her brother, either by word of mouth, or letter, or messenger? Will you, I say, bind yourself, upon your oath, to this?'

'No, Madam!' answered Ellis, with returning recollection and courage; 'no peril can be so tremendous as such a sacrifice!'

Mrs Howel, rising, said, 'Enough! abide by the consequence.'

She was leaving the room; but Ellis, affrighted, exclaimed, 'Ah, Madam, before you adopt any violent measures against me, deign to reflect that I may be innocent, and not merit them!'

'Innocent?' repeated Mrs Howel, with an air of inexorable ire; 'without a name, without a home, without a friend?—Innocent? presenting yourself under false appearances to one family, and under false pretences to another? No, I am not such a dupe. And if your bold resistance make it necessary, for the safety of my young friends, that I should lodge an information against you, you will find, that people who enter houses by names not their own, and who have no ostensible means of existence; will be considered only as swindlers; and as swindlers be disposed of as they deserve.'

Ellis, turning pale, sunk upon a chair.

Mrs Howel, stopping, with a voice as hard as her look was implacable, added; 'This is your last moment for repentance. Will you give your promise, upon oath?'

'No, Madam! again no!' cried Ellis, starting up with sudden energy: 'What I have suffered shall teach me to suffer more, and what I have escaped, shall give me hope for my support! But never will I plight myself, by willing promise, to avoid those whose virtuous goodness and compassion offer me the only consolation, that, in my desolate state, I can receive!'

"Tis well!' said Mrs Howel, 'You have yourself, then, only to thank for what ensues.'

She now steadily went on, opened the door, and left the room, though Ellis, mournfully following her, called out: Ah, Madam!—ah, Mrs Howel!—if ever you know more of me—which, at least, is not impossible, you will look back to this period with no pleasure!—or with pleasure only to that part of it, in which you received me at your house with politeness, hospitality, and kindness!'

Mrs Howel was not of a nature to relent in what she felt, or to retract from what she said: the distress, therefore, of Ellis, produced not the smallest effect upon her; and, with her head stiffly erect, and her countenance as unmoved as her heart, she descended the stairs, and issued, aloud, her commands that the horses should immediately be put to the chaise.

Ellis shut herself in her room, almost overpowered by the shock of this attack, so utterly unexpected, from a lady in whose character the leading feature seemed politeness, and who always appeared to hold that quality to be pre-eminent to all others. But the experience of Ellis had not yet taught her, how distinct is the politeness of manner, formed by the habits of high life, to that which springs spontaneously from benevolence of mind. The first, the product of studied combinations, is laid aside, like whatever is factitious, where there is no object for acting a part: the second, the child of sympathy, instructs us how to treat others, by suggesting the treatment we desire for ourselves; and this, as its feelings are personal, though its exertions are external, demands no effort, waits no call, and is never failingly at hand.

The gloomy sadness of Ellis was soon interrupted, by enquiries that reached her from the hall, whether the trunks of Lady Aurora were ready. Is she so nearly gone? Ellis cried; Ah! when may I see her again?—To the hall, to wait in the hall, she longed to go herself, to catch a last view, and to snatch, if possible, a kind parting word; but the tremendous Mrs Howel!—she shrunk from the idea of ever seeing her again.

Soon afterwards, she heard the carriages drive up to the house. She now went to the window, to behold, at least, the loved form of Lady Aurora as she mounted the chaise. Perhaps, too, she might turn round, and look up. Fixt here, she was inattentive to the opening of her own room-door, concluding that the house-maid came to arrange her fire, till a soft voice gently articulated: 'Miss Ellis!' She hastily looked round: it was Lady Aurora; who had entered, who had shut herself in, and who, while one hand covered her eyes, held out the other, in an attitude of the most inviting affection.

Ellis flew to seize it, with joy inexpressible, indescribable, and would have pressed it to her lips; but Lady Aurora, flinging both her arms round the neck of her new friend, fell upon her bosom, and wept, saying, 'You are not, then, angry, though I, too, must have seemed to behave to you so cruelly?'

'Angry?' repeated Ellis, sobbing from the suddenness of a delight which broke into a sorrow nearly hopeless; 'O Lady Aurora! if you could know how I prize your regard! your goodness!—what a balm it is to every evil I now experience, your gentle and generous heart would be recompensed for all the concern I occasion it, by the pleasure of doing so much good!'

'You can still, then, love me, my Miss Ellis?'

'Ah, Lady Aurora! if I dared say how much!—but, alas, in my helpless situation, the horror of being suspected of flattery—'

'What you will not say, then,' cried Lady Aurora, smiling, 'will you prove?'

'Will I?—Alas, that I could!'

'Will you let me take a liberty with you, and promise not to be offended?'

She put a letter into her hand, which Ellis fondly kissed, and lodged near her heart.

The words 'Where is Lady Aurora?' now sounded from the staircase.

'I must stay,' she said, 'no longer! Adieu, dear Miss Ellis! Think of me sometimes—for I shall think of you unceasingly!'

'Ah, Lady Aurora!' cried Ellis, clinging to her, 'shall I see you, then, no more? And is this a last leave-taking?'

'O, far from it, far, far, I hope!' said Lady Aurora: 'if I thought that we should meet no more, it would be impossible for me to tell you how unhappy this moment would make me!'

'Where is Lady Aurora?' would again have hurried her away; but Ellis, still holding by her, cried, 'One moment! one moment!—I have not, then, lost your good opinion? Oh! if that wavers, my firmness wavers too! and I must unfold—at all risks—my unhappy situation!'

'Not for the world! not for the world!' cried Lady Aurora, earnestly: 'I could not bear to seem to have any doubt to remove, when I have none, none, of your perfect innocence, goodness, excellence!'

Overpowered with grateful joy, 'Angelic Lady Aurora!' was all that Ellis could utter, while tears rolled fast down her cheeks; and she tenderly, yet fervently, kissed the hand of the resisting Lady Aurora, who, extremely affected, leant upon her bosom, till she was startled by again hearing her name from without. 'Go, then, amiable Lady Aurora!' Ellis cried; 'I will no longer detain you! Go!—happy in the happiness that your sweetness, your humanity, your kindness bestow! I will dwell continually, upon their recollection; I will say to myself, Lady Aurora believes me innocent, though she sees me forlorn; she will not think me unworthy, though she knows me to be unprotected; she will not conclude me to be an adventurer, though I dare not tell her even my name!'

'Do not talk thus, my dear, dear Miss Ellis! Oh! if I were my own mistress—with what delight I should supplicate you to live with me entirely! to let us share between us all that we possess; to read together, study our musick together, and never, never to part!'

Ellis could hardly breathe: her soul seemed bursting with emotions, which, though the most delicious, were nearly too mighty for her frame. But the melting kindness of Lady Aurora soon soothed her into more tranquil enjoyment; and when, at length, a message from Mrs Howel irresistibly compelled a separation, the warm gratitude of her heart, for the consolation which she had received, enabled her to endure it with fortitude. But not without grief. All seemed gone when Lady Aurora was driven from the door; and she remained weeping at the window, whence she saw her depart, till she was roused by the entrance of Mrs Greaves, the housekeeper.

Her familiar intrusion, without tapping at the door, quickly brought to the recollection of Ellis the authority which had been vested in her hands. This immediately restored her spirit; and as the housekeeper, seating herself, was beginning, very unceremoniously, to explain the motives of her visit, Ellis, without looking at her, calmly said, 'I shall go down stairs now to breakfast; but if you have time to be so good as to make up my packages, you will find them in those drawers.'

She then descended to the parlour, leaving the housekeeper stupified with amazement. But the forms of subordination, when once broken down, are rarely, with common characters, restored. Glad of the removal of a barrier which has kept them at a distance from those above them, they revel in the idea that the fall of a superiour is their own proper elevation. Following, therefore, Ellis to the breakfast-room, and seating herself upon a sofa, she began to discourse with the freedom of addressing a disgraced dependent; saying, 'Mrs Maple will be in a fine taking, Miss, to have you upon her hands, again, so all of the sudden.'

This speech, notwithstanding its grossness, surprised from Ellis an exclamation, 'Does not Mrs Maple, then, expect me?'

'How should she, when my lady never settled what she should do about you herself, till after twelve o'clock last night? However, as to sending you back without notice, she had no notion, she says, of standing upon any ceremony with Mrs Maple, who made so little of popping you upon her and Lady Aurora in that manner.'

Ellis turned from her with disdain, and would reply to nothing more; but her pertinacious stay still kept the bosom letter unopened.

Grievously Ellis felt tormented with the prospect of what her reception might be from Mrs Maple, after such a blight. The buoyant spirit of her first escape, which she had believed no after misfortune could subdue, had now so frequently been repressed, that it was nearly borne down to the common standard of mortal condition, whence we receive our daily fare of good and of evil, with the joy or the grief that they separately excite; independently of that wonderful power, believed in by the youthful and inexperienced, of hoarding up the felicity of our happy moments, as a counterpoise to future sorrows and disappointments. The past may re-visit our hearts with renewed sufferings, or our spirits with gay recollections; but the interest of the time present, even upon points the most passing and trivial, will ever, from the pressure of our wants and our feelings, predominate.

Mrs Greaves, unanswered and affronted, was for some minutes silenced; but, presently, rising and calling out, 'Gemini! something has happened to my Lady, or to Lady Aurora? Here's My Lord gallopped back!' she ran out of the room.

Affrighted by this suggestion, Ellis, who then perceived Lord Melbury from the window, ran herself, after the housekeeper, to the door, and eagerly exclaimed, as he dismounted, 'O, My Lord, I hope no accident—'

'None!' cried he, flying to her and taking and kissing both her hands, and drawing, rather than leading, her back to the parlour, 'none!—or if any there were, what could be the accident that concern so bewitching would not recompense?'

Ellis felt amazed. Lord Melbury had never addressed her before in any tone of gallantry; had never kissed, never touched her hand; yet now, he would scarcely suffer her to withdraw it from his ardent grasp.

'But, My Lord,' said Mrs Greaves, who followed them in, 'pray let me ask Your Lordship about my Lady, and My Lady Aurora, and how—'

'They are perfectly well,' cried he, hastily, 'and gone on. I am ridden back myself merely for something which I forgot.'

'I was fearful,' said Ellis, anxious to clear up her eager reception, 'that something might have happened to Lady Aurora; I am extremely happy to hear that all is safe.'

'And you will have the charity, I hope, to make me a little breakfast? for I have tasted nothing yet this morning.'

Again he took both her hands, and led her to the seat which she had just quitted at the table.

She was extremely embarrassed. She felt reluctant to refuse a request so natural; yet she was sure that Mrs Howel would conclude that they met by appointment; and she saw in the face of the housekeeper the utmost provocation at the young Lord's behaviour: yet neither of these circumstances gave her equal disturbance, with observing a change, indefinable yet striking, in himself. After an instant's reflection, she deemed it most advisable not to stay with him; and, saying that she was in haste to return to Lewes, she begged that Mrs Greaves would order the chaise that Mrs Howel had mentioned.

'Ay, do, good Greaves!' cried he, hurrying her out, and, in his eagerness to get her away, shutting the door after her himself.

Ellis said that she would see whether her trunk were ready.

'No, no, no! don't think of the trunk,' cried he: 'We have but a few minutes to talk together, and to settle how we shall meet again.'

Still more freely than before, he now rather seized than took her hand; and calling her his dear charming Ellis, pressed it to his lips, and to his breast, with rapturous fondness.

Ellis, struck, now, with terrour, had not sufficient force to withdraw her hand; but when she said, with great emotion, 'Pray, pray My Lord!—' he let it go.

It was only for a moment: snatching, it then, again, as she was rising to depart, he suddenly slipt upon one of her fingers a superb diamond ring, which he took off from one of his own.

'It is very beautiful, My Lord;' said she, deeply blushing; yet looking at it as if she supposed he meant merely to call for her admiration, and returning it to him immediately.

'What's this?' cried he: 'Won't you wear such a bauble for my sake? Give me but a lock of your lovely hair, and I will make myself one to replace it.'

He tried to put the ring again on her finger; but, forcibly breaking from him, she would have left the room: he intercepted her passage to the door. She turned round to ring the bell: he placed himself again in her way, with a flushed air of sportiveness, yet of determined opposition.

Confounded, speechless, she went to one of the windows, and standing with her back to it, looked at him with an undisguised amazement, that she hoped would lead him to some explanation of his behaviour, that might spare her any serious remonstrance upon its unwelcome singularity.

'Why, what's this?' cried he gaily, yet with a gaiety not perfectly easy; 'do you want to run away from me?'

'No, my lord,' answered she, gravely, yet forcing a smile, which she hoped would prove, at once, a hint, and an inducement to him to end the scene as an idle and ill-judged frolic; 'No; I have only been afraid that your lordship was running away from yourself!'

'And why so?' cried he, with quickness, 'Is Harleigh the only man who is ever to be honoured with your company tête-à-tête?'

'What can your lordship mean?'

'What can the lovely Ellis blush for? And what can Harleigh have to offer, that should obtain for him thus exclusively all favour? If it be adoration of your charms, who shall adore them more than I will? If it be in proofs of a more solid nature, who shall vie with me? All I possess shall be cast at your feet. I defy him to out-do me, in fortune or in love.'

Ellis now turned pale and cold: horrour thrilled through her veins, and almost made her heart cease to beat. Lord Melbury saw the change, and, hastily drawing towards her a chair, besought her to be seated. She was unable to refuse, for she had not strength to stand; but, when again he would have taken her hand, she turned from him, with an air so severe of soul-felt repugnance, that, starting with surprise and alarm, he forbore the attempt.

He stood before her utterly silent, and with a complexion frequently varying, till she recovered; when, again raising her eyes, with an expression of mingled affliction and reproach, 'And is it, then,' she cried, 'from a brother of the pure, the exemplary Lady Aurora Granville, that I am destined to receive the most heart-rending insult of my life?'

Lord Melbury seemed thunderstruck, and could not articulate what he tried to say; but, upon again half pronouncing the name of Harleigh, Ellis, standing up, with an air of dignity the most impressive, cried, 'My lord, Mr Harleigh rescued me from the most horrible of dangers, in assisting me to leave the Continent; and his good offices have befriended me upon every occasion since my arrival in England. This includes the whole of our intercourse! No calumny, I hope, will make him ashamed of his benevolence; and I have reaped from it such benefit, that the most cruel insinuations must not make me repent receiving it; for to whom else, except to Lady Aurora, do I owe gratitude without pain? He knows me to be indigent, my lord, yet does not conclude me open to corruption! He sees me friendless and unprotected, yet offers me no indignity!'

Lord Melbury now, in his turn, looked pale. 'Is it possible—' he cried, 'Is it possible, that—' He stammered, and was in the utmost confusion.

She passed him, and was quitting the room.

'Good Heaven!' cried he, 'you will not go?—you will not leave me in this manner?—not knowing what to think, what to judge, what to do?'

She made no answer but by hastening her footsteps, and wearing an aspect of the greatest severity; but, when her hand touched the lock, 'I swear to you,' he cried, 'Miss Ellis, if you will not stay—I will follow you!'

Her eyes now shot forth a glance the most indignant, and she resolutely opened the door.

He spread out his arms to impede her passage.

Offended by his violence, and alarmed by this detention, she resentfully said, 'If you compel me, my lord, to summon the servants—' when, upon looking at him again, she saw that his whole face was convulsed by the excess of his emotion.

She stopt.

'You must permit me,' he cried, 'to shut the door; and you must grant me two minutes audience.'

She neither consented nor offered any opposition.

He closed the door, but she kept her place.

'Tell—speak to me, I beseech you!' he cried, 'Oh clear the cruel doubts—'

'No more, my lord, no more!' interrupted Ellis, scorn taking possession of every feature; 'I will neither give to myself the disgrace, nor to your lordship the shame, of permitting another word to be said!'

'What is it you mean?' cried he, planting himself against the door; 'you would not—surely you would not brand me for a villain?'

She determined to have recourse to the bell, and, with the averted eyes of disdain, resolutely moved towards the chimney.

He saw her design, and cast himself upon his knees, calling out, in extreme agitation, 'Miss Ellis! Miss Ellis! you will not assemble the servants to see me groveling upon the earth?'

Greatly shocked, she desisted from her purpose. His look was aghast, his frame was in a universal tremour, and his eyes were wild and starting. Her wrath subsided at this sight, but the most conflicting emotions rent her heart.

'I see,' he cried, in a tremulous voice, and almost gnashing his teeth, 'I see that you have been defamed, and that I have incurred your abhorrence!—I have my own, too, completely! You cannot hate me more than I now hate—than I shrink from myself! And yet—believe me, Miss Ellis! I have no deliberate hardness of heart!—I have been led on by rash precipitance, and—and want of thought!—Believe me, Miss Ellis!—believe me, good Miss Ellis!—for I see, now, how good you are!— believe me—'

He could find no words for what he wished to say. He rose, but attempted not to approach her. Ellis leant against the wainscot, still close to the bell, but without seeking to ring it. Both were silent. His extreme youth, his visible inexperience, and her suspicious situation; joined to his quick repentance, and simple, but emphatic declaration, that he had no hardness of heart, began not only to offer some palliation for his conduct, but to soften her resentment into pity.

He no sooner perceived the touching melancholy which insensibly took place, in her countenance, of disgust and indignation, than, forcibly affected, he struck his forehead, exclaiming, 'Oh, my poor Aurora!—when you know how ill I have acted, it will almost break your gentle heart!'

This was an apostrophe to come home quick to the bosom of Ellis: she burst into tears; and would instantly have held out to him her hand, as an offering of peace and forgiveness, had not her fear of the impetuosity of his feelings checked the impulse. She only, therefore, said, 'Ah, my lord, how is it that with a sister so pure, so perfect, and whose virtues you so warmly appreciate, you should find it so difficult to believe that other females may be exempt, at least, from depravity? Alas! I had presumed, my lord, to think of you as indeed the brother of Lady Aurora; and, as such, I had even dared to consider you as a succour to me in distress, and a protector in danger!'

'Ah! consider me so again!' cried he, with sudden rapture; 'good—excellent Miss Ellis! consider me so again, and you shall not repent your generous pardon!'

Ellis irresistibly wept, but, by a motion of her hand, forbad his approach.

'Fear, fear me not!' cried he, 'I am a reclaimed man for the rest of my life! I have hitherto, Miss Ellis, been but a boy, and therefore so easily led wrong. But I will think and act, now, for myself. I promise it you sincerely! Never, never more will I be the wretched tool of dishonourable impertinence! Not that I am so unmanly, as to seek any extenuation to my guilt, from its being excited by others;—no; it rather adds to its heinousness, that my own passions, violent as they sometimes are, did not give it birth. But your so visible purity, Miss Ellis, had kept them from any disrespect, believe me! And, struck as I have been with your attractions, and charmed with your conversation, it has always been without a single idea that I could not tell to Aurora herself; for as I thought of you always as of Aurora's favourite, Aurora's companion, Aurora's friend, I thought of you always together.'

'Oh Lord Melbury!' interrupted Ellis, fresh tears, but of pleasure, not sorrow, gushing into her eyes; 'what words are these! how penetrating to my very soul! Ah, my lord, let this unhappy morning be blotted from both our memories! and let me go back to the morning of yesterday! to a partiality that made, and that makes me so happy! to a goodness, a kindness, that revive me with heart-consoling gratitude!'

'Oh, incomparable—Oh, best Miss Ellis!' cried Lord Melbury, in a transport of joy, and passionately advancing; but retreating nearly at the same instant, as if fearful of alarming her; and almost fastening himself against the opposite wainscoat; 'how excessive is your goodness!'

A sigh from Ellis checked his rapture; and she entreated him to explain what he meant by his allusion to 'others.'

His complexion reddened, and he would have evaded any reply; but Ellis was too urgent to be resisted. Yet it was not without the utmost difficulty that she could prevail upon him to be explicit. Finally, however, she gathered, that Ireton, after the scene produced by the letter for L.S., had given vent to the most sneering calumnies, chiefly pointed at Harleigh, to excite the experiment of which he had himself so shamefully, yet foolishly, been the instrument. He vowed, however, that Ireton should publicly acknowledge his slanders, and beg her pardon.

Ellis earnestly besought his lordship to let the matter rest. 'All public appeals,' cried she, 'are injurious to female fame. Generously inform Mr Ireton, that you are convinced he has wronged me, and then leave the clearing of his own opinion to time and to truth. When they are trusted with innocence, Time and Truth never fail to do it justice.'

Lord Melbury struggled to escape making any promise. His self-discontent could suggest no alleviation so satisfactory, as that of calling Mr Ireton to account for defamation; an action which he thought would afford the most brilliant amends that could be offered to Miss Ellis, and the best proof that could blazon his own manliness. But when she solemnly assured him, that his compliance with her solicitation was the only peace-offering she could accept, for sinking into oblivion the whole morning's transaction, he forbore any further contestation.

Mrs Greaves now brought information, that a chaise was at the door, and that a groom was in readiness. Lord Melbury timidly offered Ellis his hand, which she gracefully accepted; but neither of them spoke as he led her to the carriage.

CHAPTER XVI

From all the various sufferings of Ellis, through the scenes of this morning, the predominant remaining emotion, was that of pity for her penitent young offender; whom she saw so sorely wounded by a sense of his own misconduct, that he appeared to be almost impenetrable to comfort.

But all her attention was soon called to the letter of Lady Aurora.

'To Miss Ellis.

'I cannot express the grief with which I have learnt the difficulties that involve my dear Miss Ellis. Will she kindly mitigate it, by allowing me, from time to time, the consolation of offering her my sympathy? May I flatter myself that she has sufficient regard for me, to let the enclosed trifle lead the way to some little arrangement during her embarrassment? Oh! were I in similar distress, I would not hesitate to place in her a similar trust! Generously, then, sweet Miss Ellis, confide in my tender regard.

'AURORA GRANVILLE.'

'At Lord Denmeath's, Portman Square.'

The 'enclosed trifle' was a bank-note of twenty pounds.

Most welcome to the distress of Ellis was this kindness and this succour; and greatly she felt revived, that, severe as had been her late conflicts, they thus terminated in casting her, for all pecuniary perplexities, upon the delicate and amiable Lady Aurora.

Uncertain what might prove her reception, she desired, upon approaching Lewes, that the groom would ride on, and enquire whether she could have the honour of seeing Mrs Maple. The man then said, that he had a note for that lady, from Mrs Howel.

After being detained at the gate a considerable time, a servant came to acquaint Miss Ellis, that the ladies were particularly engaged, but begged that she would walk up stairs to her room.

There, again established, she had soon a visit from Selina, who impatiently demanded, how she had parted from Lady Aurora; and, when satisfied that it had been with the extremest kindness, she warmly embraced her, before she related, that Aunt Maple had, at first, declared, that she would never, again, let so unknown a pauper into her house; but, when she had read the note of Mrs Howel, she changed her tone. That lady had written word, that she was hastening to consign Lord Melbury and Lady Aurora to their uncle; in order to be acquitted of all responsibility, as to any continuance of this amazing acquaintance, now that, at last, she was apprized of its unfitness. She conceived that she had some claim, however, to desire, that Mrs Maple would, for the present, receive the person as usual; since if any dismissal, or disgrace, were immediately to follow her return from Howel House, it might publish to the world what an improper character had been admitted there; a mortification from which she thought that she had some right to be exempted.

Mrs Maple was by no means the less offended, by the pride and selfishness of this note, because those qualities were familiar to her own practice. It is the wise and good alone that make allowance for defects in others. Her resentment, however, endowed her with rancour, but not with courage;

she complied, therefore, with the demand which she did not dare dispute; but her spleen against its helpless object was redoubled; and she sent her a message, by Selina, to order that she would complain of a sore throat, as an excuse for not quitting her room, nor expecting any of the ladies to visit her: yet charged her to be careful, at the same time, to say, that it was very slight, lest the people in the neighbourhood, or the servants themselves, should wonder at not seeing a physician.

Ellis could by no means repine at a separation, that saved her from the pride and malevolence of Mrs Maple and of Ireton, and from the distressing incongruities of Elinor.

Her spirits being thus freed from immediate alarm, she was able to ruminate upon her situation, and upon what efforts she might make for its amelioration. Her letter from abroad enjoined her still to live in concealment, with respect to her name, circumstances, and story: all hope, therefore, of any speedy change was blown over; and many fears remained, that this helpless obscurity might be of long duration. It was necessary that she should form some plan, to accommodate her mode of life to her immediate condition; and to liberate, if possible, her feelings, from the continual caprices to which she was now subject.

To live upon charity, was hostile to all her notions, though the benefaction of Lady Aurora had soothed, not mortified, her proudest sensations. But Lady Aurora was not of an age to be supposed already free from controul, in the use of her income; and still less was she of a character, to resist the counsel, or even wishes of her friends. Ellis was determined not to induce her to do either: nor could she endure to give a mercenary character to a grateful affection, which languished to shew that its increase, as well as its origin, sprang from disinterested motives. All her thoughts, therefore, turned upon making the present offering suffice.

Yet she was aware how short a time she could exist upon twenty pounds; and while a residence at Mrs Maple's would be now more than ever unpleasant, recent circumstances had rendered it, more than ever, also, unlikely.

To acquire that sort of independence, that belongs, physically, to sustaining life by her own means, was her most earnest desire: Her many accomplishments invited her industry, and promised it success; yet how to bring them into use was difficult. She had no one with whom she could consult. Elinor, though, at times, cordially her friend, seemed, in other minutes, her enraged foe. Selina was warmly good natured, but young in every sense of the word; and Mrs Maple considered her always with such humiliating ideas, that to ask her advice would be to invite an affront.

The occupation for which she thought herself most qualified, and to which, from fondness for young people, she felt herself most inclined, was that of governess to some young lady, or ladies; and, finally, she settled, that she would endeavour to employ herself in that capacity.

This arrangement mentally made, she communicated it, in a letter of the tenderest and most grateful thanks, to Lady Aurora; entreating her ladyship's kind and valuable aid, to enable her to leave, in future, for other distressed objects, such marks of benevolence as she had last received; and to owe, personally, those, only, of esteem and regard; which she prized beyond all power of expression.

The next day, again, very unexpectedly, Selina skipt into her room. 'We have had a most terrible fuss:' she cried; 'Do you know Lord Melbury's come on purpose to see you!'

'Lord Melbury? Is he not gone to town?'

'Mrs Howel wrote word so, and aunt thought so; but he only went a little way; and then came back to spend two or three days with Sir Lyell Sycamore, at Brighthelmstone. He asked after you, when he came in, and said that he begged leave to be allowed to speak with you, a few minutes, upon a commission from Lady Aurora. Aunt was quite shocked, and said, that she hoped his lordship would excuse her, but she really could not consent to any such acquaintance going on, in her house, now he knew so well what a nobody you were; if not worse. Upon which he said he did not doubt your being a well brought up young lady, for he was certain that you were modesty itself. And then he begged so hard, and said so many pretty and civil things to Aunt, that she was brought round; only it was upon condition, she said, that there should be a witness; and she proposed Mrs Fenn. Lord Melbury was as red as fire, and said that would not be treating Miss Ellis with the respect which he was sure was her due; and he could not be so impertinent as to desire to see her, upon such terms. So, after a good deal more fuss, it was settled, at last, that Sister Elinor should be present. So now you are to come down to her dressing-room.'

Ellis, though startled at the effect that might be produced by his remaining at Brighthelmstone, was sensibly touched by these public and resolute marks of his confirmed and undoubting esteem.

Elinor, presently, with restored good humour, and an air of the most lively pleasure, came to fetch her. 'Lord Melbury,' she cried, 'certainly adores you. You never saw a man's face of so many colours in your life, as when Aunt Maple speaks of you irreverently. If you manage well, you may be at Gretna Green in a week.'

They descended, without any answer made by Ellis, to the dressing-room.

The air of Lord Melbury was far less dejected than when they had last parted; yet it had by no means regained its natural spring and vivacity; and he advanced to pay his compliments to Ellis, with a look of even studious deference. He would detain her, he said, but a few minutes; yet could not leave the country, without informing her of two visits, which he had made the day before: both of which had ended precisely with the amity that she had wished.

Elinor, enchanted in believing, from this opening, that a confidential intercourse was already arranged, declared, that her aunt must look elsewhere for a spy, as she would by no means play that part; and then ran into the adjoining room. Lord Melbury and Ellis would have detained, but could not follow her, as it was her bed-chamber.

Lord Melbury then, who saw that Ellis was uneasy, promised to be quick. 'I demanded,' said he, 'yesterday, an interview with Mr Harleigh. I told him, without reserve, all that had passed. I cannot paint to you the indignation he shewed at the aspersions of Ireton. He determined to go to him directly, and I resolved to accompany him. Don't look pale, Miss Ellis: I repeated to Mr Harleigh the promise you had exacted from me, and he confessed himself to be perfectly of your opinion, that all angry defence, or public resentment, must necessarily, in such a case, be injurious. Yet to let the matter drop, might expose you to fresh abominations. Ireton received us with a mixture of curiosity and carelessness; very inquisitive to know what had passed, but very indifferent whether it were good or bad. We both, by agreement, affected to treat the matter lightly, gravely as we both thought of it: I thanked him, therefore, for the salutary counsel, by which he had urged me to procure myself so confounded a rap of the knuckles, for my assurance; and Mr Harleigh made his acknowledgements in the same tone, for the compliment paid to his liberality, of supposing that a person, who, in any manner, should be thought under his protection, could be in a state of penury. We both, I hope, made him ashamed. He had not, he owned, reflected deeply upon the subject; for which, Mr Harleigh told me, afterwards, there was a very cogent reason, namely, that he did not know how! Mr Harleigh, when we were coming away, forcibly said, "Ireton, placing Lord Melbury and myself wholly apart in this business, ask your own sagacity, I beg, how a female, who is young, beautiful, and accomplished, can suffer from pecuniary distress, if her character be not unimpeachable?" Upon that, struck with the truth of the remark, he voluntarily protested that he would make you all the amends in his power. So ended our visit; and I cannot but hope that it will release you from all similar persecutions.'

Ellis expressed her sincere and warm gratitude; and Lord Melbury, with an air of penetrated respect, took his leave; evidently much solaced, by the consciousness of serving one whom he had injured.

Ellis had every reason to be gratified by this attention, which set her mind wholly at rest upon the tenour of Lord Melbury's regard: while Elinor was so much delighted, to find the acquaintance advance so rapidly to confidence, that she embraced Ellis, wished her joy, mocked all replies of a disclaiming nature, and, accompanying her back to her room, made her a long, social, lively, and entertaining visit; hearing and talking over her project of becoming a governess, but laughing at it, as a ridiculous idea, for the decided wife elect of Earl Melbury.

She was succeeded by Selina, who exultingly came to acquaint Ellis, that Mr Ireton had just made a formal renunciation of all ill opinion of her; and had told Mrs Maple, that he had indubitable proofs that she was a person of the very strictest character. 'So now,' cried she, 'Lady Aurora and I may vow our friendship to you for life.'

This was a very solid satisfaction to Ellis, to whom the calumny of Ireton had been almost insupportable. She now hoped that Mrs Maple would favour her new scheme, and that she might remain tranquilly in the house till it took place; and equip herself, from the donation of Lady Aurora, for her immediate appearance in the situation which she sought. She resolved to seize the first opportunity for returning Harleigh his bank notes, and the Miss Joddrels their half-guineas. She wished, also, to repay the guinea of the worthy Admiral, and to repeat to him her grateful acknowledgements: his name and address she concluded that she might learn from Harleigh; but she deferred this satisfaction till more secure of success.

The next day, Selina ran upstairs to her again. 'Who do you think,' she cried, 'came into the parlour in the middle of breakfast? Mr Dennis Harleigh! He arrived at Brighthelmstone last night. Sister Elinor turned quite white, and never spoke to him; she only just made a sort of bow to his asking how she did, and then swallowed her tea burning hot, and left the room. He can stay only one day, for he must be in London to-morrow night. He is come for his final answer; for he's quite out of patience.'

Selina had hardly descended the stairs, when Elinor herself mounted them. She entered the chamber precipitately, her face colourless, and her eyes starting from her head. 'Ellis!' she cried, 'I must speak with you!'

She seated herself, made Ellis sit exactly opposite to her, and went on: 'There are two things which I want to say to you; or, rather, to demand of you. Have you fortitude enough to tell truth, even though it should wound your self-love? and honour enough to be trusted with a commission a thousand times more important than life or death? and to execute it faithfully, though at the risk of seeing the greatest idiot that ever existed, shew sufficient symptoms of sense to run mad?'

Alarmed by her ghastly look, and frightened at the abruptness of questions utterly incomprehensible, Ellis gently entreated to be spared any request with which she could not comply.

'I do not mean,' cried Elinor, with quickness, 'to make any call upon your confidence, or to put any fetters upon your conduct. You will be as free after you have spoken as before. I want merely to ascertain a fact, of which my ignorance distracts me! If you have to give me a negative, your vanity alone can suffer; if an affirmative—' She put her hand upon her forehead, and then rapidly added, 'the suffering will not be yours!—give it, therefore, boldly! 'Twill be heaven to me to end this suspense, be it how it may!'

Starting up, but preventing Ellis from rising, by laying a hand upon each of her shoulders, she gazed upon her eyes with a fixed stare, of almost frantic impatience, and said, 'Speak! say Yes, or No, at once! Give me no phrase—Let me see no hesitation!—Kill me, or restore me to life!—Has Harleigh—' she gasped for breath—'ever made you any declaration?'

'None!' steadily, forcibly, and instantly Ellis answered.

'Enough!' cried she, recovering some composure.

She then walked up and down the room, involuntarily smiling, and her lips in a motion, that shewed that she was talking to herself. Then stopping, and taking Ellis by the hand, and half laughing, 'You will think me,' she cried, 'crazy; but I assure you I had never a more exquisite enjoyment of my senses. I see everything to urge, and nothing to oppose my following the bent of my own humour; or, in other words, throwing off the trammels of unmeaning custom, and acting, as well as thinking, for myself.'

Again, then, walking up and down the chamber, she pursued her new train of ideas, with a glee which manifested that she found them delightful.

'My dear Ellis,' she cried, presently, 'have you ever chanced to hear of such a person as Dennis Harleigh?'

Ellis wished to avoid answering this question, on account of her informant, Selina; but her embarrassment was answer sufficient. 'I see yes!' cried Elinor, 'I see that you have heard of that old story. Don't be frightened,' added she, laughing, 'I am not going to ask who blabbed it. I had as lieve it were one impertinent fool as another. Only never imagine me of the tribe of sentimental pedants, who think it a disgrace to grow wiser; or who suppose that they must abide by their first opinions, for fear the world should know that they think twice upon one subject. For what is changing one's mind, but taking the pro one time, and the con another?'

'But come,' continued she, 'this is no time for rattling. Two years I have existed upon speculation; I must now try how I shall fare upon practice. Is it not just, Ellis, that it should be you who should drag me out of the slough of despond, since it was you who flung me into it?—However, now for your commission. Do you feel as if you could execute it with spirit?'

'With willingness, certainly, if I see any chance of success.'

'No ifs, Ellis. I hate the whole tribe of dubiosity. However, that you may not make any blunder, I shall tell you my story myself; for all that you have heard from others, you must set down to ignorance or prejudice. Nobody knows my feelings, and nobody understands my reasons. So everybody is at war against me in the dark.

'Now hearken!

'Just as I came of age, and ought to have shaken off the shackles of Aunt Maple, and to have enjoyed my independence and my fortune together, accident brought into my way a young lawyer—this Dennis Harleigh—of great promise in the only profession in the world that gives wit fair play. And I thought him, then, mark me, Ellis, then!—of a noble appearance. He delighted to tell me his causes, state their merits, and ask my opinions. I always took the opposite side to that which he was employed to plead, in order to try his powers, and prove my own. The French Revolution had just then burst forth, into that noble flame that nearly consumed the old world, to raise a new one, phoenix like, from its ashes. Soon tired of our every day subjects and contests, I began canvassing with him the Rights of Man. He had fallen desperately in love with me, either for my wit or my fortune, or both; and therefore all topics were sure to be approved. Enchanted with a warfare in which I was certain to be always victorious, I grew so fond of conquest, that I was never satisfied but when combating; and the joy I experienced in the display of my own talents, made me doat upon his sight. The truth is, our mutual vanity mutually deceived us: he saw my pleasure in his company, and concluded that it was personal regard: I found nothing to rouse the energies of my faculties in his absence, and imagined myself enamoured of my vanquished antagonist. Aunt Maple did her little best—for everything she does is little—to forward the connexion; because, though his fortune is trifling, his professional expectations are high; and though he is a younger brother, he is born of a noble family: and that sort of mean old stuff is always in her head; for if the whole world were revolutionized, you could never make her conceive a new idea. And the great fact of all is, she cannot bear I should leave her house before I marry, because, she is sure, in one of my own, I shall adopt some new system of life. Thus, in the toils of my self-love, I became entangled; poor Dennis called himself the happiest of men; the settlements were all drawn up; and we were looking about us for a house to our fancy, and all that sort of stuff, when Dennis introduced his family to us. Now the rest, I suppose, you can divine?'

This was, indeed, not difficult; but Ellis durst not risk any reply.

With a rapidity scarcely intelligible, and in a manner wholly incoherent, she then went on: 'Ellis, I pretend not to any mystery. Why is one person adorable, and another detestable, but to call forth our love and our hatred? to give birth to all that snatches us from mere inert existence; to our passions, our energies, our noblest conceptions of all that is towering and sublime? Whether you have any idea of this mental enlargement I cannot tell; but with it I see human nature endowed with capabilities immeasurable of perfection; and without it, I regard and treat the whole of my race as the mere dramatis personæ of a farce; of which I am myself, when performing with such fellow-actors, a principal buffoon.'

Nearly out of breath, she stopt a moment; then, looking earnestly at Ellis, said, 'Do you understand me?'

Ellis, in a fearful accent, answered, 'I ... I am not quite sure.'

'Remove your doubts, then!' cried she, impatiently; 'I despise what is obscure, still more than I hate what is false. Falsehood may at least approach to that degree of grandeur which belongs to crime; but obscurity is always mean, always seeking some subterfuge, always belonging to art.'

Again she stopt; but Ellis, uncertain whether this remark were meant to introduce her confidence, or to censure her own secrecy, waited an explanation in silence. Elinor was evidently, however, embarrassed, though anxious to persuade herself, as well as Ellis, that she was perfectly at her ease. She walked a quick pace up and down the room; then stopt, seemed pausing, hemmed to clear her voice for speech; and then walked backwards and forwards before the window, which she frequently opened and shut, without seeming to know that she touched it; till, at length, seized with sudden indignation against herself, for this failure of courage, she energetically exclaimed, 'How paltry is shame where there can be no disgrace!—I disdain it!—disclaim it!—and am ready to avow to the whole world, that I dare speak and act, as well as think and feel for myself!'

Yet, even thus buoyed up, thus full fraught with defiance, something within involuntarily, invincibly checked her, and she hastily resumed her walks and her ruminations.

'What amazing, unaccountable fools,' she cried, 'have we all been for these quantities of centuries! Worlds seem to have a longer infancy taken out of the progress of their duration, even than the long imbecility of the childhood of poor mortals. But for the late glorious revolutionary shake given to the universe, I should, at this very moment, from mere cowardly conformity, be the wife of Dennis!—In spite of my repentance of the engagement, in spite of the aversion I have taken to him, and in spite of the contempt I have conceived—with one single exception—for the whole race of mankind, I must have been that poor man's despicable wife!—O despicable indeed! For with what sentiments could I have married him? Where would have been my soul while I had given him my hand? Had I not seen—known—adored—his brother!'

She stopt, and the deepest vermillion overspread her face; her effort was made; she had boasted of her new doctrine, lest she should seem impressed with confusion from the old one which she violated; but the struggle being over, the bravado and exultation subsided; female consciousness and native shame took their place; and abashed, and unable to meet the eyes of Ellis, she ran out of the room.

In the whole of this scene, Ellis observed, with mingled censure and pity, the strong conflict in the mind of Elinor, between ungoverned inclination, which sought new systems for its support; and an innate feeling of what was due to the sex that she was braving, and the customs that she was scorning.

She soon re-appeared, but with a wholly new air; lively, disengaged, almost sportive. Her heart was lightened by unburthening her secret; the feminine delicacies which opposed the discovery, once broken through, oppressed her no more; and the idea of passing, now, straight forward, to the purposes for which she had done herself this violence, re-animated her spirit, and gave new vigour to her faculties.

She laughed at herself for having run away, without explaining the meaning of her communication; and for charging Ellis with a commission, of which she had not made known even the nature. She then more clearly stated her situation.

From the time of her first interview with Albert, her whole mind had recoiled from all thought of union with his brother; yet the affair was so far advanced, and she saw herself so completely regarded by Albert as a sister, though treated by him with an openness, a frankness, and an affection the most captivating, that she had not courage to proclaim her change of sentiment.

The conflict of her mind, during this doubting state, threatened to cast her into a consumption. She was ordered to the south of France. And there, happily arrived, new scenes, a new world, rather, opened to her a code of new ideas, that soon, she said, taught her to scoff at idle misery: and might even, from the occupation given to her feelings, by the glorious confusion, and mad wonders around her, have recovered her from the thraldom of an over-ruling propensity, had not Dennis, unable, from professional engagements, to quit his country, been so blind, upon hearing that her health was re-established, as to persuade his brother to cross the Channel, in order to escort the two travellers home. From the moment, the fated moment, that Albert arrived to be her guide and her guard, he became so irresistibly the master of her heart, that her destiny was determined. Whether good or ill, she knew not yet; but it was fixed. Ill had not occurred to her sanguine expectations, nor doubt, nor fear, till the eventful meeting with Ellis: till then, she had believed her happiness secure, for she had supposed that nothing stood in her way, save a little brotherly punctilio. But, since the junction of Ellis, the spontaneous interest which Albert had taken in her fate, and her affairs, had appeared to be so marvellous, that, at every new view of his pity, his respect, or his admiration, she was seized with the most uneasy feelings; which sometimes worked her up into pangs of excruciating jealousy; and, at others, seemed to be so ill founded, that, recollecting a thousand instances of his general benevolence, she laughed her own surmises to scorn. How the matter still stood, with regard to his heart, she confessed herself unable to form any permanent judgment. The time, however, was now, happily, arrived, to abolish suspense, for even Dennis, now, could bear it no longer. She expected, she said, a desperate scene, but, at least, it would be a final one. She had only, for many months past, been restrained from giving Dennis his dismission, lest Albert should drop all separate acquaintance, from the horrour of seeming treacherously to usurp the place of his brother. Nevertheless, she would frankly have ended her disturbance, by an avowal of the truth, had not Albert been the eldest brother, and, consequently, the richest; and the disgraceful supposition, that she might be influenced to desire the change from mercenary motives, would have had power to yoke her to Dennis, for the rest of her weary existence, had not her mind been so luminously opened to its own resources, and inherent right of choice, by her continental excursion.

'The grand effect,' she continued, 'of beholding so many millions of men, let loose from all ties, divine or human, gave such play to my fancy, such a range to my thoughts, and brought forth such new, unexpected, and untried combinations to my reason, that I frequency felt as if just created, and ushered into the world—not, perhaps, as wise as another Minerva, but equally formed to view and to judge all around me, without the gradations of infancy, childhood, and youth, that hitherto have prepared for maturity. Every thing now is upon a new scale, and man appears to be worthy of his faculties; which, during all these past ages, he has set aside, as if he could do just as well without them; holding it to be his bounden duty, to be trampled to the dust, by old rules and forms, because all his papas and uncles were trampled so before him. However, I should not have troubled myself, probably, with any of these abstruse notions, had they not offered me a new road for life, when the old one was worn out. To find that all was novelty and regeneration throughout the finest country in the universe, soon infected me with the system-forming spirit; and it was then that I conceived the plan I am now going to execute; but I shall not tell it you in its full extent, as I am uncertain what may be your strength of mind for measures of force and character; and perhaps they may not be necessary. So now to your commission.

'I am fixed to cast wholly aside the dainty common barriers, which shut out from female practice all that is elevated, or even natural. Dennis, therefore, shall know that I hate him; Albert ... Ah, Ellis! that I hate him not!'

'My operations are to commence thus: Act I. Scene I. Enter Ellis, seeking Albert. Don't stare so; I know perfectly well what I am about. Scene II. Albert and Ellis meet. Ellis informs him that she must hold a confabulation with him the next day; and desires that he will remain at Lewes to be at hand. '

'Oh, Miss Joddrell!' interrupted Ellis, 'you must, at least, give me leave to say, that it is by your command that I make a request so extraordinary!'

'By no means. He must not suspect that I have any knowledge of your intention. The truth, like an explosion of thunder, shall burst upon his head at once. So only shall I truly know whether it will shake him with dismay—or magnetize him by its sublimity.'

'Yet how, Madam, under what pretence, can I take such a liberty?'

'Pho, pho; this is no time for delicate demurs. If he be not engaged to stay before I turn his brother adrift, he will accompany him to town, as a thing of course, to console him in his willowed state. The rest of my plot is not yet quite ripe for disclosure. But all is arranged. And though I know not whether the catastrophe will be tragic or comic, I am prepared in my part for either.'

She then went away.


CHAPTER XVII

Elinor returned almost instantly. 'Hasten, hasten,' she cried, 'Ellis! There is no time to be lost. Scene the first is all prepared. Albert Harleigh, at this very moment, is poring over the county map in the hall. Run and tell him that you have something of deep importance to communicate to him to-morrow.'

'But may he not—if he means to go—desire to hear it immediately?'

Elinor, without answering, forced her away. Harleigh, whose back was to the stair-entrance, seemed intently examining some route. The distress of Ellis was extreme how to call for his notice, and how to execute her commission when it should be obtained. Slowly and unwillingly approaching a little nearer, 'I am afraid,' she hesitatingly said, 'that I must appear extremely importunate, but—'

The astonishment with which he turned round, at the sound of her voice, could only be equalled by the pleasure with which he met her eyes; and only surpassed, by the sudden burst of clashing ideas with which he saw her own instantly drop; while her voice, also, died away; her cheeks became the colour of crimson; and she was evidently and wholly at a loss what to say.

'Importunate?' he gently repeated, 'impossible!' yet he waited her own explanation.

Her confusion now became deeper; any sort of interrogation would have encouraged and aided her; but his quiet, though attentive forbearance seemed the result of some suspension of opinion. Ashamed and grieved, she involuntarily looked away, as she indistinctly pronounced, 'I must appear ... very strange ... but I am constrained.... Circumstances of which I am not the mistress, force me to ... desire—to request—that to-morrow morning—or any part of to-morrow ... it might be possible that I could ... or rather that you should be able to ... to hear something that ... that....'

The total silence with which he listened, shewed so palpably his expectation of some competent reason for so singular an address, that her inability to clear herself, and her chagrin in the idea of forfeiting any part of an esteem which had proved so often her protection, grew almost insupportably painful, and she left her phrase unfinished; yet considered her commission to be fulfilled, and was moving away.

'To-morrow,' he said, 'I meant to have accompanied my brother, whose affairs—whatever may be his fate—oblige him to return to town: but if ... if to-morrow—'

He had now, to impede her retreat, stept softly between her and the staircase, and perceived, in her blushes, the force which she had put upon her modesty; and read, in the expression of her glistening eyes, that an innate sense of delicacy was still more wounded, by the demand which she had made, even than her habits of life. With respect, therefore, redoubled, and an interest beyond all calculation increased, he went on; 'If to-morrow ... or next day—or any part of the week, you have any commands for me, nothing shall hurry me hence till they are obeyed.'

Comforted to find herself treated with unabated consideration, however shocked to have the air of detaining him purposely for her own concerns, she was courtsying her thanks, when she caught a glance of Elinor on the stairs, in whose face, every passion seemed with violence at work.

Ellis changed colour, not knowing how to proceed, or how to stop. The alteration in her countenance made Harleigh look round, and discern Elinor; yet so pre-occupied was his attention, that he was totally unmindful of her situation, and would have addressed her as usual, had she not abruptly re-mounted the stairs.

Harleigh would then have asked some directions, relative to the time and manner of the purposed communication; but Ellis instantly followed Elinor; leaving him in a state of wonder, expectation, yet pleasure indescribable; fully persuaded that she meant to reveal the secret of her name and her history; and forming conjectures that every moment varied, yet every moment grew more interesting, of her motives for such a confidence.

Ellis found Elinor already in her chamber, and, apparently, in the highest, though evidently most factitious spirits: not, however, feigned to deceive Ellis, but falsely and forcibly elated to deceive, or, at least, to animate herself. 'This is enchanting!' she cried, 'this is delectable! this is every thing that I could wish! I shall now know the truth! All the doubts, all the difficulties, that have been crazing me for some time past, will now be solved: I shall discover whether his long patience in waiting my determination, has been for your sake, or for mine. He will not go hence, till he has obeyed your commands!—Is he glad of a pretence to stay on my account? or impelled irresistibly upon yours? I shall now know all, all, all!'

The lengthened stay of Albert being thus, she said, ascertained, she should send Dennis about his business, without the smallest ceremony.

What she undertook, she performed. Early in the evening she again visited Ellis, exultingly to make known to her, that Dennis was finally dismissed. She had assigned no reason, she said, for her long procrastination, reserving that for his betters, alias Albert; but she had been so positive and clear in announcing her decision, and assuring him that it proceeded from a most sincere and unalterable dislike, both to his person and mind, that he had shewn spirit enough to be almost respectable, having immediately ordered his horse, taken his leave of Aunt Maple, and set off upon his journey. Albert, meanwhile, had said, that he had business to transact at Brighthelmstone, which might detain him some days; and had accepted an invitation to sleep at Lewes, during that period, from poor Aunt Maple; whose provocation and surprise at all that had passed were delightful.

'To-morrow morning, therefore,' she continued, 'will decide my fate. What, hitherto, Albert has thought of me, he is probably as ignorant as I am myself; for while he has considered me as the property of my brother, his pride is so scrupulous, and his scruples are so squeamish, that he would deem it a crime of the first magnitude, to whisper, even in his own ear, How should I like her for myself? He is suspicious of some sophistry in whatever is not established by antiquated rules; and, with all his wisdom, and all his superiority, he is constantly anxious not to offend that conceited old prejudice, that thinks it taking a liberty with human nature, to suppose that any man can be so indecent as to grow up wiser, and more knowing, than his grandpapa was before him.

'Trifling, however, apart, all my real alarm is to fathom what his feelings are for you! Are they but of compassion, playing upon a disengaged mind? If nothing further, the awakening a more potent sentiment will plant them in their proper line of subordination. This is what remains to be tried. He has not made you any declaration; he is free, therefore, from any entanglement: his brother is discharged, and for ever out of the question; he knows me, therefore, also, to be liberated from all engagement. When I said that you had given me life, I did not mean, that merely to hear that nothing had yet passed, was enough to secure my happiness:—Ah no!—but simply that it inspired me with a hope that gives me courage to resolve upon seeking certitude. And now, hear me!

'The second act of the comedy, tragedy, or farce, of my existence, is to be represented to-morrow. The first scene will be a conference between Ellis and Albert, in which Ellis will relate the history of Elinor.'

Suddenly, then, looking at her, with an air the most authoritative, 'Ellis!' she added, 'there is one article to which you must answer this moment! Would you, should the choice be in your power, sacrifice Lord Melbury to Harleigh? No hesitation!'

'Miss Joddrel,' answered Ellis, solemnly, 'I have neither the hope, nor the fear, that belongs to what might be called sacrifice relative to either of them: I earnestly desire to preserve the esteem of Mr Harleigh; and the urbanity—I can call it by no other name—of Lord Melbury; but I am as free from the thought as from the presumption, of expecting, or coveting, to engage any personal, or particular regard, from either.'

Elinor, appeased, said, 'You are such a compound of mystery, that one extraordinary thing is not more difficult to credit in you, than another. My design, as you will find, in making you speak instead of myself, is a stroke of Machievalian policy; for it will finish both suspences at once; since if, when you talk to him of me, he thinks only of my agent, how will he refrain, in answering your embassy, to betray himself? If, on the contrary, when he finds his scruples removed about his brother, he should feel his heart penetrated by the cause of that brother's dismission—Ah Ellis!—But let us not anticipate act the third. The second alone can decide, whether it will conclude the piece with an epithalamium—or a requiem!'

She then disappeared.

Ellis saw her no more till the next morning, when, entering the chamber, breathless with haste and agitation, 'The moment,' she cried, 'is come! I have sent out Aunt Maple, and Selina, upon visits for the whole morning; and I have called Harleigh into my dressing-room. There, wondering, he waits; I shall introduce you, and wait, in my turn, till, in ten minutes' time, you follow, to give me the argument of the third and last act of my drama.'

Ellis, alarmed at what might be the result, would again have supplicated to be excused; but Elinor, proudly saying, 'Fear no consequences for me! Those who know truly how to love, know how to die, as well as how to live!' forcibly dragged her down to the dressing-room; through which she instantly passed herself, with undisguised trepidation, to her inner apartment.

The astonishment of Harleigh was inexpressible; and Ellis, who had received no positive directions, felt wholly at a loss what she was to relate, how far she ought to go, and what she ought to require. Hastily, therefore, and affrighted at her task, she tapped at the bedroom door, and begged a moment's audience. Elinor opened it, in the greatest consternation. 'What!' cried she, taking her to the window, 'is all over, without a word uttered?'

No; Ellis answered; she merely wished for more precise commands what she should say.

'Say?' cried Elinor, reviving, 'say that I adore him! That since the instant I have seen him, I have detested his brother; that he alone has given me any idea of what is perfection in human nature! And that, if the whole world were annihilated, and he remained ... I should think my existence divine!'

She then pushed her back, prohibiting any reply.

Harleigh, to whom all was incomprehensible, but whose expectations every moment grew higher, of the explanation he so much desired, perceiving the embarrassment of Ellis, gently advanced, and said, 'Shall I be guilty of indiscretion, if I seize this hurried, yet perhaps only moment, to express my impatience for a communication of which I have thought, almost exclusively, from the moment I have had it in view? Must it be deferred? or—'

'No; it admits of no delay. I have much to say—and I am allowed but ten minutes—'

'You have much to say?' cried he, delighted; 'ten minutes to-day may be followed by twenty, thirty, as many as you please, to-morrow, and after to-morrow, and whenever you command.'

'You are very good, Sir, but my commission admits as little of extension as of procrastination. It must be as brief as it will be abrupt.'

'Your commission?' he repeated, in a tone of disappointment.

'Yes; I am charged by ... by ... by a lady whom I need not name—to say that ... that your brother—'

She stopt, ashamed to proceed.

'I can have no doubt,' said he, gravely, 'that Miss Joddrel is concerned, for the length of time she has wasted in trifling with his feelings; but this is all the apology her conduct requires: the breach of the engagement, when once she was convinced, that her attachment was insufficient to make the union as desirable to herself as to him, was certainly rather a kindness than an injury.'

'Yes, but, her motives—her reasons—'

'I conceive them all! she wanted courage to be sooner decided; she apprehended reproach—and she gathered force to make her change of sentiments known, only when, otherwise, she must have concealed it for ever. Pardon this presumptuous anticipation!' added he, smiling; 'but when you talk to me of only ten minutes, how can I suffer them to be consumed in a commission?'

He spoke in a low tone, yet, Ellis, excessively alarmed, pointed expressively to the chamber-door. In a tone, then, still softer, he continued: 'I have been anxious to speak to you of Lord Melbury, and to say something of the indignation with which I heard, from him, of the atrocious behaviour of Ireton. Nothing less than the respect I feel for you, could have deterred me from shewing him the resentment I feel for myself. I should not, however, have been your only champion; Lord Melbury was equally incensed; but we both acknowledged that our interests and our feelings ought to be secondary to yours, and by yours to be regulated. The matter, therefore, is at an end. Ireton is convinced that he has done you wrong; and, as he never meant to be your enemy, and has no study but his own amusement, we must pity his want of taste, and hope that the disgrace necessarily hanging upon detected false assertion, may be a lesson not lost upon him. Yet he deserves one far more severe. He is a pitiful egotist, who seeks nothing but his own diversion; indifferent whose peace, comfort, or reputation pays its purchase.'

'I am infinitely obliged,' said Ellis, 'that you will suffer the whole to drop; but I must not do the same by my commission!—You must let me, now, enter more particularly upon my charge, and tell you—'

'Forgive, forgive me!' cried he, eagerly: 'I comprehend all that Miss Joddrel can have to say. But my impatience is irrepressible upon a far different subject; one that awakens the most lively interest, that occupies my thoughts, that nearly monopolizes my memory; and that exhausts—yet never wearies my conjectures. That letter you were so good as to mention to me?—and the plan you may at length decide to pursue?—permit me to hope, that the communication you intend me, has some reference to those points?'

'I should be truly glad of your counsel, Sir, in my helpless situation: but I am not at this moment at liberty to speak for myself;—Miss Joddrel—'

Her embarrassment now announced something extraordinary; but it was avowedly not personal; and Harleigh eagerly besought her to be expeditious.

'You must make me so, then,' cried she, 'by divining what I have to reveal!'

'Does Miss Joddrel relent?—Will she give me leave to summon my brother back?'

'Oh no! no! no!—far otherwise. Your brother has been indifferent to her ... ever since she has known him as such!'

She thought she had now said enough; but Harleigh, whose faculties were otherwise engaged, waited for further explanation.

'Can you not,' said Ellis, 'or will you not, divine the reason of the change?'

'I have certainly,' he answered, 'long observed a growing insensibility; but still—'

'And have you never,' said Ellis, deeply blushing, 'seen, also, its reverse?'

This question, and yet more the manner in which it was made, was too intelligible to admit of any doubt. Harleigh, however, was far from elated as the truth opened in his view: he looked grave and disturbed, and remained for some minutes profoundly silent. Ellis, already ashamed of the indelicacy of her office, could not press for any reply.

'I am hurt,' he at length said, 'beyond all measure, by what you intimate; but since Miss Joddrel has addressed you thus openly, there can be no impropriety in my claiming leave, also, to speak to you confidentially.'

'Whatever you wish me to say to her, Sir, '

'And much that I do not wish you to say to her,' cried he, half smiling, 'I hope you will hear yourself! and that then, you will have the goodness, according to what you know of her intentions and desire, to palliate what you may deem necessary to repeat.'

'Ah, poor Miss Joddrel!' said Ellis, in a melancholy tone, 'and is this the success of my embassy?'

'Did you, then, wish—' Harleigh began, with a quickness of which he instantly felt the impropriety, and changed his phrase into, 'Did you then, suspect any other?'

'I was truly sorry to be entrusted with the commission.'

'I easily conceive, that it is not such a one as you would have given! but there is a dangerous singularity in the character of Miss Joddrel, that makes her prone to devote herself to whatever is new, wild, or uncommon. Even now, perhaps, she conceives that she is the champion of her sex, in shewing it the road, a dangerous road!—to a new walk in life. Yet, these eccentricities set apart, how rare are her qualities! how powerful is her mind! how sportive her fancy! and how noble is her superiority to every species of art or artifice!'

'Yet, with all this,' said Ellis, looking at him expressively, 'with all this....' she knew not how to proceed; but he saw her meaning. 'With all this,' he said, 'you are surprised, perhaps, that I should look for other qualities, other virtues in her whom I should aspire to make the companion of my life? I beseech you, however, to believe, that neither insolence nor ingratitude makes me insensible to her worth; but, though it often meets my admiration, sometimes my esteem, and always my good will and regard, it is not of a texture to create that sympathy without which even friendship is cold. I have, indeed ... till now....'

He paused.

'Poor, poor, Miss Joddrel!' exclaimed Ellis, 'If you could but have heard, or if I knew but how to repeat, even the millionenth part of what she thinks of you!—of the respect with which she is ready to yield to your opinions; of the enthusiasm with which she honours your character; of the devotion with which she nearly worships you—'

She stopt short, ashamed; and as fearful that she had been now too urgent, as before that she had been too cold.

Harleigh heard her with considerable emotion. 'I hope,' he said, 'your feelings, like those of most minds gifted with strong sensibility, have taken the pencil, in this portrait, from your cooler judgment? I should be grieved, indeed, to suppose—but what can a man suppose, what say, upon a subject so delicate that may not appear offensive? Suffer me, therefore, to drop it; and have the goodness to let that same sensibility operate in terminating, in such a manner as may be least shocking to her, all view, and all thought, that I ever could, or ever can, entertain the most distant project of supplanting my brother.'

'Will you not, at least, speak to her yourself?'

'I had far rather speak to you!—Yet certainly yes, if she desire it.'

'Give me leave, then, to say,' cried Ellis, moving towards the bedroom door, 'that you request an audience.'

'By no means! I merely do not object to it. You may easily conceive what pain I shall be spared, if it may be evaded. All I request, is a few moments with you! Hastily, therefore, let me ask, is your plan decided?'

'To the best of my power, of my ideas, rather, yes. But, indeed, I must not thus abandon my charge!'

'And will you not let me enquire what it is?'

'There is one thing, only, in which I have any hope that my exertions may turn to account; I wish to offer myself as a governess to some young lady, or ladies.'

'I beseech you,' cried he, with sudden fervour, 'to confide to me the nature of your situation! I know well I have no claim; I seem to have even no pretext for such a request; yet there are sometimes circumstances that not only excuse, but imperiously demand extraordinary measures: perhaps mine, at this moment, are of that sort! perhaps I am at a loss what step to take, till I know to whom I address myself!'

'O Sir!' cried Ellis, holding up her hands in act of supplication, 'you will be heard!'

Harleigh, conscious that he had been off all guard, silenced himself immediately, and walked hastily to the window.

Ellis knew not whether to retire, at once, to her own room; or to venture into that of Elinor; or to require any further answer. This last, however, Harleigh seemed in no state to give: he leant his forehead upon his hand, and remained wrapt in thought.

Ellis, struck by a manner which shewed that he felt, and apparently, repented the possible meaning that his last words might convey, was now as much ashamed for herself as for Elinor; and not wishing to meet his eyes, glided softly back to her chamber.

Here, whatever might be the fulness of her mind, she was not allowed an instant for reflection: Elinor followed her immediately.

She shut the door, and walked closely up to her. Elinor feared to behold her; yet saw, by a glance, that her eyes were sparkling, and that her face was dressed in smiles. 'This is a glorious day for me!' she cried; ''tis the pride of my life to have brought such a one into the history of my existence!'

Ellis officiously got her a chair; arranged the fire; examined if the windows were well closed; and sought any occupation, to postpone the moment of speaking to, or looking at her.

She was not offended; she did not appear to be hurried; she seemed enchanted with her own ideas; yet she had a strangeness in her manner that Ellis thought extremely alarming.

'Well,' she cried, when she had taken her seat, and saw that Ellis could find no further pretext for employing herself in the little apartment; 'what garb do you bring me? How am I to be arrayed?'

Ellis begged to know what she meant.

'Is it a wedding-garment?' replied she, gaily; 'or ...' abruptly changing her tone into a deep hoarse whisper, 'a shroud?'

Ellis, shuddering, durst not answer. Elinor, catching her hand said, 'Don't be frightened! I am at this moment equal to whatever may be my destiny: I am at a point of elevation, that makes my fate nearly indifferent to me. Speak, therefore! but only to the fact. I have neither time nor humour for narratory delays. I tried to hear you; but you both talked so whisperingly, that I could not make out a sentence.'

'Indeed, Miss Joddrel,' said Ellis, trembling violently, 'Mr Harleigh's regard—his affection—'

'Not a word of that trite class!' cried Elinor, with sudden severity, 'if you would not again work all my passions into inflammation involve me no more in doubt! Fear nothing else. I am no where else vulnerable. Set aside, then, all childish calculations, of giving me an inch or two more, or an inch or two less of pain, and be brief and true!'

Ellis could not utter a word: every phrase she could suggest seemed to teem with danger; yet she felt that her silence could not but indicate the truth which it sought to hide; she hung her head, and sighed in disturbed perplexity. Elinor looked at her for some time with an examining eye, and then, hastily rising, emphatically exclaimed, 'You are mute?—I see, then, my doom! And I shall meet it with glory!'

Smiles triumphant, but wild, now played about her face. 'Ellis,' she cried, 'go to your work, or whatever you were about, and take no manner of heed of me. I have something of importance to arrange, and can brook no interruption.'

Ellis acquiesced, returning to the employment of her needle, for which Mrs Fenn took especial care that she should never lack materials.

Elinor spoke to her no more; but her ruminations, though undisturbed by her companion, were by no means quiet, or silent. She paced hastily up and down the room; sat, in turn, upon a chair, a window seat, and the bed; talked to herself, sometimes with a vehemence that made several detached words, though no sentences, intelligible; sometimes in softer accents, and with eyes and gestures of exultation; and, frequently, she went into a corner by the side of the window, where she looked, in secret, at something in a shagreen case that she held in her hand, and had brought out of her chamber; and to which she occasionally addressed herself, with a fervency that shook her whole frame, and with expressions which, though broken, and half pronounced, denoted that she considered it as something sacred.

At length, with an air of transport, she exclaimed, 'Yes! that will produce the best effect! what an idiot have I been to hesitate!' then, turning with quickness to Ellis: 'Ellis,' she cried, 'I have withheld from any questions relative to yourself, because I abominate all subterfuge; but you will not suppose I am contented with my ignorance? You will not imagine it a matter of indifference to me, to know how I have failed?'

She reddened; passion took possession of every feature, and for a moment nearly choaked her voice: she again walked, with rapid motion, about the room, and then ejaculated, 'Let me be patient! let me not take away all grandeur from my despair, and reduce it to mere common madness!—Let me wait the fated moment, and then—let the truth burst, blaze, and flame, till it devour me!

'Ellis,' she presently added, 'find Harleigh; tell him I wish him a good journey from the summer-house in the garden. Not a soul ever enters it at this time of the year. Bid him go thither directly. I shall soon join him. I will wait in my room till you call me. Be quick!'

Ellis required not to have this order repeated: to place her under the care of Harleigh, and intimate to him the excess of her love, with the apprehensions which she now herself conceived of the dangerous state of her mind, was all that could be wished; and where so essential a service might be rendered, or a mischief be prevented, personal punctilio was out of the question.

He was not in the hall; but, from one of the windows, she perceived him walking near the house. A painful sensation, upon being obliged again, to force herself upon his notice, disturbed, though she would not suffer it to check her. He was speaking with his groom. She stopt at the hall-door, with a view to catch his eye, and succeeded; but he bowed without approaching her, and continued to discourse with his groom.

To seem bent upon pursuing him, when he appeared himself to think that he had gone too far, and even to mean to shun her, dyed her cheeks of the deepest vermilion; though she compelled herself, from a terrour of the danger of delay, to run across the gravel-walk before the house, to address him. He saw her advance, with extreme surprise, but by no means with the same air of pleasure, that he had manifested in the morning. His look was embarrassed, and he seemed unwilling to meet her eyes. Yet he awaited her with a respect that made his groom, unbidden, retire to some distance; though to await her at all, when he might have met her, struck her, even in this hurried and terrified moment, as offering the strongest confirmation which she had yet received, that it was not a man of pleasure or of gallantry, but of feeling and of truth, into whose way she was thus singularly and frequently cast: and the impression which she had made upon his mind, had never, to her hitherto nearly absorbed faculties, appeared to be so serious or so sincere, as now, when he first evidently struggled to disguise a partiality, which he seemed persuaded that he had, now, first betrayed. The sensations which this discovery might produce in herself were unexamined: the misery with which it teemed for Elinor, and a desire to relieve his own delicacy, by appearing unconscious of his secret, predominated: and she assumed sufficient self-command, to deliver the message of Elinor, with a look, and in a voice, that seemed insensible and unobservant of every other subject.

He soon, now, recovered his usual tone, and disengaged manner. 'She must certainly,' he said, 'be obeyed; though I so little expected such a summons, that I was giving directions for my departure.'

'Ah, no!' cried Ellis, 'rather again defer it.'

'You would have me again defer it?' he repeated, with a vivacity he tried still more, though vainly, to subdue than to disguise.

The word again did not make the cheeks of Ellis paler; but she answered, with eagerness, 'Yes, for the same purpose and same person!—I am forced to speak explicitly—and abruptly. Indeed, Sir, you know not, you conceive not, the dreadfully alarming state of her nerves, nor the violence of her attachment. You could scarcely else—' she stopt, for he changed colour and looked hurt: she saw he comprehended that she meant to add, you could scarcely else resist her: she finished, therefore, her phrase, by 'scarcely else plan leaving her, till you saw her more composed, and more reconciled to herself, and to the world.'

'You may imagine,' said he, pensively, 'it is any thing rather than my inclination that carries me hence ... but I greatly fear 'tis the only prudent measure I can pursue.'

'You can best judge by seeing her,' said Ellis: 'her situation is truly deplorable. Her faculties are all disordered; her very intellects, I fear, are shaken; and there is no misfortune, no horrour, which her desperation, if not softened, does not menace.'

Harleigh now seemed awakened to sudden alarm, and deep concern; and Ellis painfully, with encreasing embarrassment, from encreasing consciousness, added, 'You will do, I am sure, what is possible to snatch her from despair!' and then returned to the house: satisfied that her meaning was perfectly comprehended, by the excess of consternation into which it obviously cast Harleigh.

CHAPTER XVIII

Comforted, at least, for Elinor, whose situation in being known, seemed to lose its greatest danger, Ellis, with less oppression upon her spirits, returned to the dressing-room.

Elinor was writing, and too intently occupied to heed the opening of the door. The motion of her hand was so rapid, that her pen seemed rather to skim over, than to touch her paper. Ellis gently approached her; but, finding that she did not raise her head, ventured not even to announce that her orders had been executed.

At length, her paper being filled, she looked up, and said, 'Well! is he there?'

'I have delivered to him, Madam, your commands.'

'Then,' cried she, rising with an exulting air, 'the moment of my triumph is come! Yes, Harleigh! if meanly I have offered you my person, nobly, at least, I will consecrate to you my soul!'

Hastily rolling up what she had been writing, and putting it into a desk, 'Ellis!' she added, 'Mark me well! should any accident betide me, here will be found the last and unalterable codicil to my will. It is signed, but not witnessed: it is not, however, of a nature to be disputed; it is to desire only that Harleigh will take care that my bones shall be buried in the same charnel-house, in which he orders the interment of his own. All that remains, finally, of either of us, there, at least, may meet!'

Ellis turned cold with horrour. Her first idea was to send for Mrs Maple; yet that lady was so completely without influence, that any interference on her part, might rather stimulate than impede what it was meant to oppose. It seemed, therefore, safest to trust wholly to Harleigh.

The eyes of Elinor were wild and fierce, her complexion was livid, her countenance was become haggard; and, while she talked of triumph, and fancied it was what she felt, every feature exhibited the most tortured marks of impetuous sorrow, and ungoverned disappointment.

She took from her bureau the shagreen case which she had so fondly caressed, and which Ellis concluded to contain some portrait, or cherished keep-sake of Harleigh; and hurried down stairs. Ellis fearfully followed her. No one happened to be in the way, and she was already in the garden, when, turning suddenly round, and perceiving Ellis, 'Oh ho!' she cried, 'you come unbidden? you are right; I shall want you.'

She then precipitately entered the summer-house, in which Harleigh was awaiting her in the keenest anxiety.

His disturbance was augmented upon observing her extreme paleness, though she tried to meet him with a smile. She shut and bolted the door, and seated herself before she spoke.

Assuming then a mien of austerity, though her voice betrayed internal tremour, 'Harleigh!' she cried, 'be not alarmed. I have received your answer!—fear not that I shall ever expect—or would, now, even listen to another! 'Tis to vindicate, not to lower my character that I am here. I have given you, I am aware, a great surprise by what you conceive to be my weakness; prepare yourself for a yet greater, from an opposite cause. I come to explain to you the principles by which I am actuated, clearly and roundly; without false modesty, insipid affectation, or artful ambiguity. You will then know from what plan of reasoning I adopt my measures; which as yet, believing to be urged only by my feelings, you attribute, perhaps, like that poor scared Ellis, to insanity.'

Ellis forced a smile, and, seating herself at some distance, tried to wear the appearance of losing her apprehensions; while Harleigh, drawing a chair near Elinor, assured her that his whole mind was engaged in attention to what she might disclose.

Her voice now became more steady, and she proceeded.

'You think me, I know, tarnished by those very revolutionary ideas through which, in my own estimation, I am ennobled. I owe to them that I dare hold myself intellectually, as well as personally, an equal member of the community; not a poor, degraded, however necessary appendent to it: I owe to them my enfranchisement from the mental slavery of subscribing to unexamined opinions, and being governed by prejudices that I despise: I owe to them the precious privilege, so shamefully new to mankind, of daring to think for myself. But for them—should I not, at this moment, be pining away my lingering existence, in silent consumption? They have rescued me from that slow poison!'

'In what manner,' said Harleigh, 'can I presume—'

She interrupted him. 'Imagine not I am come to reproach you! or, still less, to soften you!' She stopt, confused, rose, and again seated herself, before she could go on. 'No! littleness of that description belongs not to such energies as those which you have awakened! I come but, I repeat, to defend myself, from any injurious suspicion, of having lightly given way to a mere impulse of passion. I come to bring you conviction that reason has guided my conduct; and I come to solicit a boon from you, a last boon, before we separate for ever!'

'I am charmed if you have anything to ask of me,' said Harleigh, 'that my zeal, my friendship, my attachment, may find some vent; but why speak of so solemn a separation?'

'You will grant, then, what I mean to request?'

'What can it be I could refuse?'

'Enough! You will soon know. Now to my justification. Hear me, Harleigh!'

She arose, and, clasping her hands, with strong, yet tender, emotion, exclaimed. 'That I should love you—' She stopt. Shame crimsoned her skin. She covered her face with both her hands, and sunk again upon her chair.

Harleigh was strongly and painfully affected. 'O Elinor!' he cried, and was going to take her hand; but the fear of misinterpretation made him draw back; and Elinor, almost instantly recovering, raised her head, and said, 'How tenacious a tyrant is custom! how it clings to our practice! how it embarrasses our conduct! how it awes our very nature itself, and bewilders and confounds even our free will! We are slaves to its laws and its follies, till we forget its usurpation. Who should have told me, only five minutes ago, that, at an instant such as this; an instant of liberation from all shackles, of defiance to all forms; its antique prescriptions should still retain their power to confuse and torment me? Who should have told me, that, at an instant such as this, I should blush to pronounce the attachment in which I ought to glory? and hardly know how to articulate.... That I should love you, Harleigh, can surprise no one but yourself!'

Her cheeks were now in flames; and those of Harleigh were tinted with nearly as high a colour. Ellis fixed her eyes stedfastly upon the floor.

Shocked, in despite of her sunk expectations, that words such as these could be heard by Harleigh in silence, she resumed again the haughty air with which she had begun the conference.

'I ought not to detain you so long, for a defence so unimportant. What, to you, can it matter, that my valueless preference should be acknowledged from the spur of passion, or the dictates of reason?— And yet, to the receiver, as well as to the offerer, a sacrifice brings honour or disgrace, according to its motives. Listen, therefore, for both our sakes, to mine: though they may lead you to a subject which you have long since, in common with every man that breathes, wished exploded, the Rights of woman: Rights, however, which all your sex, with all its arbitrary assumption of superiority, can never disprove, for they are the Rights of human nature; to which the two sexes equally and unalienably belong. But I must leave to abler casuists, and the slow, all-arranging ascendence of truth, to raise our oppressed half of the human species, to the equality and dignity for which equal Nature, that gives us Birth and Death alike, designs us. I must spend my remaining moments in egotism; for all that I have time to attempt is my personal vindication. Harleigh! from the first instant that I saw you—heard you—knew you—'

She breathed hard, and spoke with difficulty; but forced herself on.

'From that first instant, Harleigh! I have lived but to cherish your idea!'

Her features now regained their highest expression of vivacity; and, rising, and looking at him with a sort of wild rapture, 'Oh Harleigh!' she continued, 'have I attained, at last, this exquisite moment? What does it not pay of excruciating suspense, of hateful, laborious forebearance and unnatural self-denial? Harleigh! dearest Harleigh! you are master of my soul! you are sovereign of my esteem, my admiration, my every feeling of tenderness, and every idea of perfection!—Accept, then, the warm homage of a glowing heart, that beats but for you; and that, beating in vain, will beat no more!'

The crimson hue now mounted to her forehead, and reddened her neck: her eyes became lustrous; and she was preparing, with an air of extacy, to open the shagreen case, which she had held folded to her bosom, when Harleigh, seizing her hand, dropt on one knee, and, hardly conscious of what he did, or what he felt, from the terrible impression made by a speech so full of love, despair, and menace, exclaimed, 'Elinor! you crown me, then, with honours, but to kill me with torture?'

With a look of softness new to her features, new to her character, and emanating from sensations of delight new to her hopes, Elinor sunk gently upon her chair, yet left him full possession of her hand; and, for some instants, seemed silent from a luxury of inward enjoyment. 'Is it Harleigh,' she then cried, 'Albert Harleigh, I see at my feet? Ah! what is the period, since I have known him, in which I would not joyfully have resigned all the rest of my life, for a sight, a moment such as this! Dear, dear, delicious poison! thrill, thrill through my veins! throb at my heart! new string every fibre of my frame! Is it, then, granted me, at last, to see thee thus? and thus dare speak to thee? to give sound to my feelings; to allow utterance of my love? to dare suffer my own breath to emit the purest flame that ever warmed a virgin heart?—Ah! Harleigh! proud Harleigh!—'

Harleigh, embarrassed had risen, though without quitting her hand, and re-seated himself.

'Proud, proud Harleigh!' she continued, angrily snatching away her hand; 'you think even this little moment of sympathy, too long for love and Elinor! you fear, perhaps, that she should expect its duration, or repetition? Know me, Harleigh, better! I come not to sue for your compassion, I would not accept it!—Elinor may fail to excite your regard, but she will never make you blush that you have excited hers. My choice itself speaks the purity of my passion, for are not Harleigh and Honour one?'

She paused to recover some composure, and then went on.

'You have attached neither a weak, giddy, unguarded fool, nor an idly wilful or romantic voluptuary. My defence is grated upon your character as much as upon my own. I could divide it into many branches; but I will content myself with only striking at its root, namely, the Right of woman, if endowed with senses, to make use of them. O Harleigh! why have I seen you wiser and better than all your race; sounder in your judgment, more elegant in your manners, more spirited in your conduct;—lively though benevolent, gentle, though brilliant, Oh Albert! Albert! if I must listen to you with the same dull ears, look at you with the same unmarking eyes, and think of you with the same unmeaning coldness, with which I hear, see, and consider the time-wearing, spirit-consuming, soul-wasting tribe, that daily press upon my sight, and offend my understanding? Can you ask, can you expect, can you wish to doom half your species to so degraded a state? to look down upon the wife, who is meant for the companion of your existence; and upon the mother, of whose nature you must so largely partake; as upon mere sleepy, slavish, uninteresting automatons? Say! speak! answer, Harleigh! can such be your lordly, yet most unmanly desire?'

'And is it seriously that Elinor would have me reply to such a question?'

'No, Harleigh! your noble, liberal nature answers it in every word, in every look! You accord, then, you conceive, at least, all that constitutes my defence, in allowing me the use of my faculties; for how better can I employ them than in doing honour to excellence? Why, for so many centuries, has man, alone, been supposed to possess, not only force and power for action and defence, but even all the rights of taste; all the fine sensibilities which impel our happiest sympathies, in the choice of our life's partners? Why, not alone, is woman to be excluded from the exertions of courage, the field of glory, the immortal death of honour, not alone to be denied deliberating upon the safety of the state of which she is a member, and the utility of the laws by which she must be governed:—must even her heart be circumscribed by boundaries as narrow as her sphere of action in life? Must she be taught to subdue all its native emotions? To hide them as sin, and to deny them as shame? Must her affections be bestowed but as the recompence of flattery received; not of merit discriminated? Must everything that she does be prescribed by rule? Must everything that she says, be limited to what has been said before? Must nothing that is spontaneous, generous, intuitive, spring from her soul to her lips?—And do you, even you, Harleigh, despise unbidden love!'

'No, Elinor, no!—if I durst tell you what I think of it—'

He stopt, embarrassed.

'I understand you, Harleigh; you know not how to find expressions that may not wound me? Well! let me not pain you. Let us hasten to conclude. I have spoken all that I am now capable to utter of my defence; nothing more remains but the boon I have to beg. Harleigh!—if there be a question you can resolve me, that may mitigate the horrour of my destiny, without diminishing its glory—for glory and horrour go hand in hand! would you refuse me—when I solicit it as a boon?—would you refuse, Harleigh, to satisfy me, even though my demand should be perplexing? could you, Harleigh, refuse me?—And at such a moment as this?'

'No, certainly not!'

'Tell me, then, and fear not to be sincere. Is it to some other attachment—' a sort of shivering fit stopt her for a moment, but she recovered from it by a pride that seemed to burn through every vein, as she added, 'or is it to innate repugnance that I owe your dislike?'

'Dislike? repugnance?' Harleigh repeated, with quickness, 'can Elinor be, at once, so generous and so unjust? Can she delineate her own feelings with so touching and so glowing a pencil, yet so ill describe, or so wilfully fail in comprehending mine?'

'Dare, then, to be ingenuous, and save me, Harleigh, if with truth you can, the depression, the shame, of being rejected from impenetrable apathy! I ought, I know, to be above such narrow punctilio, and to allow the independence of your liberty; but I did not fall into the refining hands of philosophy, early enough to eradicate wholly from my mind, all dregs of the clinging first impressions of habit and education. Say, then, Harleigh, if it be in your power so to say, that it is not a free heart which thus coldly disdains me; that it is not a disengaged mind which refuses me its sympathy! that it is not to personal aversion, but to some previous regard, that I owe your insensibility! To me the event will be the same, but the failure will be less ignoble.'

'How difficult, O Elinor!—how next to impossible such a statement makes every species of answer!'

'At a period, Harleigh, awful and finite to our intercourse like this, fall not into what I have hitherto, with so much reverence, seen you, upon all occasions, superiour to, subterfuge and evasion! Be yourself, Harleigh!—what can you be more noble? and plainly, simply let me into the cause, since you cannot conceal from me the effect. Speak, then! Is it but in the sullen majesty of masculine superiority,

'Lord of yourself, uncumber'd by a wife,'[8]

that you fly all marriage-bonds, with insulated, haughty singleness? or is it that, deceived by my apparent engagement, your heart never asked itself the worth of mine, till already all its own pulsations beat for another object?'

[Footnote 8: Dryden.]

Harleigh tried to smile, tried to rally, tried to divert the question; all in vain; Elinor became but more urgent, and more disordered. 'O Harleigh!' she cried, 'is it too much to ask this one mark of your confidence, for a creature who has cast her whole destiny at your feet? Speak!—if you would not devote me to distraction! Speak!—if you would not consign me to immediate delirium!'

'And what,' cried he, trembling at her vehemence, 'would you have me say?'

'That it is not Elinor whom you despise—but another whom you love.'

'Elinor! are you mad?'

'No, Harleigh, no!—but I am wild with anguish to dive into the full depth of my disgrace; to learn whether it were inevitable, from the very nature of things, from personal antipathy, gloss it over as you will with esteem, regard, and professions;—or whether you had found that you, also, had a soul, before mine was laid open to you. No evasion—no delay!' continued she, with augmenting impetuosity; 'you have promised to grant my boon, speak, Harleigh, speak!—was it my direful fate, or your insuperable antipathy?'

'It was surely not antipathy!' cried he, in a tone the most soothing; yet with a look affrighted, and unconscious, till he had spoken, of the inference to which his words might be liable.

'I thank you!' cried she, fervently, 'Harleigh, I thank you! This, at least, is noble; this is treating me with distinction, this is honouring me with trust. It abates the irritating tinglings of mortified pride; it persuades me I am the victim of misfortune, not of contempt.'

Suddenly, then, turning to Ellis, whose eyes, during the whole scene, had seemed rivetted to the floor, she expressively added, 'I ask not the object!'

Harleigh breathed hard, yet kept his face in an opposite direction, and endeavoured to look as if he did not understand her meaning. Ellis commanded her features to remain unmoved; but her complexion was not under the same controul: frequent blushes crossed her cheeks, which, though they died away almost as soon as they were born, vanished only to re-appear; evincing all the consciousness that she struggled to suppress.

A pause ensued, to Harleigh unspeakably painful, and to Ellis indescribably distressing; during which Elinor fell into a profound reverie, from which, after a few minutes, wildly starting, 'Harleigh,' she cried, 'is your wedding-day fixed?'

'My wedding-day?' he repeated, with a forced smile, 'Must not my wedding itself be fixed first?'

'And it is not fixed?—Does it depend upon Ellis?'

He looked palpably disconcerted; while Ellis, hastily raising her head, exclaimed, 'Upon me, Madam? no, indeed! I am completely and every way out of the question.'

'Of you,' said Elinor, with severity, 'I mean not to make any enquiry! You are an adept in the occult sciences; and such I venture not to encounter. But you, Harleigh, will you, also, practise disguise? and fall so in love with mystery, as to lose your nobler nature, in a blind, infatuated admiration of the marvellous and obscure?'

Ellis resentfully reddened; but her cheeks were pale to those of Harleigh. Neither of them, however, spoke; and Elinor continued.

'I cannot, Harleigh, be deceived, and I will not be trifled with. When you came over to fetch me from France; when the fatal name of sister gave me a right to interrogate you, I frankly asked the state of your heart, and you unhesitatingly told me that it was wholly free. Since that period, whom have you seen, whom noticed, except Ellis! Ellis! Ellis! From the first moment that you have beheld her, she has seemed the mistress of your destiny, the arbitress of your will. My boon, then, Harleigh, my boon! without a moment's further delay! Appease the raging ferment in my veins; clear away every surmize; and generously, honestly say 'tis Ellis!—or it is another, and not Ellis, I prefer to you!'

'Elinor! Elinor!' cried Harleigh, in a universal tremour, 'it is I that you will make mad!' while Ellis, not daring to draw upon herself, again, the rebuke which might follow a single declaiming word, rose, and turning from them both, stood facing the window.

'It is surely then Ellis! what you will not, Harleigh, avow, is precisely what you proclaim—it is surely Ellis!'

Ellis opened the window, and leant out her head; Harleigh, clapping his hand upon his crimsoned forehead, walked with hasty steps round the little apartment.

Losing now all self-command, and wringing her hands, in a transport of ungovernable anguish, 'Oh, Harleigh! Harleigh!' Elinor cried, 'to what a chimera you have given your heart! to an existence unintelligible, a character unfathomable, a creature of imagination, though visible! O, can you believe she will ever love you as Elinor loves? with the warmth, with the truth, with the tenderness, with the choice? can she show herself as disinterested? can she prove herself as devoted?—'

'She aims, Madam, at no rivalry!' said Ellis, gravely, and returning to her seat: while Harleigh, tortured between resentment and pity, stood still; without venturing to look up or reply.

'Rivalry?' repeated Elinor, with high disdain: 'No! upon what species of competition could rivalry be formed, between Elinor, and a compound of cold caution, and selfish prudence? Oh, Harleigh! how is it you thus can love all you were wont to scorn? double dealing, false appearances, and lurking disguise! without a family she dare claim, without a story she dare tell, without a name she dare avow!'

A deep sigh, which now burst from Ellis, terminated the conflict between indignation and compassion in Harleigh, who raised his eyes to meet those of Elinor, with an expression of undisguised displeasure.

'You are angry?' she cried, clasping her hands, with forced and terrible joy; 'you are angry, and I am thankful for the lesson. I meant not to have lingered thus; my design was to have been abrupt and noble.'

Looking at him, then, with uncontrolled emotion, 'If ever man deserved the sacrifice of a pure heart,' she continued, ''tis you, Harleigh, you! and mine, from the period it first became conscious of its devotion to you, has felt that it could not survive the certitude of your union with another. All else, of slight, of failure, of inadequate pretensions, might be borne; for where neither party is happy, misery is not aggravated by contrast, nor mortification by comparison. But to become the object of insolent pity to the happy!—to make a part of a rival's blessings, by being offered up at the shrine of her superiority—No, Harleigh, no! such abasement is not for Elinor. And what is the charm of this wretched machine of clay, that can pay for sustaining its burthen under similar disgrace? Let those who prize support it. For me, my glass is run, my cup is full, I die!'

'Die?' repeated Ellis, with a faint scream, while Harleigh looked petrified with horrour.

'Die, yes!' answered Elinor, with a smile triumphant though ghastly; 'or sleep! call it which you will! so animation be over, so feeling be past, so my soul no longer linger under the leaden oppression of disappointment; under sickness of all mortal existence; under incurable, universal disgust:—call it what you please, sleep, rest, or death; termination is all I seek.'

'And is there, Elinor, no other name for what follows our earthly dissolution?' cried Harleigh, with a shuddering frown. 'What say you if we call it immortality?'

'Will you preach to me?' cried she, her eyes darting fire; 'will you bid me look forward to yet another life, when this, short as it is deemed, I find insupportable? Ah, Harleigh! Harleigh!' her eyes suffusing with sudden tenderness; 'were I your's—I might wish indeed to be immortal!'

Harleigh was extremely affected: he approached her, took her hand, and soothingly said, 'My dear Elinor, compose your spirits, exert your strength of mind, and suffer us to discuss these subjects at some length.'

'No, Harleigh; I must not trust myself to your fascinations! How do I know but they might bewitch me out of my reason, and entangle me, again, in those antique superstitions which make misery so cowardly? No, Harleigh! the star of Ellis has prevailed, and I sink beneath its influence. Else, only sometimes to see you, to hear of you, to watch you, and to think of you always, I would still live, nay, feel joy in life; for still my imagination would gift you, ultimately, with sensibility to my regard. But I anticipate the union which I see to be inevitable, and I spare my senses the shock which I feel would demolish them. Harleigh!—dearest Harleigh, Adieu!'

A paleness like that of death overspread her face.

'What is it,' cried Harleigh, inexpressibly alarmed, 'what is it Elinor means?'

'To re-conquer, by the courage of my death, the esteem I may leave forfeited by my jealousy, my envy, my littleness in life! You only could have corrected my errours; you, by your ascendance over my feelings, might have refined them into virtues. Oh, Harleigh! weigh not alone my imperfections when you recollect my attachment! but remember that I have loved you so as woman never loved!'

Her voice now faultered, and she shook so violently that she could not support herself. She put her hand gently upon the arm of Harleigh, and, gliding nearly behind him, leant upon his shoulder. He would have spoken words of comfort, but she seemed incapable of hearing him. 'Farewell!' she cried, 'Harleigh! Never will I live to see Ellis your's!—Farewell!—a long farewell!'

Precipitately she then opened the shagreen case, and was drawing out its contents, when Ellis, darting forward, caught her arm, and screamed, rather than articulated, 'Ellis will never be his!—Forbear! Forbear!—Ellis never will be his!'

The astonished Harleigh, who, hitherto, had rigorously avoided meeting the eyes of Ellis, now turned towards her, with an expression in which all that was not surprise was resentment; while Elinor, seeming suddenly suspended, faintly pronounced, 'Ellis—deluding Ellis!—what is it you say?'

'I am no deluder!' cried Ellis, yet more eagerly: 'Rely, rely upon my plighted honour!'

Harleigh now looked utterly confounded; but Ellis only saw, and seemed only to breathe for Elinor, who recovering, as if by miracle, her complexion, her voice, and the brightness of her eyes, rapturously exclaimed, 'Oh Harleigh!—Is there, then, sympathy in our fate? Do you, too, love in vain?'—And, from a change of emotion, too sudden and too mighty for the shattered state of her nerves, she sunk senseless upon the floor.

The motive to the strange protestations of Ellis was now apparent: a poniard dropt from the hand of Elinor as she fell, of which, while she spoke her farewell, Ellis had caught a glance.

Harleigh seemed himself to require the aid that he was called upon to bestow. He looked at Elinor with a mixture of compassion and horrour, and, taking possession of the poniard, 'Unhappy Elinor!' he cried, 'into what a chaos of errour and of crime have these fatal new systems bewildered thee!'

The revival of Elinor was almost immediate; and though, at first, she seemed to have lost the remembrance of what had happened, the sight of Ellis and Harleigh soon brought it back. She looked from one to the other, as if searching her destiny; and then, with quick impatience, though somewhat checked by shame, cried, 'Ellis! have you not mocked me?'

Ellis, covered with blushes and confusion, addressing herself to Harleigh, said, 'Pardon, Mr Harleigh, my seeming presumption, where no option has been offered me; and where such an option is as wide from my expectations as it would be from my desert. This terrible crisis must be my apology.'

A shivering like that of an ague-fit again shook the agitated Elinor, who, ejaculating, 'What farce is this?—Fool! fool! shall I thus sleepily be duped?' looked keenly around for her lost weapon.

'Duped? no, Madam,' cried Ellis, in a tone impressive of veracity: 'if I had the honour to be better known to Miss Joddrel, one assertion, I flatter myself, would suffice: my word is given; it has never yet been broken!'

While this declaration, though softened by a sigh the most melancholy, struck cold to the heart of Harleigh, its effect upon Elinor was that of an extacy which seemed the offspring of frenzy. 'Do I awake, then,' she cried, 'from agony and death—agony, impossible to support! death, willing and welcome! to renewed life? to an interesting, however deplorable, existence? is my fate in harmony with the fate of Harleigh? Has he, even he! given his soul, his noble soul!—to one who esteems and admires him, yet who will not be his? Can Harleigh love in vain?'

Tears now rolled fast and unchecked down her cheeks, while, in tones of enthusiasm, she continued, 'I hail thee once again, oh life! with all thy arrows! Welcome, welcome, every evil that associates my catastrophe with that of Harleigh!—Yet I blush, methinks, to live!—Blush, and feel little, nearly in the same proportion that I should have gloried to die!'

With these words, and recoiling from a solemn, yet tender exhortation, begun by Harleigh, she abruptly quitted the little building; and, her mind not more highly wrought by self-exaltation, than her body was weakened by successive emotions, she was compelled to accept the fearfully offered assistance of Ellis, to regain, with tottering steps, the house.


CHAPTER XIX

Ellis entered into the chamber with Elinor; who, equally exhausted in body and in mind, flung herself upon her bed, where she remained some time totally mute: her eyes wide open, yet looking at nothing, apparently in a state of stupefaction; but from which, in a few minutes, suddenly starting, and taking Ellis by the hand, with a commanding air, she abruptly said, 'Ellis, are you fixed to marry Lord Melbury?'

Ellis positively disclaimed any such idea.

'What am I to infer?' cried Elinor, with returning and frightful agitation; 'Will you be firm to your engagement? Is it truly your decision to refuse the hand of Harleigh, though he were to offer it you?'

Ellis shuddered, and looked down; but answered, 'I will surely, Madam, never forget my engagement!'

The most perfect calm now succeeded to the many storms which had both impelled and shattered Elinor; and, after swallowing a copious draught of cold water, she laid her head upon her pillow, and fell into a profound and heavy, though not tranquil sleep.

Ellis, unable to conjecture in what frame of mind she might wake, did not dare leave her. She sat watchfully by her side, amazed to see, that, with such energy of character, such quickness of parts, such strength of comprehension, she not only gave way to all her impulses like a child, but, like a child, also, when over-fatigued, could suddenly lose her sufferings and her remembrance in a sort of spontaneous slumber.

But the balmy rest of even spirits, and a composed mind, was far from Elinor; exhausted nature claimed some respite from frantic exertion, and obtained it; but no more. She awoke then; yet, though it was with a frightful start, even this short repose proved salutary, not only to her nerves, but to her intellects. Her passions became less inflamed, and her imagination less heated; and, though she remained unchanged in her plans, and impenitent in her opinions, she acknowledged herself sensible to the strangeness of her conduct; and not without shame for its violence. These, however, were transitory sensations: one regret alone hung upon her with any serious weight: this was, having suffered her dagger to be seen and seized. She feared being suspected of a mere puerile effort, to frighten from Harleigh an offer of his hand, in menacing what she had not courage, nor, perhaps, even intention to perform.

This suggestion was intolerable: she blushed with shame as it crossed her mind. She shook with passion, as she considered, that such might be the disgraceful opinion, that might tarnish the glory that she meant to acquire, by dying at the feet of the object of her adoration, at the very moment of yielding to the happier star of an acknowledged rival; a willing martyr to successless, but heroick love.

She was now tempted to prove her sincerity by her own immediate destruction. 'And yet,' she cried, 'shall I not bear what Harleigh bears? Shall I not know the destiny of Harleigh?'

This idea again reconciled her to present life, though not to her actual situation; and she ruminated laboriously, for some time, in gloomy silence; from which, however, breaking with sudden vivacity, 'No, no!' she cried: 'I will not risk any aspersing doubt; I will shew him I have a soul that strenuously emulates the nobleness of his own. He shall see, he shall confess, that no meanness is mixt with the love of Elinor. He shall not suppose, because she glories in its undisguised avowal, that she waits in humble hope for a turn in her favour; that she is a candidate for his regard; a supplicant for his compassion! No! he shall see that she is frank without weakness, and free from every species of dissimulation or stratagem.'

She then rushed out of the room, shutting the door after her, and commanding Ellis not to follow: but Ellis fearing every moment some dreadful catastrophe, softly pursued her, till she saw her enter the servants' hall; whence, after giving some orders, in a low voice and hurried manner, to her own footman, she re-mounted to her chamber; into which, without opposition, or even notice, Ellis also glided.

Here, eagerly seizing a pen, with the utmost rapidity, though with many blots, and frequent erazures, she wrote a long letter, which she read and altered repeatedly before she folded; she then wrote a shorter one; then rang for her maid, to whom she gave some secret directions, which she finished by commanding that she would find out Mr Harleigh, and desire that he would go immediately to the summer-house.

In about a quarter of an hour, which she spent in reading, revising, sealing, and directing her letters, the maid returned; and, after a long whisper, said, that she had given the message to Mr Harleigh.

Turning now to Ellis, with a voice and air of decision, that seemed imperiously to forbid resistance, she put into her hand the long letter which she had just written, and said, 'Take this to him immediately; and, while he reads it, mark every change of his countenance, so as to be able to deduce, and clearly to understand, the sensations which pass in his mind.'

When Ellis expostulated upon the utter impropriety of her following Mr Harleigh, she sternly said, 'Give the letter, then, to whatever other person you judge most proper to become a third in my confidence!'

She then nearly forced her out of the room.

Ellis did not dare venture to keep the letter, as she wished, till some opportunity should offer for presenting it quietly, lest some high importance should be annexed to its quick delivery; yet she felt that it would be cruel and indelicate to make over such a commission to another; in opposition, therefore, to the extremest personal repugnance, she compelled herself, with fearful and unwilling, yet hasty steps, to proceed again to the summer-house.

She found Harleigh, with an air at once pensive and alarmed, waiting for Elinor; but at the unexpected sight of Ellis, and of Ellis alone, every feature brightened; though his countenance, his manner, his whole frame, evinced increased agitation.

Anxious to produce her excuse, for an intrusion of which she felt utterly ashamed, she instantly presented him the letter, saying, 'Miss Joddrel would take no denial to my being its bearer. She has even charged me to remain with you while you read it.'

'Were that,' said he, expressively, 'the severest pain she inflicts upon me, I should soon become her debtor for feelings that leave pain apart!—Urgent, indeed, was my desire to see you again, and without delay; for after what has passed this morning, silence and forbearance are no longer practicable.'

'Yet, at this moment,' said Ellis, striving but ineffectually to speak without disturbance; 'it will be impossible for me to defer returning to the house.'

'Yet if not now, when?'

'I know not—but she will be very impatient for some account of her letter.'

'She will, at least, not be desperate, since she expects, and therefore will wait for you; how, then, can I hope to find a more favourable opportunity, for obtaining a few instants of your time?'

'But, though she may not be desperate just now, is it not possible, Sir, that my staying may irritate, and make her so?'

'That unhappily, is but too true! There is no relying upon the patience, or the fortitude, of one so completely governed by impulse; and who considers her passions as her guides to glory, not as the subtlest enemies of every virtue! Nevertheless, what I feel for her is far beyond what, situated as I now am with her, I dare express—Yet, at this moment—'

'Will you not read her letter?'

'That you may run away?' cried he, half smiling; 'no, at this moment I will not read her letter, that you may be forced to stay!'

'You cannot wish me to make her angry?'

'Far, far from it! but what chance have I to meet you again, if I lose you now? Be not alarmed, I beg: she will naturally conclude that I am studying her letter; and, but for an insuperable necessity of—of some explanation, I could, indeed think of no other subject: for dreadful is the impression which the scene that I have just had with her has made upon my nerves. Ah! how could she imagine such a one calculated to engage my heart? How wide is it from all that, to me, appears attractive! Her spirit I admire; but where is the sweetness I could love? I respect her understanding; but where is the softness that should make it charm while it enlightens? I am grateful for her partiality; but where is the dignity that might ennoble it, or the delicacy that might make it as refined as it is flattering? Where—where the soul's fascination, that grows out of the mingled excellencies, the blended harmonies, of the understanding with the heart and the manners?'

Vainly Ellis strove to appear unconscious of the comparison, and the application, which the eyes of Harleigh, yet more pointedly than his words, marked for herself in this speech: her quickly rising blushes divulged all that her stillness, her unmoved features tried to disguise; and, to get rid of her confusion, she again desired that he would open the letter, and with an urgency which he could not resist. He merely stipulated that she would wait to hear his answer; and then read what follows.

'For Albert Harleigh.

'I am sick of the world, yet still I crawl upon its surface. I scorn and defy the whole human race, yet doom myself to be numbered in its community. While you, Albert Harleigh, you whom alone, of all that live and breath, I prize, you, even your sight, I, from this moment, eternally renounce! Such the mighty ascendance of the passion which you have inspired, that I will sooner forego that only blessing—though the universe without it is a hateful blank to my eyes—than risk opposing the sway of your opinion, or suffer you to think me ignoble, though you know me to be enslaved. O Harleigh! how far from all that is vile and debasing is the flame, the pure, though ardent flame that you have kindled! To its animating influence I am indebted for one precious moment of heavenly truth; and for having snatched from the grave, which in its own nothingness will soon moulder away my frame, the history of my feelings.

'I have conquered the tyrant false pride; I have mocked the puerilities of education; I have set at nought and defeated even the monster custom; but you, O Harleigh! you I obey, without waiting for a command; you, I seek to humour, without aspiring to please! To you, my free soul, my liberated mind, my new-born ideas, all yield, slaves, willing slaves, to what I only conceive to be your counsel, only conjecture to be your judgment; that since I have failed to touch your heart, after having opened to you my own, a total separation will be due to my fame for the world, due to delicacy for myself....

'Be it so, Albert ... we will part! Though my fame, in my own estimation, would be elevated to glory; by the publication of a choice that does me honour; though my delicacy would be gratified, would be sanctified, by shewing the purity of a passion as spotless as it is hopeless—yet will I hide myself in the remotest corner of the universe, rather than resist you even in thought. O Albert! how sovereign is your power! more absolute than the tyranny of the controlling world; more arbitrary than prescription; more invincible than the prejudices of ages! You, I cannot resist! you, I shall only breathe to adore! to bear all you bear, the tortures of disappointment, the abominations of incertitude; to say, Harleigh himself endures this! we suffer in unison! our woes are sympathetic! O word to charm all the rigour of calamity!.... Harleigh, I exist but to know how your destiny will be fulfilled, and then to come from my concealment, and bid you a last farewell! to leave upon the record of your memory the woes of my passion; and then consign myself for ever to my native oblivion. Till then, adieu, Albert Harleigh, adieu!

'ELINOR JODDREL.'

Harleigh read this letter with a disturbance that, for a while, wholly absorbed his mind in its contents. 'Misguided, most unfortunate, yet admirable Elinor!' he cried, 'what a terrible perversion is here of intellect! what a confusion of ideas! what an inextricable chaos of false principles, exaggerated feelings, and imaginary advancement in new doctrines of life!'

He paused, thoughtfully and sadly, till Ellis, though sorry to interrupt his meditations, begged his directions what to say upon returning to the house.

'What her present plan may be,' he answered, 'is by no means clear; but so boundless is the licence which the followers of the new systems allow themselves, that nothing is too dreadful to apprehend. Religion is, if possible, still less respected than law, prescriptive rights, or any of the hitherto acknowledged ties of society. There runs through her letter, as there ran through her discourse this morning, a continual intimation of her disbelief in a future state; of her defiance of all revealed religion; of her high approbation of suicide. The fatal deed from which you rescued her, had no excuse to plead from sudden desperation; she came prepared, decided, either to disprove her suspicions, or to end her existence!—poor infatuated, yet highly gifted Elinor!—what can be done to save her; to recall her to the use of her reason, and the exercise of her duties?'

'Will you not, Sir, see her? Will you not converse with her upon these points, in which her mind and understanding are so direfully warped?'

'Certainly I will; and I beg you to entreat for my admission. I must seek to dissuade her from the wild and useless scheme of seclusion and concealment. But as time now presses, permit me to speak, first, upon subjects which press also, press irresistibly, unconquerably!—Your plan of becoming a governess—'

'I dare not stay, now, to discuss any thing personal; yet I cannot refrain from seizing a moment that may not again offer, for making my sincerest apologies upon a subject—and a declaration—I shall never think of without confusion. I feel all its impertinence, its inutility, its presumption; but you will make, I hope, allowance for the excess of my alarm. I could devise no other expedient.'

'Tell me,' cried he, 'I beg, was it for her ... or for me that it was uttered? Tell me the extent of its purpose!'

'You cannot, surely, Sir, imagine—cannot for a moment suppose, that I was guided by such egregious vanity as to believe—' She stopt, extremely embarrassed.

'Vanity,' said he, 'is out of the question, after what has just passed; spare then, I beseech, your own candour, as well as my suspense, all unnecessary pain.'

'I entreat, I conjure you, Sir,' cried Ellis, now greatly agitated, 'speak only of my commission!'

'Certainly,' he answered, 'this is not the period I should have chosen, for venturing upon so delicate—I had nearly said so perilous a subject; but, so imperiously called upon, I could neither be insincere, nor pusillanimous enough, to disavow a charge which every feeling rose to confess!—Otherwise—just now, my judgment, my sense of propriety, all in the dark as I am—would sedulously, scrupulously, have constrained my forbearance, till I knew—' He stopt, paused, and then expressively, yet gently added, 'to whom I addressed myself!'

Ellis coloured highly as she answered, 'I beg you, Sir, to consider all that was drawn from you this morning, or all that might be inferred, as perfectly null—unpronounced and unthought.'

'No!' cried he with energy, 'no! To have postponed an explanation would have been prudent, nay right:—but every sentiment of my mind, filled with trust in your worth, and reverence for your virtues, forbids now, a recantation! Imperious circumstances precipitated me to your feet—but my heart was there already!'

So extreme was the emotion with which Harleigh uttered these words, that he perceived not their effect upon Ellis, till gasping for breath, and nearly fainting, she sunk upon a chair; when so livid a paleness overspread her face, and so deadly a cold seemed to chill her blood, that, but for a friendly burst of tears, which ensued, her vital powers appeared to be threatened with immediate suspension.

Harleigh was instantly at her feet; grieved at her distress, yet charmed with a thousand nameless, but potent sensations, that whispered to every pulse of his frame, that a sensibility so powerful could spring only from too sudden a concussion of pleasure with surprise.

He had hardly time to breathe forth a protestation, when the sight of his posture brought back the blood to her cheeks, and force to her limbs; and, hastily rising, with looks of blushing confusion, yet with a sigh that spoke internal anguish, 'I cannot attempt,' she cried, 'Mr Harleigh, I could not, indeed, attempt—to express my sense of your generous good opinion!—yet—if you would not destine me to eternal misery, you must fly me—till you can forget this scene—as you would wish me to fly perdition!'

She rose to be gone; but Harleigh stopt her, crying, in a tone of amazement, 'Is it possible, can it be possible, that with intellects such as yours, clear, penetrating, admirable, you can conceive eternal misery will be your portion, if you break a forced engagement made with a mad woman?—and made but to prevent her immediate self-destruction?'

Shaking her head, but averting her eyes, Ellis would neither speak not be detained; and Harleigh, who durst not follow her, remained confounded.


Frances Burney – A Short Biography

Frances Burney was born on June 13th, 1752 in Lynn Regis (now King's Lynn).

Her mother, Esther, was described as of "warmth and intelligence," the daughter of a French refugee, she had been brought up a Catholic.

Frances's father, Charles Burney, was a noted musician, musicologist and composer as well as being a man of letters.

In 1760 the family moved to Poland Street, In London's Soho, giving them an entrée to a wider circle of the cultural elite.

A difficult situation arose in 1766 when Charles Burney eloped to marry for a second time. Elizabeth Allen, was the wealthy widow of a King's Lynn wine merchant and already the mother of three children.

The two families were now merged into one and tensions were always simmering as Elizabeth established her rules in an overbearing way, always with the threat of anger near to the surface.

Her father had always favoured her sisters Esther and Susanna over Frances. By the age of 8 Frances had still not learned the alphabet and couldn't read. Her sisters were sent to be educated in Paris whilst Frances educated herself, reading from the family library, which she then devoured as her ambitions began to take hold. She now also began her own 'scribblings'.

In 1762, her mother, Esther, died and it was a loss that Frances was to feel deeply for the rest of her life.

However, there was one family friend who had spotted Frances's talents. He was Samuel Crisp. He encouraged Frances to write, mainly by requesting frequent journal-letters from her that recounted the family goings-on and also that of her social circle in London.

Frances was fifteen by the time her father eventually remarried in 1767. Pressure was also being exerted for her to give up writing; it was "unladylike" and "might vex Mrs. Allen."

Feeling that she had been improper, she burnt her first manuscript, The History of Caroline Evelyn, which she had written in secret. However, Frances did keep an account of the emotions that led up to this in her diaries which she thereafter continued to write, a practice she kept faith with for 72 years.

Frances was a talented storyteller with a strong sense of character, she often wrote these "journal-diaries" as correspondence to her family and friends, recounting events from her life and her observations upon them. Her diary contains the extensive reading in her father's library, as well the visits and behaviour of the various important arts personalities who came to their home. Frances and her sister Susanna were particularly close, and it was to her that Frances would correspond throughout her adult life, in the form of such journal-letters.

In 1775 Frances received a proposal from Thomas Barlow, whom she had met only once before, and which she recounts amusingly in her journals.

By 1778 Frances Burney was ready to be acknowledged as an author. The publication that year of Evelina or the History of a Young Lady's Entrance into the World, was published anonymously in 1778, without her father's knowledge or permission, by Thomas Lowndes, who, after reading the first volume, agreed to publish it upon receipt of the finished work.

This was a time when having a novel published by a young woman was almost unthinkable. In fact, she had her brother pose as its author. Unfortunately, he was also the negotiator and despite its critical success and praise from such luminaries as Edmund Burke and Dr Johnson she received only twenty guineas.

Its comic depictions of English society and realistic use of accents among the working class brought it to the attention of her father who was at first surprised and then supportive that his daughter had published a novel and enhanced the family's standing. With the books rare use of a female teenage protagonist Frances was already pushing the boundaries of the novel.

It also brought Frances an invitation to the home of patron of the arts Hester Thrale. Here she met Dr Johnson, who would remain her friend and correspondent throughout the period of her visits, from 1779 to 1783. Mrs Thrale wrote to Dr Burney on July 22nd, stating that: "Mr. Johnson returned home full of the Prayes of the Book I had lent him, and protesting that there were passages in it which might do honour to Richardson: we talk of it for ever, and he feels ardent after the dénouement; he could not get rid of the Rogue, he said." Dr Johnson's best compliments were eagerly transcribed in Frances's diary.

Sojourns at Streatham could occupy months at a time, and on several occasions the guests, including Frances, made trips to Brighton and Bath. As with other notable events, these experiences were faithfully recorded.

In 1779, encouraged by the public's warm reception of comic material in Evelina, and with offers of help from Arthur Murphy and Richard Brinsley Sheridan, Frances began to write a dramatic comedy called The Witlings. The play satirised London society, including the literary world and its pretensions.

It was not published at the time as her father and Samuel Crisp thought it would offend some of the public by seeming to mock the Bluestockings, and also their reservations about the propriety of a woman writing comedy. The play is the story of Celia and Beaufort, lovers kept apart by their families due to "economic insufficiency".

In 1781 Samuel Crisp died. Much of her subsequent work, Cecilia, or Memoirs of an Heiress, was written after much discussion with Crisp. The novel was published the following year. Her advance was now £250 and the first edition ran to 2000 copies, the first of several printings that year alone.

The narrative of Cecilia tells of Cecilia Beverley, whose inheritance from her uncle comes on the condition that she marries but keeps the family name.

In 1784 one of her greatest supporters, and her frequent correspondent, Dr Johnson, died. Her promising relationship with a clergyman, George Owen Cambridge, was also over. Frances was 33 years old but she had made a great deal of her life already.

In 1785, thanks to her association with Mary Granville Delany, a woman influential in both literary and royal circles, Frances travelled to the court of King George III and Queen Charlotte. There she was offered the post of "Keeper of the Robes", and a salary of £200 per annum. Frances hesitated. She had no wish to be separated from her family, nor to anything that would restrict her time in writing. But, unmarried at 34, she felt obliged to accept and thought that improved social status and income might allow her greater freedom to write.

She developed a warm relationship with the queen and princesses that lasted into her later years, yet her worries were prophetic: the position exhausted her and left her little, if any, time to write. She was unhappy and her feelings were amplified by a poor relationship with her colleague, Elizabeth Schwellenburg, co-Keeper of the Robes.

But despite writing little in the way of novels she still kept at her journals recounting life at court and the various political and social events.

By 1790, frustrated at her lack of writing, her further failed relationships, and with her health failing she asked to be released from service. The request was granted.

She returned to her father's house in Chelsea, but continued to receive a yearly pension of £100. She maintained a friendship with the royal family and received letters from the princesses until her death.

Between 1790–91 Frances wrote four blank-verse tragedies: Hubert de Vere, The Siege of Pevensey, Elberta and Edwy and Elgiva. Only the last was performed but met with public failure and played for only one night.

The French Revolution which had begun in 1789 brought support from many English literates for the ideals of equality and social justice. It was now that Frances became acquainted with a group of French exiles known as "Constitutionalists", who had fled France and were living at Juniper Hall, near Mickleham, where Frances's sister Susanna lived.

Frances quickly became attached to General Alexandre D'Arblay, an artillery officer who had been adjutant-general to Lafayette, a hero of the French Revolution.

Frances's father disapproved because of Alexandre's poverty, his Catholicism, and his ambiguous social status as an émigré. In spite of these objections they were married on July 28th, 1793.

On December 18th, 1794, Frances gave birth to their only child, a son, Alexander.

The impoverished couple were saved from poverty in 1796 by the publication of her next novel Camilla, or a Picture of Youth, a story of frustrated love and impoverishment. She made £1000 on the novel and sold the copyright for another £1000. This was enough to enable them to build a house in Westhumble; Camilla Cottage. Their life was now happy on all fronts.

Sadly, the news that her sister Susanna and her family were moving to Ireland that year caused her, and her father, some consternation, as did her sister Charlotte's remarriage in 1798 to the pamphleteer Ralph Broome.

Between 1797–1801 Frances wrote three further comedies; Love and Fashion, A Busy Day and The Woman Hater. All were unpublished during her lifetime.

The illness and death of Susanna in 1800 brought an end to their lifelong correspondence. Frances was devastated and only resumed her journal writing at the request of her husband, for the benefit of their son.

In 1801 D'Arblay was offered service with the government of Napoleon in France, and in 1802 Frances and her son followed him to Paris, where they expected to remain for a year. The outbreak of the war between France and England meant their stay extended for ten years. Although the conditions of their time left her isolated from her family, Frances was supportive of her husband's decision to move.

In August 1810 Frances developed pains in her breast. Her husband suspected breast cancer. Through her royal network of acquaintances, she was treated by leading physicians and, a year later, on September 30th, 1811, she underwent a mastectomy performed by "7 men in black". The operation was performed by M. Dubois, the accoucheur (midwife or obstetrician) to the Empress Marie Louise, Duchess of Parma, and widely considered the best doctor in France. Frances was later able to write about the operation in detail, since she was conscious through most of it, anesthetics not yet being in use.

Frances survived, even though she was still in recovery and not back to full health, returned to England in 1812 to visit her ailing father and also to avoid young Alexander's conscription into the French army

In 1814, Frances published her fourth novel, The Wanderer or, Female Difficulties, a few days before her father's death. A story of love and misalliance set in the French Revolution", it criticises the English treatment of foreigners during the war.

Frances made £1500 from the first run, but it did not go into a second English printing, although it met her immediate financial needs.

In 1815 Napoleon escaped from Elba. D'Arblay was then serving with the King's Guard, and he became involved in the military actions that followed. Frances joined her wounded husband at Trèves, and together they returned to Bath, England. Frances wrote an account of this and of her Paris years in her Waterloo Journal, written between 1818 and 1832. D'Arblay was rewarded with promotion to lieutenant-general but died shortly afterwards, in 1818, of cancer.

Frances now moved to London to be nearer to her son, a fellow at Christ's College. In honour of her father she gathered and in 1832 published, in three volumes, the Memoirs of Doctor Burney. The memoirs overly praised her father's accomplishments and character. Always protective of her father and the family's reputation, she deliberately destroyed evidence of facts that were painful or unflattering.

She now lived almost in retirement, outliving her son, Alexander, who died in 1837, and her sister, Charlotte, who died in 1838.

Frances continued to receive many visits from younger members of the Burney family, who gathered to listen to her fascinating accounts and her talents for imitating the people she described. She continued to write in her journals but alas her canon of novels and plays received no further additions.

Frances Burney died on January 6th, 1840.

She was buried with her son and her husband in Walcot cemetery in Bath.

There is a Royal Society of Arts blue plaque to record her period of residence at 11 Bolton Street, Mayfair.


Frances Burney – A Concise Bibliography

Fiction
The History of Caroline Evelyn, (manuscript destroyed by author, 1767.)
Evelina: or, The History of a Young Lady's Entrance into the World. 1778.

Cecilia: or, Memoirs of an Heiress. 1782.
Camilla: or, A Picture of Youth. 1796.
The Wanderer: or, Female Difficulties. 1814.

Non Fiction
Brief Reflections Relative to the French Emigrant Clergy. 1793.
Memoirs of Doctor Burney. 1832.

Journals & Letters
The Early Diary of Frances Burney 1768–1778. 2 volumes. 1889.
The Diary and Letters of Madame D'Arblay. 1904.
The Diary of Fanny Burney.
Dr. Johnson & Fanny Burney by Fanny Burney.
The Early Journals and Letters of Fanny Burney, 1768–1786. 5 volumes.
The Court Journals and Letters of Frances Burney. 4 volumes. (to date).
The Journals and Letters of Fanny Burney (Madame D'Arblay) 1791–1840. 12 volumes.

Plays
The Witlings, 1779 (satirical comedy).
Edwy and Elgiva, 1790 (verse tragedy). Produced at Drury Lane, 21 March 1795.
Hubert de Vere, 1788–91 (verse tragedy).
The Siege of Pevensey, 1788–91 (verse tragedy).
Elberta, (fragment) 1788–91 (verse tragedy).
Love and Fashion, 1799 (satirical comedy).
The Woman Hater, 1800–1801 (satirical comedy).
A Busy Day, 1800–1801 (satirical comedy).

Made in the USA
Las Vegas, NV
01 December 2020

11831194R00072